Praise for the par
Joyce and Jim La

MW00936778

Taxi for the Dead Paranormal Mysteries:

~ Unique, light paranormal cozy with an underlying depth . . . I loved the Lavene's Telltale Turtle and their Missing Pieces series, so when I saw this self-published paranormal cozy, I snatched it up right away. Broken Hearted Ghoul is a light, fun read. It does not go as in depth into characters and motivations as in the Missing Pieces series, but it is exactly the kind of book I need when I am in between complex urban fantasies and my nerves need to cool down. There is still lots of action and character interaction, and a unique concept to boot. Despite its light nature, it is not fluff. There are deep underlying concepts that raise the question of how we (were we to be in Skye Mertz's shoes) would choose to live life, and how we would choose to die.

~ By Alice in Vunderland

Renaissance Faire Mysteries:

"Murderous Matrimony is the first book Ren Faire Mysteries that I have read. It is not only a cozy mystery, but full of surprises. It is charming, silly, fantasy, history, romantic, haunted and crazy. You are not sure what to believe is real, and what parts are not. The characters are a variety of fun and crazy people. They have wizards, a fortune teller, and more fun characters waiting for you in every chapter."

~ R. Laney

Missing Pieces Mysteries:

"Readers will find themselves drawn into the investigation of the death. Throw in a little ghostly activity, the promise of a pirates' treasure, and the reader will be hooked." ~ Fresh Fiction

"Paranormal amateur sleuth fans will enjoy observing Dae use cognitive and ESP mental processes to uncover a murderer...Readers will enjoy."

~ Midwest Book Review

Sweet Pepper Fire Brigade Mysteries:
"This series just keeps getting better and better! I love Stella, she is such a strong character. I also like her relationship with Eric, who happens to be ghost! This book absolutely left me guessing and I had no idea in which direction it was going to go. Great job!
~ Melina Mason
Our Paranormal Mysteries:

Dead Girl Blues

A Taxi for the Dead Paranormal Mystery

By

Joyce and Jim Lavene

Chapter One

"So what do you think?" Debbie Hernandez put her twenty dollar bill on the sunbaked dash of the old van. "I think she'll run, Skye."

I pulled out my binoculars and surveyed the old homestead in Murfreesboro, Tennessee. The house was in good condition, a two-story frame building that sat quietly in a pretty valley. It was surrounded by thick green grass and a few tall oaks. The whole effect was like a picture from a calendar.

"I think she'll be okay. She's got this pretty house, and there are kids who play here—see the swings and bikes? She won't run and upset them." I put my twenty dollars on the dash next to Debbie's.

It was midsummer, hot and dry. Clouds of dust filled the air instead of pollen as people cut their grass. The rivers and streams were lower than they had been in twenty years, or so they said on TV. Newscasters pleaded with residents of the state to moderate their water usage.

Me?

I just wished my old van had air conditioning. I didn't feel the cold much since I'd died, but I suffered in the heat. Even sitting with the windows open to catch any spare breeze wasn't much help. In a job like ours, we waited a lot. It would've been nice if we were waiting in a little comfort.

But the money I made picking up Abraham Lincoln Jones's LEP workers (that's Life Extended People – Abe doesn't like it when I call them zombies) never went as far as I would've liked. It was enough to keep the house in one piece and pay for food, clothes, and my daughter's swimming lessons. That was about it.

"Is that her, Skye?" Debbie adjusted the thin strap on her red tank top for the tenth time. "Is she married?"

Debbie liked to dress sexy in her thin, low-cut tops and short-shorts. She was pretty—early thirties, with a round face, chocolate brown eyes, and thick, shoulder-length hair. She was shorter than me, but her plump curves were in all the right places.

I was tall, thin, and a little older. Not so many curves. My short blond hair was wild most of the time since it tended to curl. I used to put all kinds of gels and stuff on it to keep it in place when my husband was alive.

Now I was dead, and so was he. I didn't care so much anymore. My T-shirt and shorts were utilitarian—like the Beretta I carried in a lightweight shoulder holster. Whatever I needed to get the job done.

I looked down at the peaceful picture before us. A white-haired woman in jeans and a yellow T-shirt was coming out of the house. She was laughing and talking with an older man. They leaned together as they spoke, as couples do who have been together for many years.

They were headed toward an old pickup that needed a wash as bad as my van. Someone had even written 'wash me' in the dust on the side of the truck. Probably one of the kids.

"Abe never gives us that kind of information." I started the engine. "We're supposed to cajole, remind, and if necessary, drag his late workers back to the mortuary. He doesn't consider knowledge about their lives important."

Most of what should have been important to our job, Abe didn't consider necessary information. I'd worked as a police officer in Nashville for ten years. If they'd been so stingy with info, I wouldn't have made it that long. No one would.

But that's another story. Another lifetime.

"Here we go." Debbie took out the tranquilizer gun and inserted a dart into it. "I'm telling you. She's a runner."

Long hours of waiting for the people we were supposed to take back with us had developed this game. I'd worked for Abe by myself the first two years after I'd taken him up on his offer of another twenty years of life so I could raise my daughter.

Debbie had come onboard in the last year to save her husband's life. Some days it was better having her to talk to while I waited. Some days it wasn't.

The old white van rattled down the washboard gravel driveway. It effectively blocked the pickup from leaving unless it went airborne over the creek that surrounded the property.

"Put that away," I told her. "We're here to offer a ride to the mortuary, not threaten her."

Debbie shrugged. "They almost always run. We might as well take something with us for when it happens."

"That's not the way Abe wants it done. When it's your time, do you want someone to show you some respect or just shoot you down?"

She gently put the dart gun on the seat between us. "Okay. But I think Abe needs to work it into his contract that if his people want respect at the end of their twenty years, they shouldn't try to run us down, throw things at us, or any of the other things they do to keep from going back."

And to think she was so meek and mild when she first started. "You could stay in the van if that works better for you."

"Okay. I get your point. I'm sorry. I won't think about it that way." Debbie opened her door and stepped out into the slowly fading daylight.

The man and woman coming out of the house saw us. They kissed briefly and whispered a few quick words. I hoped that meant that she was coming with us quietly. Usually the people who had made plans for this day were the easy ones. They'd told the people around them what was going to happen. There might be some tears and anguish, but they accepted their fate, grateful for the extra time Abe had given them.

That's how I wanted to be. I had seventeen years left before my time was up. That was borrowed time that Abe had given me the night I'd died. I wouldn't be here if it wasn't for him and his offer. My daughter, Kate, would have been alone for the past three years, since she was five. I would've been in a cemetery resting quietly alongside my husband, Jacob, who'd died in the same wreck that had killed me.

"Good evening." I raised my voice, pleasantly, as I approached the couple. "Mrs. Jane Darcy? I'm Skye Mertz, and this is my partner, Debbie Hernandez. We're here to offer you a ride to Nashville. Abe sent for you. It's your time."

"Thank you." Mrs. Darcy had a very sweet smile. She looked about sixty, but that may have been her age at the time of her death. Abe's people didn't age.

I glanced at Debbie with a knowing look in my blue eyes. Mrs. Darcy was going to be fine. Sometimes winning that twenty dollars from her was easy pickings.

And sometimes not.

The man beside Jane Darcy pulled out an old shotgun. He fired a few rounds at me and Debbie. Not a great shot, but we hit the ground as Mrs. Darcy sprinted toward the back of the old house.

Mrs. Darcy had a plan in place for this day all right. I sighed. It just wasn't to accept what she'd been given and come along peacefully. Life was hard to give up.

Debbie laughed. "I told you. You can't go by where they live. As a matter of fact, it seems to me that the nicer the place, the faster they run."

"Yeah, well, you won the twenty. Now shut up and get the tranq gun. I'll handle Mr. Darcy."

She kept snickering as she sneaked back into the van and pulled out the gun. I got behind a large rock that had a holly bush growing out of it and took my Beretta 9mm revolver from its holster. This wasn't going to be pretty.

"What about your kids, Mr. Darcy?" I tried to talk him out of shooting his way through this. "I don't think you and your wife want them to see you this way."

"You don't care anything about us," he snapped back as he fired off another round. "If you care about our kids and grandkids, go away. Leave us alone. Forget you saw Jane here. We'll leave. You'll never see us again."

I could hear the quiver in his voice. He was wiping away tears by the time he'd finished his speech.

A moment later, I heard the high-pitched whine of a small horse power engine. I glanced around the holly bush and saw Jane taking off across the meadow behind their house on a four- wheeler. There were duffel bags, and a shot gun, strapped on the back.

It seemed they had a *really* good plan.

"There she goes," Debbie yelled out. "We can't catch her on foot."

"We can't catch her with the van either, not on this terrain. I have an idea."

I rushed at Jane's husband, firing the Beretta. As I'd thought, planning something and executing it are two different things. He fell apart as I shot at him, finally dropping to the dry ground and putting his hands over his head.

"Please," he whimpered. "Please let her stay with us. She didn't know what was going to happen when she signed that contract with the devil. Don't take her away."

"If we don't take her, someone else will. She can't stay after twenty years. Believe me, I've seen what happens. You don't want that either. She wouldn't be your wife anymore."

I snatched up the shotgun.

Debbie ran toward us as the shots stopped. I handed her the Beretta and took the tranq gun from her. "Watch him. I'm going to get her."

The keys were in the old pickup, as I'd thought. The van couldn't handle the rocks and uneven ground, but the pickup could. I started it up and took off after Jane.

I could still see the four-wheeler racing across the meadow. It was going to hit the bend in the stream—unless they'd thought of that in their escape plans too. She couldn't get across the deep ditch even though there was only a trickle of water running through it.

The pickup was faster than the four-wheeler. The rocks and ruts jarred my teeth, but it was only a few minutes until I was on her. I'd been right—the Darcys *had* thought of everything, including a small wood bridge across the stream. Jane waved and laughed because she knew the truck couldn't get across the bridge or through the deep ditch. I waved back because I knew something she didn't.

As she crossed the bridge, I revved the truck engine and forced the vehicle to jump the ditch. A tire flew off and rolled away on the passenger side when I landed, but the momentum from the jump kept the truck moving. Several pieces of the tailpipe dropped on the ground. I felt the back axle give way.

I didn't care. I pushed open the driver door and jumped out into the half-dead meadow grass, rolling until I got to my feet.

Jane's face was a mask of astonishment. She wouldn't have done what I did because she valued the old truck. That was my secret.

That, and I didn't have to worry about dying. She didn't either since she was technically already dead. Most of Abe's people just didn't get it.

I ran close to her as she tried to speed up after leaving the bridge. She couldn't quite reach the shot gun that was tied on the back. I aimed the tranq gun at her and fired a dart that hit her in the shoulder.

The four-wheeler rolled over as she lost control of it while trying to remove the dart. By that time, it was too late. She'd dropped off the vehicle as the fast-acting tranquilizer took effect. It crashed into an old elm tree as she rolled on the ground, almost asleep at my feet.

There were tears in her blue eyes as she stared pitifully up at me. "Why? Why couldn't you leave me alone?"

"I'm sorry. It has to be this way. You don't realize it, but you can't stay undead for more than the twenty years Abe gave you." I knelt beside her. "Be glad you didn't get away. You would've come back and killed everyone you cared about."

Chapter Two

The truck was scrap, but I got the four-wheeler running again. I called Debbie's cell phone and then tossed Jane's unconscious body across my lap as I left the meadow. The van was waiting on the road.

"That was rough." Debbie helped me with Jane. "Why do people run? They made the deal. They got the twenty years. They should honor it."

I made sure Jane was comfortable on the seat and that she wouldn't roll off. "They made the deal with Abe for the extra time in the first place. They didn't want to die. They don't want to leave now either. I hope I won't be the same when my time comes, but who knows?"

Abe gave us a bonus, besides our salary, for every person we brought home to him. It was less when we brought them in unconscious. It bothered him for us to use any kind of force. We bargained with them when we could—threatened or knocked them out when we had to. The job was hard when you understood how much each person was leaving behind.

But it had to be done. I'd seen the ghouls the LEPs became when their time was up. I hoped never to see one again.

It was dark by the time we'd reached Nashville. Jane was awake and bleakly staring out the window in the backseat. She hadn't tried to get away again. Debbie was listening to music with headphones—we'd had a few strong disagreements on music.

"Doesn't this ever get to you?" Jane asked as we passed the Welcome to Nashville sign.

"All the time, but it has to be done." I caught her eyes in the rearview mirror. "If it makes you feel any better, it'll happen to me one day too. I'm a zombie just like you."

"I'd tried to kill myself the day Abe saved me." She shook her head. "I'd just found out my husband of twenty-two years was cheating on me. He'd said he was leaving. My kids were grown. I wanted to die."

"At least you thought you wanted to die, right?"

"That's right. When you're lying there, and everything starts getting dim, you realize how precious life is. I would've done anything to take back what I'd done." She held her wrist scars up for my inspection. "That's why I agreed to work for Abe."

"What did you do for him?"

She shrugged. "I worked at a nuclear power station. I gave him reports. It wasn't much."

I wasn't surprised. The zombies—LEPs— came from all over and did a variety of jobs. Some of the workers made sense—accountants, stock brokers, lawyers, and police officers. Some of them, only he understood. I couldn't imagine why Abe needed someone who worked at a power station.

"What did you do before?" she asked. "How did you die?"

"I was a Nashville police officer. My husband and I died in a car wreck. He didn't make it long enough to be offered the deal. My little girl would've been left alone if I hadn't taken Abe's offer. Now I pick people up in my taxi for the dead when it's their time. Go figure." I stared at the lights of the city around us.

Most of the people Abe brought back worked at their past employment. I was almost the only one who didn't. I'd fought with him about it. He said he needed a resourceful driver to pick up his people, not another cop.

But what I did made me feel more like a bounty hunter. She lowered her gaze. "I'm sorry. I guess we only see our own problems."

"That's okay. I don't regret staying for her. I guess things got better for you when you came back."

"Yes. My husband has been faithful for the past twenty years. Our children have had grandchildren. Life has been sweet." She began sobbing quietly again.

"You've had your time. Someone else gets to have their twenty years now. It's fair."

Headlights flashed toward us, but not from the direction they should have been. A heavy, older vehicle was rushing toward us, no slowing down. I called out a warning to Debbie and our passenger just before the car T-boned the van.

Debbie squealed as she was pushed against the door. We were propelled sideways into a brick wall. The heavy van rocked once or twice before the engine died and steam started sputtering out from under the hood.

"What the hell?" A trickle of blood slid down from my forehead. There was a sharp pain in my wrist. The car backed up and the headlights came our way again.

I took out my Beretta.

"It's my husband," Jane yelled. "This was the second part of our plan in case I couldn't get away at the house. I'll stop him. He doesn't understand. Please don't hurt him."

She wasn't tied up. The seatbelt slipped from her quickly, and she scrambled out the back door.

"Yeah. Like I believe that." My seatbelt was stuck. It was one of the old kind that was just a lap belt. I cut it with the Swiss Army knife I always kept in my pocket, the material easily giving way.

My door was another thing. It was too crushed to open. "What are you gonna do?" Debbie asked as she stumbled into the backseat. Her door was pinned closed against the building. She couldn't get out that way. "You can't kill her."

Debbie and I got out the back door. Jane was making good on her promise to stop her husband. She stood between the van and his car, silhouetted in the bright headlights. Even though she was keeping the car from hitting the van again, that didn't mean her protection would last.

"The plan hasn't changed," I told Debbie. "We're still a few blocks away from the mortuary. We'll get her and walk."

But it appeared Jane had changed her mind. Once she convinced her husband not to slam his older Mercedes into the van again, she climbed into the car beside him, and they took off.

"She's gone," Debbie sighed. "How are we going to find her again in this traffic?"

"Call Abe and let him know there's been a snag." I spied a motorcycle parked on the side of the street close next to us. It took me a few minutes, but I hot-wired it and got behind Jane and her husband in the heavy mass of cars.

Despite their lead time, it was easy to catch them and keep up. Cars and trucks were bumper to bumper as police tried to clear an accident. I stayed with them, waiting for traffic to slow and stop as it reached the blue and red flashing lights ahead of us.

I impatiently wiped the blood still running down my face. This might be a messy pickup, but Abe better have a bonus waiting when I got Jane back to the mortuary.

Horns blew, impatience bringing out the worst in everyone. One good thing about a motorcycle was being able to weave in and out of traffic. I got up beside the Mercedes on the sidewalk. As soon as it stopped for the accident, I abandoned the motorcycle for a more direct approach.

Walking up to the side of the car, I shot out both tires on the passenger's side. They weren't going anywhere now.

Jane yelped when I opened the car door and pulled her out. "I understand why it's important for me to go back to Abe. I just can't convince my husband."

It was a weak excuse, but I could see the terror in her eyes. It ended up being a diversion as her husband got out of the Mercedes and stalked around to us with a pistol in his hand.

"Leave her alone. Let her go—or I swear I'll kill you."

I stared into his terrified eyes. "You can't kill me. I'm already dead, just like your wife. You have to let this happen. You don't have any choice."

He was desperate enough to shoot me. I didn't want him to do that even though I'd heal. It still hurt. I didn't want to shoot him either. And it wasn't only because I'd lose my bonus.

People were starting to notice what was happening even with the heavy traffic. It wasn't long before we heard sirens approaching.

"Good," he mocked me. "The police will sort this out. I don't think they'll believe that my wife is dead. But they'll believe that you attacked us without provocation."

I felt sorry for the Darcys. They had no idea what was going on and probably believed the police would get them out of this. But Abe had people everywhere. There was no going back to the life they'd known.

I holstered my weapon and raised my hands as the police officers swarmed over us. They took all of us to the nearest police station. We were separated, and I was detained in a small room by myself.

There were voices in the hall, and phones were ringing. They'd taken my cell phone so I amused myself by reading the scribbling on the walls for about thirty minutes. I knew it wouldn't be long before the right police officer—one of Abe's people—finally figured out what was going on.

The door opened, and a handsome young cop nodded to me. "You're free to go. Abe wants to see you right away."

"What about Jane Darcy?"

"That's already been taken care of."

Which meant no bonus for me and Debbie.

I walked into the hall, ready for this day to be over. Mr. Darcy was seated inside another small room with the door partially open. Jane wasn't with him. He was sobbing, his head bent forward.

What could I say that hadn't been said? I hated it, but he saw me.

"All we wanted was a few more months," he said. "Our youngest granddaughter is about to graduate from college. Jane just wanted to see her finish. Was that so much to ask?"

I had no answer to his sorrow or mine for that matter. I needed a drink, and I needed to see my daughter. I left him there without a word.

Chapter Three

I was surprised to see Debbie waiting outside the police station. The weather had turned, and heavy clouds hung over the mountains in the distance. No doubt people were praying for rain.

Sometimes I felt so far from the normal, everyday aspects of life that nothing seemed to mean anything. I didn't care if there was a drought or there was flooding. I didn't follow the Tennessee State Volunteers anymore. I got through Christmas for my daughter. It was as though part of me never came back to life at all.

I'd decided it was my heart, thinking about it through many long, sleepless nights. The organ was still beating in my chest, but it was empty of emotions. It was the twenty-first century. We all knew emotions came from some part of your brain. But it was my heart that felt dark and lifeless.

"Abe sent me back for you." She shrugged. "What are we gonna do about the van?"

"He'll have it fixed like he always does."

"Why doesn't he buy you a new one? I'm sure he could afford it. You know he must be rich after all these years."

We started walking up the sidewalk together toward Simon's Mortuary and Deadly Ink, Abe's tattoo shop next door. Traffic was still heavy. People rushed by us on the sidewalk with their heads down, destinations and plans for the evening in mind. Women clutched their bags, and men held their briefcases close to them.

"I don't speculate on Abe's finances," I told her. "As long as he pays me, I don't care. I suppose if the van is ever wrecked badly enough he'll get a new one or at least another used one."

"Yeah, but how are we supposed to get home?"

"He'll think of something. He always does. You gotta figure he's been at this for a long time. His first drivers must've had wagons and horses. Who knows what will come after us?"

Having a free moment, Debbie started her daily diatribe on what was happening with her husband. "So things have gotten even weirder with Terry. I'm not sure what to do."

She'd agreed to take on the twenty-year service for Terry, a cop, after he'd been shot and killed at a convenience store robbery. Debbie was the only LEP that I knew of that had done such a thing.

Abe had visions of them being together—we all knew it. Debbie was devoted to her husband and two children. I didn't see them having a relationship any time soon. Still Abe courted her in his weird way. I was glad I didn't have to face that problem.

But again, like Abe's magic affected his dead workers after twenty years, something unusual had begun happening with Debbie's husband too.

"He won't eat anything but raw meat now," she continued. "It has to be really bloody too. I had to start going to a friend of ours who hunts. The meat in the store was too clean and old for him. What do you think of that?"

Considering the last time I'd seen Terry, his legs had become shorter and covered in thick hair, I didn't know what to say. He was going through some sort of transformation—into what I wasn't sure. I knew Debbie was frightened by it, but it was beyond my understanding. It wasn't like I was knowledgeable about supernatural happenings before this. I'd been learning about things as I went along.

"How is he doing with the kids?" I asked. Debbie had a daughter, Raina, who was eight like my daughter, Kate. She also had a teenage son, Bowman, who was fourteen.

"They don't seem to notice what's going on with him," she said. "Bowman doesn't want anything to do with him anymore. I think it's because he's so disappointed about Terry quitting the highway patrol. Bowman still wants to be a cop, too, even though his father was shot and killed—not that I would ever tell him about that."

I knew Terry had decided to take disability. It didn't look as though he would ever walk again, at least not in the normal sense. I'd seen him get up from the wheelchair. He *could* walk, but I didn't think he'd be able to wear a uniform—not with legs like a goat.

"And the bottom half of him, Skye." She shook her head. "He looks like an animal from the waist down. I'm not kidding. Do you think it's permanent?"

"I don't know. But we didn't get Jane Darcy to the mortuary. I'm sure Abe has something to say about that—and we won't get our bonuses."

"I know." She frowned as she scuffed her sandal along the hot sidewalk. "I was planning on taking the kids to the waterpark next week with that money."

We'd reached Deadly Ink. A few of Abe's rowdy crowd of zombies jostled us as they left. The building was one of those older ones that made you wonder what was holding it up. The old red bricks looked as though they'd been there hundreds of years trying to survive the wind, rain, and sun.

Abe lived on the top floor of the three-story building. I'd never gone up that far. He was very private about his personal life. I didn't want to know that much about him anyway.

He was a frightening man.

They said he was born in 1863 when his mother named him for President Lincoln after the Emancipation Proclamation. He'd fallen in love with a witch who'd killed him and made him her slave. The story went on to say how he'd killed the witch and began his own zombie army.

He'd never acknowledged that any of it was true—at least not to me. And he wasn't a man I wanted to have that conversation with.

His past was his, as far as I was concerned. I wasn't interested in his mythology. I was only here for Kate.

The tattoo shop was busy, as it always was. Abe had a keen interest in tattoos even though he didn't have any ink that I'd ever seen.

On the night I'd died, a pale blue tattoo that looked like an A inside a circle, was put on my heel. All of the LEPs had them. It seemed like a possessive thing to me, although people said it was just Abe's magic that was part of keeping us alive.

But come on—an A when his name was Abe? I thought it was more that he wanted us to know that he owned us.

We had an instinct for finding each other too, Abe's people. Maybe that was part of the magic too. I could look across the room and easily pick up on who was living and who was dead. To me the dead had a kind of blue glow about them.

Abe kept a dozen or so young, tough guys around the tattoo shop. What were their jobs? I could only imagine where they went and what they did when they left Deadly Ink in groups with small handguns tucked into their waistbands.

But I kept my imagination on a short leash. It was none of my business.

"He's waiting to see you." The new head tough guy sat on a tall stool behind the counter, scrolling through his phone. He jerked his head toward the back office—like we didn't know where to find Abe. I ignored him.

Debbie gave him her new killer look and then turned to me nervously. "Should I go in with you? I already saw him. He just told me to get you."

"You're involved too," I reminded her, admiring a full-torso tattoo of a gold dragon on a man's chest. The color was wonderful. Even though the image wasn't finished, it was still incredible.

"Okay. But I have to get home soon."

"Me too. Let's hope what he has to say doesn't take too long."

I understood Debbie's reluctance to face Abe. Besides being a scary person, he'd made it clear that he wanted her in his bed. I tried to stay out of that issue and focus on our jobs. That other part was between him and her. They were both consenting adults.

If we were going to be taken down a notch or two for the botched attempt to bring Jane Darcy in, I wanted Debbie there too. She'd been my partner long enough to claim bonuses when things worked out. She'd also been there long enough to listen to Abe tell us what a bad job we did on a day like today.

His door was open. He was sitting behind his big desk, staring at his cell phone. Like many other people, he was obsessed with it. He changed brands frequently but always kept the old phones going too. Maybe he was afraid one of them would stop working.

He looked up as we walked in, hastily donning his usual sunglasses. Unlike the rest of us who looked like normal, living people, Abe had no pupils or irises. His eyes were white and empty. I wasn't sure if he wore the sunglasses to attempt to look normal or if he was embarrassed and didn't want us to ask a lot of questions. He didn't have to worry about me.

"Ladies. Please take a seat." He gestured toward the two, older leather chairs in front of his desk. Abe rarely raised his voice or seemed to get upset about anything. He sat back in his chair with his fingers in a pyramid in front of his face. Of course there had been the time Abe was so upset with me that he lifted me straight off the floor with one hand. And the time I'd seen him kill a man with the same calm demeanor. Abe's still waters ran deeper than most, but that was to be expected after being alive for more than a hundred and fifty years.

"Close the door, Skye. We don't need an audience."

Debbie squirmed in her seat, pouting like a child who knew they'd done wrong. "It wasn't our fault," she blurted. "They had it all set up. We did the best we could."

"I'm sure you did." Abe's teeth were very white against his shiny black skin. "Nevertheless, the absence of your bonus will speak louder than my words."

I closed the door and took my seat. I'd worked for him long enough to know that there was more going on than a botched pickup. There had been many LEPs I couldn't bring back. He was right. The worst that had ever happened was that I didn't get a bonus.

"What's going on?" I asked, almost belligerently. "No one died. You don't call me in for making a mess."

"The van was wrecked," Debbie reminded him. "Is that why we're here?"

"That is being seen to. I'll let you know when it's ready." He sat forward, the scent of cloves and other spices wafting across from him. "Something else is amiss that I hope you ladies will be able to help me with, especially you, Skye, though I imagine it will be good for Debbie to learn something of what you know as well."

"Okay. So, what's up?" I realized at that moment why it's police procedure to have a suspect remove their sunglasses, hats, and other things that people hide behind. It was hard to know if I was getting a straight answer from him.

Of course with no expression in his ghastly white eyes, would that even matter?

Debbie glanced anxiously at her watch. "Look at the time. I have to go soon—the kids you know."

Abe surged to his feet. He was a big man, well over six feet. His arms and chest were formidable. He didn't move lightly—more like a mountain—covered in skin like shiny black rubber.

I admit I sat back in my chair. I try to keep my distance, maintain an air of cool nonchalance. But inside, he terrifies me.

Whatever was wrong was a *big* deal for him. Debbie grabbed my arm, even more afraid than me.

Before either of us could pee our pants, one of Abe's tough guys knocked at the door and barged inside. "People are starting to ask questions about the dead magician in the alley, Abe. No one else has seen him, but they keep walking out there. What do you want us to do?"

Chapter Four

"Harold the Great is dead?" I was surprised to hear it, even though I'd seen Abe's last magic user killed right in my own backyard. I'd thought Jasper's death was a fluke and that magic users were tougher than that.

Abe's threatening posture relaxed. "That's right. I was about to explain the situation to you when Debbie reminded me of her *other* obligations besides the one she owes me."

All eyes turned to Debbie whose face had gone white. "That's okay. I can do whatever you need me to. Terry is home with the kids."

I thought Abe might spout some rhetoric about how Terry wouldn't be home with the kids at all if it wasn't for his intervention, but he only grunted and moved to the door.

It may not sound like Abe was romantically interested in Debbie, but she'd snubbed him last year, and his new scheme to win her seemed to be ignoring and badgering her. Not much of a plan. But since she had nowhere to go, it could still work. Abe was a powerful figure who held her life and death in his huge hands. That could get to her eventually.

Debbie and I followed him and his heavily tattooed assistant, Morris, out of the office. Morris was a tough-guy wannabe who didn't quite measure up. He was kind of small and thin with a crippled leg, but he had awesome tattoos across every spare scrap of his skin.

"I didn't mean to get him all riled up," Debbie whispered to me. "You never know with him. I don't know how you can joke with him, Skye."

"What's the worst he can do? I'm already dead." I shrugged and put my hands in my pockets.

"Yeah. I guess." She bit her lip and was silent as we walked back through the tattoo shop.

The crowd there parted for Abe like he was Moses. Eyes turned away. No one spoke. Even if you didn't know the true purpose of the shop and Abe's power, he was a figure to reckon with. I can't imagine anyone wanting to take him on. Surely if someone had murdered Harold, that person had no idea who the magician actually worked for.

Or he was crazy.

We went into the dark alley together. Someone had put up a few lines of limp crime scene tape that fluttered in the breeze. I could see from the lights on the buildings beside us that the Harold's body had been covered with a blue tarp. There was no sign that the police had been called—they would certainly not have left the body behind for Abe to show us.

"I want to know who murdered Harold."

"Have you called the police?" I was still a little raw, even after almost three years, about him not wanting me to take back my old job when he resurrected me. I suppose I was holding a grudge. I had loved being a cop, and I'd been good at it.

Abe's large head swiveled in my direction as his assistant turned on a spotlight that illuminated the area in the alley. "I don't want the police involved. This was not a normal murder. There was magic, *dark* magic, responsible for Harold's death."

Knowing that Harold was really Harold the Great, a stage magician that I'd once hired for my daughter's birthday party, I was less inclined to agree about the magic part. I'd been surprised when he'd gone to work for Abe and wondered how long he could pretend to be a powerful magic user.

"What makes you think there was magic involved?" I asked in a snarky tone. "I've seen a lot of murders that seemed to have no rational explanation, but good police investigation always found the truth."

"Skye—" Debbie whispered as she clutched my arm.

"You want to see the truth?" Abe grinned. "Morris—lift the tarp."

Morris grinned too. That made me more certain that I should have kept my mouth closed.

The blue tarp was flipped over, and the strong light played on the victim. Harold was dressed in ordinary street clothes, not his performance robe with stars on it and a pointy hat. Otherwise there was nothing ordinary about his death.

Snakes were crawling over him—a few had lodged themselves in his mouth and throat, clogging his nostrils, and coming out of his eyes and ears. They hissed at us but didn't move away from Harold's body. Dozens of them were twined around his legs and arms. One seemed to be in a death embrace around his chest, probably crushing his ribs.

"Oh my God!" Debbie's hands became talons on my arm. "Oh my God—who could do such a thing?"

Abe had Morris replace the tarp as he turned to us. "I'm hoping you two can come up with answers. Skye has ten years of experience dealing with solving crime, although perhaps this one is a little...closer to home."

I knew right away what he meant. "Lucas didn't kill him. He only killed Jasper because that idiot came to our house to kill *him*. What was he supposed to do—stand there and let him cut off his head?"

It had been an unfortunate situation. Abe's magic user claimed to know Lucas, a sorcerer with amnesia who I'd met by chance in Nashville. He'd followed me home, and I let him stay, not realizing that there was bad blood between them—or that Jasper would come to my home.

"Lucas killed my necromancer," Abe said. "Why should I be surprised if he killed my new magic user?"

"Lucas doesn't just go around killing necromancers, magicians, or other sorcerers. He hasn't killed anyone in a year. There's no reason to suspect that he had some part in this."

Abe chuckled in a way that made my skin crawl. "Perhaps he's changed his mind about working for me after a long year of cleaning your house and doing landscaping. He may miss his former life."

"We have no proof that Jasper was right about who Lucas is. He doesn't even do magic, and if he wasn't happy working around the inn, I'm sure he'd find something else to do."

"That is exactly why I believe you're perfect for this assignment, Skye. I suggest you question Lucas first as a suspect. Don't worry. I won't harm him. Quite the contrary. If he killed Harold, I have a place for him."

"But no police?" I asked.

He shrugged. "No police. Better for you and Lucas, I think. And better for me. Brandon will do the autopsy. Show Debbie how to do what you do. Report back to me as soon as you learn anything. That's all."

He told Morris to have Harold's body moved to the mortuary when Debbie and I were finished examining the scene.

"What are we supposed to do?" Debbie whispered with a quick backward glance at Morris who stood there smiling.

"Let's take a look around the area and see what we can find." An audience didn't bother me. I'd been working hard at becoming a homicide detective before my untimely demise. I was used to people staring at me from a crowd.

The alley seemed barren of anything that could tell us what had happened. There were no cameras on either building beside us. Debbie and I combed carefully through the debris along the edges of the cracked and dirty pavement. A few trashcans had been knocked over, but they weren't close enough to Harold's body to think they were significant.

"If this was done by dark magic," Debbie reminded me. "How can anything we find out here make a difference? We're wasting our time. You should go home and talk to Lucas. Even if he didn't kill Harold, he might have some ideas."

Even if? "He didn't kill Harold. He hasn't even been around the mortuary or Deadly Ink for months."

"But since it was done with magic—would he have to be right here to do it?"

"We're not going down that road. Lucas didn't kill Harold. He made it very clear last year that he didn't want to work for Abe. He thinks he's evil and would like me to stop working for him too."

"Really? He knows you're dead, right? What does he think would happen if you stopped working for Abe?"

"I don't know. He says he wants to remember who he is so he can save me from Abe."

As we spoke, I caught a hint of gold glitter on the ground. When I reached down for it, it was a partially smoked cigarette. There were several others close to it, as though the smoker had stood here for a while. Maybe waiting for Harold.

"See if you can find a plastic bag in the shop, will you?" I asked Debbie.

"What did you find?" She glanced into my hand. "*Eww.* Old cigarette butts? That's nasty."

"Just get a bag, will you?"

While she went for the plastic bag, I shuffled through other debris—a few drink cups from the local coffee house, and a wrapper from a bagel. Probably from the same place, though there wasn't a bag.

"I found some napkins too." Debbie handed them to me without touching my hand. "You'd better put those away and go inside for some hand sanitizer. Why do you think the cigarette butts are important?"

I used some of the napkins to separate the butts from the cup and wrapper. It wouldn't work for police procedure, but my evidence didn't have to be admissible in court. It was enough to give us a place to start that had nothing to do with magic snakes.

"Find anything?" Brandon asked from the other side of the crime scene tape. "I thought I'd have the body to work on by now."

In the pale light, he looked more like a movie-style zombie than any of the rest of us. His skin was so pale as to be almost transparent. He was as light as Abe was dark. When I'd first met him, I thought he was a teenager—short, thin, with the narrow build of a much younger man.

He didn't look his forty-two years, sixty-one if you counted the time he was dead as well. He was another LEP like me. Abe had taken him from being a murdered stockbroker and made him his morgue attendant.

"You know there are snakes all over, inside and outside this man, right?" Debbie asked with a toss of her dark brown hair.

Brandon rubbed his hands together and smiled. "I know. I can't wait to get started."

"But how are you going to—?" Debbie shuddered. "Never mind. I don't want to know."

"So he's ready to go?" Morris asked.

"Yeah." I put the plastic bag in my pocket. "I'm not looking any closer at Harold the Great until the snakes are gone. See you later, Brandon."

Chapter Five

We picked up an older green Ford Festiva from one of Abe's workers to use until the van was repaired. It ran like a thirty-year-old car and had bald tires. But it would have to do. I hoped we wouldn't have any pickups before the van was back.

I dropped Debbie off at her house. It was dark, but a welcoming porch light was shining. Her cabin was pretty, like one of those they use in the travel brochures. Debbie and Terry had kept it well-maintained. There were colorful flowers on the front overhanging porch, and the grass was green and manicured.

Debbie's kids, Raina and Bowman, always had some sports equipment outside that just seemed to add the right touch. It said a family lived here.

"Are you sure you won't come in for a minute?" Debbie asked as she got her umbrella and handbag.

I knew she wanted me to talk to Terry and figure out what was wrong with him. Sometimes I tried to help her out when he went through another change. Tonight, I was just too tired. We both knew there was something really wrong with him, but it wasn't something a doctor could fix. I didn't want to see it any more than I wanted to look at Harold's dead body.

"You know, it's late, and I'm really beat. Kate and Addie will be waiting for me."

"Are you going to ask Lucas about killing Harold?"

"Not if you mean ask him if he killed Harold. I might ask him what he thinks about someone being killed with magic snakes. He's been getting some of his memory back. It's slow, and when he does magic, it's in random spurts, like the way he killed Jasper. He didn't kill Harold."

She smiled at me, the dash light picking out glints from the diamond chip earrings she got for Christmas from Terry. "Don't be stubborn about this, Skye. I know you care about Lucas, but you owe Abe your life."

"I know." I smiled half-heartedly. "It's hard to forget that. See you tomorrow, Debbie."

I kept my foot on the gas to keep the engine running so the headlights would illuminate the path between the driveway and the porch. Bowman waved to me when he opened the front door for his mother. I waved back and then left the house.

It was getting harder for Debbie to go home each day. I knew it was because she never knew what she was going to find. One night, Terry was completely naked, running through the front yard. One night, the kids were scared of him because he'd killed a rabbit on the kitchen table. I knew she was holding on to the mess her life had become since her perfect world had ended when Terry was killed.

The back roads outside Nashville between my house and Debbie's were dark, narrow, curving country roads. The best thing I could say about them was that they were usually empty. Over the summer there was more traffic from tourists, but it also stayed light later.

Despite the lateness of the hour, I took a turn I usually avoided going home. It took me past the spot where Jacob and I had died. It had been three years, but that night would always be like yesterday in my mind.

We were coming home after a late dinner. It was dark, and the roads were empty. Jacob and I were full of plans for the future. We were happy and hopeful.

A truck was coming from the opposite direction on the narrow, winding road. The bright lights flashed into our eyes, alerting us to the danger—too late—it was in our lane.

Jacob took evasive action and swerved off the road. Our SUV bumped and bounced over rocks and small trees into the thick woods surrounding us.

I know I passed out for a few minutes. When I woke up, Jacob was getting ready to walk back to the road and find help. Our cell phones had no service, and the truck driver hadn't stopped.

He was slightly injured but nothing serious, at least to my admittedly dazed eyes. He promised he'd come back for me as soon as he could. I think I lost consciousness again. When I woke, he still wasn't back.

The police finally found me, and I was rushed to the hospital, fighting for my life.

Addie, Jacob's mother, and the doctor tried to persuade me not to look at his body, but I couldn't stay away. I didn't care if that was the shock that killed me. I had to see him to believe it was real.

He was mangled almost beyond recognition, torn to pieces, his handsome face shredded. There was no way his injuries had happened in the wreck. But though I protested and demanded an investigation, nothing happened. At that point, I'd died, and I had my own realities to deal with. I'd put Jacob's death behind me—as Abe had insisted I should. But I never forgot.

I mostly avoided the spot where we'd both died that night. It was a shortcut we'd liked to take going home. The sharp curve always re-played our last conversation in my mind. I could still see his smiling face the instant before he said he was going for help.

But it was different tonight. There were several highway patrol cars, an ambulance, and a few firefighters at the same spot where we'd had our wreck.

Addie was going to pitch a fit that I was home so late, but I couldn't stop myself from slowing down and parking on the side of the road with the emergency vehicles.

Someone was directing traffic. Flares had been set on the road to make sure no one came down the right hand side. I could see from the temporary lighting that another vehicle had gone off the road here. Small trees had been smashed to the ground and underbrush flattened.

Curious, I followed the tracks of men and machines until I came to the spot that could have been where our wreck took place. A body was being taken from a bright red pickup truck. It was already covered with a white sheet. Emergency workers were taking out a body bag.

"Can I help you?" A tall, husky highway patrolman stopped me. His badge said *Rusk*. He'd removed his flat brimmed hat. There was a spot of blood on his uniform.

"I'm sorry. I know I shouldn't be here. It's just that—"

His forehead wrinkled. "Wait. I know you."

I could see he was groping for my name. I remembered his. Tim Rusk. "Skye Mertz. I used to be a Nashville police officer. My husband and I—"

"You were involved in another accident here a few years back." His eyes widened. "I remember you and your husband. You were both NPD, right? That was a terrible shame. I'm so sorry."

Looking at his open, broad face, I realized that we had worked together before that awful night. "We worked on a project before that...to reduce wrecks in the city, wasn't it?"

"That's right! It was a few years before." He smiled kindly and held out his hand. "I'm glad we're meeting again even if this is a bad place for it. I've thought about you and your husband many times since then. I think you were unconscious when we pulled you from the wreck. You probably don't even recall me being here. Why did you stop tonight, Skye?"

"We've got another one out here," a voice called from out of the closely wooded area that surrounded us. "Jesus! What a mess. How could he have been thrown this far from the vehicle?"

Tim zeroed in on the voice in the darkness. "I gotta go. You shouldn't be here."

I looked toward the voice as other emergency workers ran into the woods. Was it the same story?

Too far to be thrown from the wreck. Never seen anything like it. Horribly mauled.

"I know." I kept the tears at bay by biting my lip. "I'm leaving. Thanks for talking with me."

He shook my hand and then joined the rest of the workers.

I walked back to my car feeling cold and numb in a way that had nothing to do with being a zombie. Something was happening out here in the dark woods. How common was it? Was the story always the same?

I waited in the car until I saw Tim leaving an hour after the rest of the emergency services people. It was close to two a.m. when I approached him. I think I startled him when I called his name.

"You still here?" He shone a flashlight in my face. "This won't help you, Skye. You know that."

I put my hands in my pockets. "I know. How long until you're off duty? I'd like to buy you a beer."

He frowned. "And pick my brain?"

"Yeah. I know an all-night place right down the hill. I'm buying."

"Okay. I've already been off duty a few hours. You know how it is."

"I do. See you there."

I got the car started after a few tries. It chugged to life and finally went down the hill to the tiny tavern where Jacob and I had met sometimes. There were two pickup trucks in front. I parked near them, and Tim parked beside me.

We went inside the dark drinking hole together. The two men at the bar glanced our way for a moment and then turned back to their beer.

"Always glad to have a lawman come in for a drink." The slight bartender who owned the place—Matt—put two coasters on the table in front of us. "Whatcha havin'?"

"I'll have a Bud and whatever the lady is having." He nodded to me.

"I'll have the same and the check. I'm buying, remember?" I smiled at the bartender. "Hi, Matt. How are you?"

"I know you," he said. "You used to come in with that other fella. Where's he tonight?" He meant Jacob. I'd never come here with anyone else.

"He couldn't be here," I said, not going into it.

"I'll get those beers."

"What do you want, Skye?" Tim put his coaster over a wet spot on the wood table. "I know when someone is looking for information."

"I'm not with Nashville PD anymore. Not since my husband died. I'm sure you can imagine what I want to know after seeing the wreck in the same spot as ours."

"That's what I thought." He gazed directly into my face. "I don't know what to tell you. There are frequent wrecks in the area. There's a blind spot coming around that curve. Sometimes people drift into the other lane. It happens."

"But does it always happen that one of the passengers in the vehicle is thrown from it, found impossibly far away from the vehicle, and mangled like Jacob was?"

The bartender put our beers on the table and left us.

Tim took a large gulp of his. "There's a pattern of it happening here, yes, Skye. I'm sure you know it already, right?"

Chapter Six

My heart beat a little faster—yes—my heart still beats.

I took a big swallow of beer to cover my excitement at the possibility that I'd found someone who could help me figure out what had really happened to Jacob. I wasn't supposed to do this, but Abe didn't own all of me. I wanted to know what happened that night.

"You're right," I agreed. "I know there have been other accidents. It happened tonight too, didn't it?"

Tim ran his hand across his worn face. "Yes. I've brought it up at several staff meetings. We all know about the blind spot in the road. The Tennessee Department of Highways is looking into doing something about it, but you know how long that takes."

"I do. What I don't understand is the other part." I leaned across the table and whispered, "My husband wasn't dead or even badly injured when he left me to get help. When I saw his body at the morgue, someone or some*thing*, had ravaged him."

He sniffed and took another drink of beer, his eyes blank. "I've read your statement. Hell, I've read a dozen statements like it from survivors. None of them impressed me like yours. The rest I could chalk up to pain and hallucination from the trauma—you know how people get when something happens to them. But you were a cop. You were trained to notice things. I still have a copy of your statement from that night."

My pulse ratcheted up a few more notches. After three years of sniffing along the edges of this, was I finally getting somewhere?

"Thanks."

"There was one other survivor from a previous wreck who told almost the same account that you did. I respected his story, too, since he'd just come back from Iraq. The man had seen action. He'd seen people blown to pieces. His statement was like yours, only it was his wife that was dead. He said she was taken from their pickup by something fast and strong. The passenger side door was ripped clean off its hinges. Craziest thing I ever saw since there was no other damage to that side of the vehicle."

Both our voices were hushed in the nearly empty bar with the streetlight shining through the dirty window beside us. One of the two men at the bar said goodnight and left. Otherwise the silence was only broken by the *swish-swish* sound of the bartender's mop on the tile floor.

"Who is he?" I tried not to sound desperate.

"I'll give you his name and address if you promise to tell me what you find. I've gone as far as I can with conventional methods. My superiors don't want to hear that something weird is happening out there in the woods, you know?"

"I can imagine. No problem. Give me your contact info, and I'll let you know what I find."

He wrote a name and address on a card from his pocket and handed it to me. "Is this why you quit NPD? They wouldn't let you look into your husband's death?"

"That was kind of it." I put the card in my pocket. "I couldn't keep doing the job."

"I hear you." He finished his beer. "Where are you working now? Do you have a way for me to reach you?"

I didn't have a card that said *Taxi for the Dead Driver and Zombie Bounty Hunter*, but I wrote my cell phone number and email on a napkin for him. "This means a lot to me. I know people thought I was crazy when I said my husband had been attacked after the wreck. No one would listen. I have a few newspaper clippings from some of the other incidents at that spot in the last three years. You've given me hope, Tim. I can't thank you enough."

We left the tavern together, and I shook his hand. I was thrilled to finally meet someone else with the same ideas.

Even though I'd kept it hidden from Abe, finding Jacob's killer was one of the things that kept me going. I was here to see my daughter into adulthood and figure out what had killed my husband. That was it. If I could accomplish those two things in the time I had, someone could pick me up and take me back to Abe when my time was up. I wouldn't complain.

I drove into the small community where I grew up. Wanderer's Lake, Tennessee, population 3,500 on a good day. It was a tiny spot on the map, picturesque in any season and likely not to become a large city because it was hard to get to. It was built around a pretty lake with barely a two-lane road going in and out of town. The main road could never be expanded unless they put a bridge over the lake.

That had kept many things the same as they had been when Jacob and I had grown up here and met in high school. It was comforting to know that some things didn't change, especially when the rest of the world around me became so different.

Five years ago, no one could have convinced me that there were sorcerers, ghosts, and undead people in the world. Those were things from movies and books. They didn't really happen. I knew better now.

Wanderer's Lake was a quiet place where everything closed by six p.m. during the week and eight p.m. on the weekends. There was bingo at the recreation center on Saturday nights and singing in the town square at Christmas. Houses were quiet, and there was no traffic as I crept through the dark streets toward Apple Betty's Inn. Jacob's parents had run the bed and breakfast for more than sixty years. It had been a popular vacation spot until Jacob's mother, Addie, had passed three years ago, just a few months after Jacob and me.

Her impending death from cancer had been one of my deciding factors in accepting Abe's proposal. Kate would have been completely alone in the world, as I had been growing up, in and out of foster homes, subject to the whims of people who didn't know or love her. I'd been determined not to let that happen.

Of course if I'd known Addie was going to come back the next day as a know-it-all ghost, I might have reconsidered.

New gravel scrunched under the wheels of the Festiva. There was also a fresh coat of white paint on the three-story inn. The newly replaced lights on the building picked out all the details of a well-cared-for-house and yard. You could actually see the base of the inn where the old bushes had been trimmed back. Lucas had brought it back to its former glory since he'd come to live with us.

Addie, my dead mother-in-law, was pleased with it—but not with me as I walked through the back door. A ghost makes a good babysitter but not always a pleasant companion. Addie and I didn't get along when Jacob was alive. Even though it was her idea for me to sign the contract with Abe, it hadn't made us any closer.

"I can't believe you're dragging in here at this time of the morning," she raged as soon as the back door was closed. "Why not just stay out all night? You're not worried about your daughter."

I removed my shoes and left them in the mud room, a habit even when it wasn't raining or snowing. "I was busy. Things went bad with my pick up. I did the best I could. Is everything okay?"

Her ghostly form wavered a little, but she had much better control now. She could lift almost anything and even ventured outside the inn sometimes to watch Lucas work.

"Everything is *not* okay when I have to tuck Kate in at night with her asking for you. You're supposed to be here for her. And don't give me that stuff about work. You decide that, my girl."

I didn't like to argue with her. Sometimes it was all I could do *not* to argue with her. I had learned to grit my teeth and keep it to myself. She'd always believed I wasn't good enough for her son and criticized my parenting skills, even while Jacob was alive. She was a tough old bird in life. Death hadn't softened her. But I didn't know what I would've done without her watching over the one thing we had in common—Kate.

"Was there a problem?" I walked carefully around her. I'd walked through her before. It wasn't pleasant. "If not, I'm tired, and I'm going upstairs."

"There wasn't a problem because Lucas was here to get notebook paper tonight at the store. Kate needed it for school tomorrow. If we'd waited for you, she'd be writing on her hand. You couldn't even bother to call and check in to see if we needed anything."

"Lucas has a car?"

"He fixed up the old truck that's been sitting in the back for the last ten years. He spent some time and a few dollars on it for this kind of emergency." She sighed. "Sometimes he reminds me of Jacob—even if he is a sorcerer or whatever. He was down on his hands and knees today scrubbing the tile in the bathrooms. That man isn't afraid to do anything that needs to be done around here."

"And to think you thought it was horrible that I brought him home." *Guess you're not right about everything, are you?*

"He's very handy and a hard worker, I'll give him that." Her already prim mouth became a thin line in her face that had lost so much of its transparency. "It's still wrong for you to sleep in his bed.

I picked up the mail from the side table. "I wish he had a credit card so he could pay some of the bills too."

"At least he's interested in the inn. We could reopen this place and make some extra money with his help. You should at least consider it, Skye. I still get letters and cards from people who want to book a reservation."

"Yeah. A ghost, a sorcerer, and a dead girl run a bed and breakfast. Sounds like the beginning of a bad joke."

"I still think you should consider it. I'd do it myself if I could."

"I'm thinking. Goodnight, Addie."

I jogged up the stairs to the second floor. Even though it was late, I had to see Kate. I quietly pushed open the door to her dark room and watched her sleep for a few minutes. She was growing up smart and strong. Not only did she get straight A's in school, she questioned everything and kept at it until she had the answer.

She was like Jacob that way and looked more like him than me too. Soft brown/blond hair. Big, soulful brown eyes. She had my nose though and my stubbornness. Sometimes that was all I could see of me, but it was enough to see so much of her father in her.

Curiosity and stubborn refusal to look the other way was why she knew everything that was going on now. I hadn't planned to tell her about my deal with Abe until she was older—at least fifteen or sixteen. Not eight. I wanted her to be prepared for the day I had to leave. She was still too young to deal with having a ghost for a grandmother and understanding that her mother was on borrowed time.

But she knew the truth, and she'd coped with it. She'd asked a few questions like why Jacob wasn't working for Abe too or why he wasn't a ghost like Addie, and that was it. I hoped she wouldn't need therapy someday because of her weird upbringing, but at least we were weird people who loved her.

I kissed her cheek before I left her. Jacob would be so proud of her. She wanted to be a forensic investigator when she grew up. She'd be safe in that field and still part of law enforcement as Jacob and I had been. I couldn't believe she even knew what that was at her age.

The light was still on upstairs. Lucas slept in the turret room on the third floor. He'd kind of taken it over since he first arrived. None of us had ever even gone up there after Addie's death, even though it had been the most popular room at the inn when it was open for tourists.

I slowly walked up the stairs. I wasn't much of a housekeeper, but Lucas never let the upstairs get full of cobwebs and dust as it had been when he'd arrived. It was no wonder Addie approved of him.

"You're late." He was sitting in front of the big stone fireplace in the turret room. Even though it was summer, Lucas was usually cold and had a fire burning up here.

Something common for sorcerers? I would probably never know.

The room was large and five-sided, with a smooth-as-satin wood floor and three tall windows overlooking the street. It was spotlessly clean and smelled of lemon oil and incense. The big wrought iron bed was plumped up and covered in clean sheets and a red velvet comforter. There was a red Persian carpet on the floor that looked old and valuable.

Lucas had brought the carpet with him from wherever he was from. Sometimes I wondered if it was a magic carpet, but those were only times when I'd had too much to drink.

There was a large, claw foot tub in one corner of the room. Candles were lit on every flat surface, like always. I wasn't sure where those came from unless he also made candles between his other chores around the inn.

It wouldn't have surprised me.

"Was there difficulty at your employment?"

Lucas had been trying hard to fit in. He'd looked and sounded like a Ren Faire character when I'd found him in Nashville. He'd learned contractions, and he'd taken over the maintenance of the inn and grounds. He'd also become our cook, dishwasher, and the one who washed and dried our clothes.

I hadn't asked him to take over those responsibilities. He was the kind of person who just saw what needed to be done and did it.

He wore Jacob's old clothes, mostly jeans on his long legs and T-shirts on his lean muscular chest. Lucas claimed that he couldn't remember anything about his past. His use of magic was limited, perhaps because of it.

It was possible he was a murderer, as Abe had accused, and one of the most feared sorcerers in history, as I'd read online about a man with his name, Lucas Trevailer. Maybe he was a French sorcerer that had vanished from 1312, ending his reign of terror—brought forward in time for some nefarious purpose.

But as yet, he hadn't done anything that wasn't good for me, Addie, and Kate. That was all I cared about.

I sat in the big, comfortable velvet chair he'd claimed as his own from the attic. "Besides a complicated runner situation that wrecked my van, Abe's new magic user was killed in the alley outside Deadly Ink."

He poked the roaring fire again before sitting closer to me. "I suppose Abe suspects me."

"You killed his last magic user, necromancer, or whatever you want to call him."

"But you explained that I had no choice in the matter since Jasper had wanted to kill me."

"For the tenth time, yes." I tried not to watch his face for signs that he was lying to me. It was an old professional habit. Maybe I wouldn't even be able to tell if a sorcerer was telling the truth. There was a lot about magic, and Lucas, that I didn't understand. "I don't think he believes me. Even worse, he still thinks you want to work for him."

Lucas got to his feet, tall and lithe. His black hair gleamed in the firelight, much shorter than it had been when he'd first arrived. His unusual green eyes—the color of jade—stared into my face. "And you, Skye. What do you believe?"

"I don't think you killed Harold the Great, but his death was from dark magic, according to Abe."

"He should know since his life swims in it." Lucas removed the blue robe he wore and slid, naked, into bed. "But tell me, what does he qualify as black magic?"

I pulled up the picture I'd taken of Harold in the alley. "This. I was skeptical at first, but I don't see any way a normal killer did this, do you?"

He still handled the cell phone as though it was made of crystal, carefully keeping his fingers on the edge of the device. "Yes. I see what you mean. Definitely magic."

"Would you be willing to come and take a look at it, at Harold? Abe wants me and Debbie to figure out who killed him."

"Of course he does. I'm sure he doesn't want to be near anyone who could do this." He handed the phone back to me. "Not tonight, surely. Are you coming to bed?"

Abe's people don't sleep. When he'd first told me that, I thought it would be a great thing. *Think of the things you could do besides sleeping.* Not to mention feeling as though I would never sleep again after Jacob's death.

But two years into my life as a zombie, I realized why people sleep—boredom and an empty feeling at night when everyone else was asleep around you. Maybe if I'd had a job at night it wouldn't have been so bad. As it was, I would have begged for just a few hours of unconsciousness.

When Lucas had come into my life, I'd found that he could provide that quiet. When I lay beside him I could close my eyes and the world faded away. It was such a blessed relief that I'd taken to being with him every night.

Addie said that I was disgracing Jacob's memory and that I was a dim-witted slut to spend my resting time with Lucas. It was the only thing she didn't like about him. In the balance of things, she found it was easier to blame me than him since he did so many other wonderful things that took care of her beloved home.

"No. Not yet. Maybe not tonight."

He searched my face. "There is more, isn't there? It involves Jacob, doesn't it?"

"Yes."

"I can help, if you'll let me."

"Thanks. But not tonight." I touched his handsome, angular face. "I'll be up when I'm done if Kate isn't awake."

He looked a little hurt that I didn't want his help and that I didn't want to sleep with him. But I needed to be alone with my thoughts about Jacob's death and the riddle of what was killing people in the woods on that curve.

Chapter Seven

Sometimes I felt as horrible and guilty as Addie always reminded me that I should by being with Lucas. I had expected to spend my twenty years mourning my husband. I hadn't expected Lucas to pop into my life.

Sometimes I even managed to feel guilty about him. I didn't know how he felt about me, but I didn't love him. I had just come to depend on him.

He'd claimed when we met that I was a witch because no one else could have yanked him from his own time and into mine. As far as I knew, he still believed that. We never talked about it anymore.

He may have been an evil sorcerer, as the Wikipedia page had claimed. Abe's necromancer, Jasper, had said the same when he'd come to the inn to kill him.

I'd seen Lucas do magic, but it was always as though it had burst from him during an emotional response. He never used magic to clean the house or trim the hedges. If he was a sorcerer, evil or otherwise, he was content living without his magic.

At least as far as I knew. Lucas was careful with what he said. I wasn't sure what he was holding back, but my cop gut told me there was something.

He claimed Abe's magic was dark and that he was taking advantage of all the LEPs. He'd promised to free me from it without taking away my time with Kate. But he'd never said how or when he was going to do it, and I hadn't asked.

I wandered through the quiet inn, listening to the sounds of the old house settling and birds sleeping in the rafters. I could close my eyes and find my way through the darkness. Light and dark were the same to me. I had seen things I'd never seen before I'd died. My senses were more acute.

Addie had kept Jacob's childhood bedroom exactly as it had been before he'd gone off to college. When we'd married, we'd shared one of the larger rooms with our own bathroom.

After Jacob's death, I'd started keeping everything I could find about the area where we'd died and the other deaths that had happened there on the desk in his old bedroom. It gave me a place to put up poster board and pin newspaper articles about other accidents and deaths on that curve. I hadn't wanted Kate to find it.

And that was the one part of our lives that I had managed to keep from her sharp little mind. She still thought her daddy had died in a car accident.

When I was in Jacob's old room, I was surrounded by his superhero posters and collectibles of everything from horses to Frankenstein. There was a globe in one corner and a hanging mobile of the solar system above me. There was so much hope for the future here, a future cut short by our tragedy.

Looking up the name Tim Rusk had given me at the bar was easy on the laptop. Gerald Linker was a decorated veteran of two tours in Iraq as well as various other military missions. I found pictures of him and his wife, Julie, on their wedding day. They'd only been married a short time when she had died. There were no children.

I studied Gerald's lean face in his army uniform and then compared it to the photo of him the day after the wreck that had killed his wife. He hadn't been shy about telling everyone that Julie's death wasn't normal. He'd spoken out for months, questioning the police findings.

He'd claimed that someone had been waiting in the woods that night and had taken her from their pickup truck. He'd gone all the way to the governor's office—no doubt getting there with good PR from his military career, but that was as far as it went.

A few days after his visit to the governor, Gerald had been thrown in jail for public drunkenness and assault. He'd gotten into a bar fight and seriously hurt the other man. After that, it was downhill for him until he was taken to a mental hospital for observation.

There was nothing mentioned about him after that.

I sat back in Jacob's old chair and looked around at his teenage belongings. No wonder Gerald had finally given up. The system could beat anyone down. I'd known that and had tried just to be grateful that I had the next twenty years to spend with Kate. I'd followed Abe's strict orders to stay away from looking into Jacob's death.

In short, I'd been a coward. Time was passing quickly, only seventeen years left to find out what had happened that night.

I saw Addie standing in the doorway and turned off the laptop. It was already six-thirty a.m. Time to get Kate up and ready for school soon.

"Did you find anything new?" she asked with the apathetic air of someone who was used to disappointment.

"Maybe." I told her what had happened. "I'm going to see Gerald Linker as soon as I can. Maybe we can compare stories and come up with some new ideas."

Her thick face was much clearer now than it had been when she'd first returned as a ghost. Lucas had been helping her become more solid, learning about her ghostly powers.

"Why not today, right away? What else do you have to do?"

"I have to investigate a magic user's death. Remember Harold the Great?"

"The magician? Sure, although I think of him as Harold the mediocre. He couldn't even make balloon animals at Kate's party. Why are you investigating his death?"

"Because Abe wants me to. Turns out he was a real sorcerer. He worked for Abe for a while. Abe thinks Lucas may have killed Harold to get his position."

"Well, that's just stupid. You can tell Abe I said that too. Ignore him. Go talk to this Gerald person. Do what you need to for my son."

I switched off the desk lamp. "I will. You know I will."

"Sometimes I wonder." She disappeared, and I ran upstairs to take a shower and change clothes.

Lucas was already up—he didn't sleep any better than I did most nights. He was in the shower already. I took off my shorts and T-shirt and jumped in with him.

"Why is the water always boiling?" I winced as the water hit my skin. "And why are you always cold? No one has a fire in the summer. Is it some magic thing?"

He handed me the soap. "I don't know. All I know is I feel cold all the time. No matter what I do, I can't get warm. Do you want me to come with you this morning to look at the dead sorcerer?"

"Yes." I grabbed the shampoo and dumped a small amount on my short blond hair. "Thanks. I know you don't like Abe."

He smiled. "But I like you, Skye, and I would do anything to repay your kindness."

"I think you've repaid that already." We switched places under the water, after I'd adjusted the temperature. "Addie loves you. So does Kate. And what's this about repairing that old rusted pickup in the yard?"

He shrugged. "The engine was very rudimentary. I traded some of Addie's apple butter for the parts I needed. Did you know her apple butter and jam are famous? They have the picture of the inn on them."

"Anyone can do that," I explained. "But I think the jam and apple butter were pretty good. People bought them like crazy when she was alive."

"And she stopped because of her death?" He shivered as he stepped out of the shower and grabbed a towel. "I shall speak with her about it. Perhaps we could continue her legacy and bring in some extra money."

I turned off the water and took the towel he offered me. "I'm sure she'd like that. Have you ever made jam or apple butter? It's one of my least favorite things to do."

"Not surprising. Addie says you're not a home-maker. I assume that means you are uninterested in anything about the home. That explains the conditions you were living in before I arrived."

"Smart ass." I flicked him with the end of the towel. "I have better things to do."

He put his arms around me. Lucas never tried to kiss me, though we frequently had sex.

"Did Jacob not require home-making skills of you as his wife?"

"No. He liked that I was a cop and didn't care that I'd never ironed a shirt in my life."

"He was an intelligent man, it seems."

"Yes." I moved away from him and scrounged in a drawer to find clean work shorts and a tank top. I could feel him watching me as I dressed and dried my hair. "Is something wrong?"

"No. I was just thinking that you are unlike any woman I have ever known. You don't require silks nor furs and jewels."

"So you remember women from your past?"

"They are like ghosts, flitting though my mind. I couldn't tell you their names or where I know them from." He put his hands to his head. "It maddens me."

I tossed the damp towel in the hamper knowing it would be washed and dried before I got home. "Maybe you shouldn't try so hard."

"You mean because I might be an evil sorcerer from the past as you read on your computer. People feared me and were glad to know that I had disappeared."

"No, because you might be putting too much pressure on yourself. The answers will come when you're ready. There's a reason you can't remember anything."

"Why aren't you afraid of me?"

"Maybe because I'm already dead." I shrugged as I ran a comb through my hair and stared into my blue eyes in the mirror. "Or maybe because you've been nice to everyone— except Jasper. I have to wake Kate. See you downstairs."

Kate was already up when I reached her bedroom. She ran to hug me, her brown eyes wide awake and looking toward the new day.

"When did you get home, Mommy?"

"I'm not sure what time it was." I hugged her. "At least you were asleep. How was school yesterday?"

"It was okay, except that the teacher put me in a group with snotty Suzy Smith." She opened her eyes wide and tossed back her light brown hair. "*I'm not doing any of this. My mother is a lawyer, and she'll have our nanny do it for me.*"

I laughed at her high-pitched, snotty-girl voice. "Did you tell the teacher she plans to cheat?"

"The teacher won't listen to me. Everyone knows about Suzy. It's just the way it is." Kate threw her pajamas on the bed and took out the shorts and T-shirt she'd chosen to wear to school.

"That's the time you should say something," I encouraged her. "Nothing should just be the way it is."

"Everything is like that, isn't it? You're dead and still walking around. Grandma is a ghost. Daddy is dead. I can't do anything about those things. They are the way they are."

I sat on the bed as she brushed her teeth and combed her hair, her earnest little face breaking my heart. "That's not the same. Some things you can change. They don't have to be the way they are."

"How do you know the difference?"

"You have to look at each situation and ask yourself if you can change it. I can't change that I'm dead. I can change what I do with my time while I'm here."

"So like I can't change that I have to go to school, but I can keep Suzy from cheating."

"Sure." I wasn't sure if that was true or not, but I didn't want her to give up on her life already without trying to make things right.

Addie appeared near the window. "Lucas is making fruit and bagels for breakfast. You should both get down there. You're running late."

Kate laughed. "Oh Grandma. Lucas can't make fruit, even if he really is a sorcerer. Fruit grows on trees." She looked at me. "Can he make bagels, or can you only get those in the store?"

"You can make them, smarty pants," Addie replied. "But I think these are from the store. Are you ready to go?"

"No. Not really," Kate replied. "I don't want to go to school today. I'd rather stay home."

"You only have a few days left before summer vacation," I reminded her. "Besides, you love school."

"It's so close to summer." Kate stared out the window. "And something feels funny."

We talked about her funny feeling all the way downstairs. Coffee was brewing, and Lucas had already toasted bagels and sliced strawberries.

"Good morning." He put a cup of Kate's favorite tea in front of her. "What's all this about funny feelings?"

Addie stood at the table as we ate. I didn't need to, but it made Kate feel better when I ate with her.

"I don't know." Kate shrugged as she crammed strawberries into her mouth, her lips red with them. "It's like something is coming. Something bad."

"Don't be silly, chicken feet," Addie chided, using her pet name for Kate who always walked on her toes. "Nothing bad is coming. You're going to finish school and have a wonderful summer."

Lucas shoveled a mound of sugar into his coffee and topped it off with heavy cream. "You shouldn't ignore her. Children have a sense of the world that adults have lost. Something bad might indeed be coming."

"I think it may be that she's about to finally lose that tooth." I frowned at Lucas, hoping he'd get the idea that we didn't want to talk about something bad coming. "If that doesn't come out soon, something bad will be me wiggling it until it falls out."

Lucas didn't say anything else about Kate's random musings until we had dropped her off at school for the day. The Festiva had died out twice while we waited in the school drop-off line. I held my tongue until we were alone.

"You can't encourage her to get morbid about her life," I told him as we started toward Nashville. "She lives with a zombie, a sorcerer, and a ghost. Her life will never be normal. The least she can have is a happy childhood."

"Even children can be unhappy," he said. "And they frequently recognize trouble when we are too busy to notice. There is magic in her, as there is in you. I can sense it. Don't ignore her prophecy, Skye. It may be important."

Chapter Eight

Even though the showers that had been anticipated the day before had never materialized, thick gray clouds hung over Nashville, obscuring the skyline in many places. Traffic was just as heavy going into the city, and drivers were just as impatient.

I made an unscheduled stop at the mechanic's shop where Abe usually had the van repaired. It was still out in the yard with no work done on it.

"I'll get to it when I can," Bernie promised from under a Honda. "I've got work piled up. I told Abe I was too busy to work on it right away. He should've sent it to one of his other mechanics."

"Just give me some kind of estimate," I coaxed. "Or maybe you have another car I can use. This thing is a piece of crap. I barely got here today."

Bernie peeked out at the old Festiva. "I ain't got nothing else, honey. You better talk to Abe. I'm sorry."

"I could take a look at it," Lucas offered. "Not the van, but the engine on the small car. I fully understand how they work."

"Let's get to the mortuary first. Maybe you can do something with it there." I glared at Bernie who shrugged and went back under the Honda. "How am I supposed to pick up zombies if the car won't get there?"

I got in the Festiva and gunned the engine. The car shuddered and coughed until it died out again. So much for anger helping the situation.

"This is as good a place as any." Lucas had me open the hood.

"I guess it can't hurt for you to look at it." I got out and watched him. "How did you learn about cars?"

He started messing around with something in the engine. "I studied the engine in the old truck since we clearly needed another tool for going places when you weren't home. It's very simple, based on electrical principles. Magic is roughly based on the same ideas."

"But you haven't been able to purposely access your magic—have you?" I studied the side of his face as he keenly went through the wiring in the engine.

"Not purposely. If there are spells or incantations, I don't recall them. But this I understand. Get back in and start it again."

I felt like it was a waste of time, but I did as he asked. The little engine started right up and purred like a kitten. I put my foot on the gas, and it revved loud and steady. It didn't even die out.

"You fixed it." No one was as surprised as me. "You could open a mechanic shop and make a lot more money than you could on jam and apple butter."

He closed the hood and got in the car. "That might be true. I hadn't considered it."

"Just kidding, Lucas. Why are you so worried about making money anyway?"

"Because there are certain needs that cannot be met by bartering in your society." He glanced out the window as a man in a gray Jag stuck his finger up at me for pulling out too slow. "I hope to help you meet those needs. Perhaps that will lessen the work you need do for Abe."

He smiled, and I glanced away, pretending to be intent on the road. He almost made my poor dead heart dance in my chest again. That bothered me. I didn't want to have those softer feelings for him. We helped each other. That was enough.

"Do you ever wonder if you'll remember who you are some day?" I asked.

"Are you concerned about it? If the spells and incantations return to me, I could become the man on the computer, the one everyone dreaded."

"I'm not worried about it, Lucas," I reassured him. "I only care about what you are now. Besides, half of that stuff from the past isn't true anyway. And we're only guessing that you're the same person."

"So you have no faith that I can spare you from the dark one's subjugation."

I knew he meant Abe. I also knew that I didn't want to be spared unless my life was going to continue. "You know I signed up for this, right?"

"After he convinced you that it was necessary to keep Kate from being alone." He stared at me when we'd stopped for a light. "He was lying."

"He's been doing this a long time." I didn't mention that Abe knew who he was and how to use his magic. That seemed rude. Lucas was doing the best he could. No point in rubbing it in.

"And we don't know anything for sure about me or my magic." He said what I was thinking. "You don't trust me."

"I trust you a lot more than any other man in my life right now. You live with us and interact with Kate. I wouldn't let that happen if I didn't trust you."

"Perhaps I meant that you don't trust my magic."

"Maybe." I smiled at him. "Maybe not so much."

"Thank you for your honesty."

I pulled the Festiva into the back parking lot at Simon's Mortuary. It was a pathetic looking place that needed a paint job and a new roof. Abe didn't seem to be big on home improvement either. There was a large, dirty window in the front of the mortuary where two older mannequins stood dressed in 1950s apparel with a casket between them.

Not that any normal humans used this facility. Only Abe's LEPs were brought here. This was where he cut the silver cord that bound us to him—the official end of our twenty borrowed years.

Brandon, who'd worked for Abe at the mortuary for almost all of his extended life, said Abe took his magic energy back when he cut the silver cord. That was why Abe could only have so many zombies at one time. His magic only extended so far. Which was why he also needed a magic user of some type to protect him.

I didn't know if Brandon had guessed that or if Abe had told him. But he was about to find out the truth since he'd been with Abe for nineteen years. I hoped he didn't run. I didn't want to be the one who had to bring him here at the end.

"Skye—" Lucas tried to continue the conversation about his magic.

I pushed open the car door, not wanting to discuss something so difficult. I'd only just begun to believe magic was possible. I couldn't knowledgeably argue with him one way or another.

Brandon came out the back door, and I didn't have to. He was a strange little man who'd been a friend to me since I'd woken up in the mortuary on a slab. He seemed to know so much more than he was sharing, claiming to be too frightened of Abe to say anything more.

"I was wondering when you were going to get here." His pale blue eyes searched the interior of the car. "Where's Debbie? And what's *he* doing here?"

"Debbie's home today, unless we have a pick up. I brought Lucas to take a look at the murder scene and the victim."

"I thought Abe wanted her to be with you while you investigated," he retorted. "I don't think he'd be happy to see Lucas here."

"Abe told me to do what was needed to figure out who killed Harold," I reminded him. "That's what I'm doing."

Brandon smiled as Lucas got out of the car. "But doesn't Abe think Lucas killed Harold?"

"If he does, he has only respect for him. I'm sure he won't mind if I tap into his skill set."

Lucas reached us and held out his hand to Brandon. "Good morning. Is there a problem?"

"No. Absolutely not." The slight breeze blew the thin blond strands of Brandon's longish hair. "Harold is right in here. See what you think."

We went inside. I could see Lucas's breath in the cold air. It didn't feel cold to me, but nothing did. Brandon led us past several closed doors to the autopsy room. I wondered if Jane Darcy was in one of those rooms.

Brandon turned on the bright overhead light and swept the green sheet off Harold's naked body. "I got the snakes out of him. Cause of death was pretty easy—the snake in his throat suffocated him. If that hadn't happened, the rest of the snakes inside him would have killed him for sure. They were everywhere—"

"We get the picture." I stopped his explanation.

Lucas glanced around the otherwise empty room. "Where are the snakes?"

"They were all dead by the time we got the body in here. I removed them and put them in separate containers just in case someone asked." Brandon grinned at him. "Would you like to take a look at them?"

"Yes," Lucas said. "Were they all living snakes, as far as you know?"

"You mean the kind you could look up and categorize?" Brandon asked as he led us into a smaller room and switched on another light. "Yes. I looked them up last night. They were from all over the world—like someone broke into a reptile house at the zoo and liberated a few. But they were real snakes."

Lucas immediately started examining the snakes in each glass container. He took them out and held them in his hands as he closed his eyes to concentrate on them.

"So how's Debbie's husband doing?" Brandon asked as we watched Lucas.

"He's getting crazier." I shrugged. "I don't know what she's going to do with him."

"Well, we know he can't die yet. He's one of Abe's people, like us. Maybe Abe can do something for him."

"I don't see that happening since Abe wants Debbie, do you?"

"Not really. Do you think Debbie will want Abe if she can't control Terry?"

"I don't know. But you better quit drooling over her before Abe notices. He might decide to terminate your contract before it's time."

"That won't happen." Brandon chuckled. "Abe's a stickler for his contracts. He never brings anyone in early."

I smiled at him and the worried frown that had appeared between his brows. "I'm sure you're right. Any plans for your last year of half-life?"

"I plan to drink, gamble, and have sex with as many people as possible. Are you busy tonight, Skye?"

He was joking—at least partially so. I had no doubt that if I'd agreed to have sex with him in one of his plush coffins, he wouldn't turn me down. I was surprised to see Lucas break his concentration to glare at Brandon for a moment before he returned his focus to the dead cobra in his hands.

"Yeah." Brandon cleared his throat. "Just razzing you, Lucas. Really. I think of Skye as a sister. A sexy sister, but you get the idea. No need to cut off my head."

Lucas put the cobra back into its jar and went to the sink to wash his hands. "And where did the man die?"

"Don't you want to examine Harold?" Brandon asked.

"It's not necessary." Lucas dried his hands. "I would like to see where he died."

"I'll take you," I volunteered. "We can walk from here."

Lucas turned to Brandon and shook his hand again. "I wouldn't suggest you consider Skye as you do Debbie, my friend. It could be unhealthy for you, even in your current dead state."

Chapter Nine

"What does that mean?" I asked as Lucas and I walked outside.

"I think Brandon and I are clear on my meaning." His brilliant green eyes stared straight ahead as we walked toward the alley.

"But I don't think I'm clear on the meaning. Maybe you could explain." I put my hand on his arm to stop his forward motion. "What you and I have—"

"Isn't to be shared with others. You have my mark of protection on you, Skye."

"But that doesn't mean I belong to you."

"Yet you have adjusted to the idea that you belong to Abe."

His gaze was riveted on mine. I had his full attention. "Not all right exactly, just necessary. But you and I don't belong to each other. We're convenient, right? We have a give and take that works for both of us. It's not romantic, right?"

"Are we not?" His voice was intense, deep. "Do we not belong to one another?"

I didn't know what to say. I'd assumed his feelings for me were the same as mine for him. He was taking our relationship more seriously than I was. Maybe that was because I still loved Jacob. If Lucas had someone in his past, he probably didn't remember. That might make it easier for him to bond with me.

"Skye?"

"I'm sorry. It's too soon for me to feel that way about anyone. I might never feel that way again." I put my hand on his face, hoping not to see some terrible sadness in his eyes. I didn't want to hurt him.

He kissed my hand and then took it in his to walk the rest of the way to the alley. "Perhaps someday."

I was glad to see Abe and Morris behind the yellow crime scene tape in the dirty alley when we arrived. Brandon must have called him.

Work was what I needed to keep from being swallowed up by grief at that moment. I understood this. It was part of me.

"Lucas!" Abe called out to him as though they were old friends. He stuck out his huge black hand. "I'm very glad to see you."

I was afraid for a moment that Lucas wouldn't shake his hand. But after a brief hesitation, he took Abe's hand for a moment. He didn't smile the way Abe did, but he was pleasant.

"Abe. I understand you have a problem."

"That's right." Abe moved closer to Lucas. "Do I have you to thank for an opening in my organization?"

"No. I haven't changed my mind about working for you. But I am here to help Skye if I can. Where was your magic user killed?"

Morris was standing right where we'd found Harold's body. He took a step back and grinned. "Right here. Cast your magic eyes this way, sorcerer."

Lucas gave him all the regard one would give a fly at a picnic. "If you will all back away, please."

Abe stood beside me with Morris on the other side of Lucas.

"And you said he can't control his magic." Abe made a humphing sound. "He looks and feels in control to me."

"I can't speak for him, but I've never seen him use magic around the house."

"No?" Abe's brows went up. "What about when he killed Jasper?"

"Like I said, that was different. He seems to be able to perform magic on combustion engines if you'd like to hire him as a mechanic. Maybe my van could get repaired faster in that case."

"Yes. I'm sorry it's taking so long. Does the car suffice?"

I took a page from Debbie's book. "You could get me a new van."

He chuckled. "I'm sure it will be repaired before that, Skye."

Lucas walked around the area where Harold's body had been. He closed his eyes and concentrated, a dark frown on his face. When he finished, he faced Abe. "I feel something here, but I don't know what it is."

Morris laughed loudly. "Good thing he doesn't want to work for you, Abe. I don't think he knows what he's doing."

"What is it you don't understand, Lucas?" Abe ignored Morris, as he usually did.

"I believe it is something about the context of the man's death. There is magic left here from the killer, but the snakes were real, perhaps enchanted."

Abe stared at me instead of Lucas. "Is he saying he doesn't know who killed Harold?"

"I think so. Sorry. I thought he might be able to help."

"Yes. I think perhaps you had better go it alone. This one seems to be as useless as you claim." Abe thanked Lucas in a loud voice for his help before he and Morris disappeared back inside the tattoo shop.

"He seemed unimpressed." Lucas smiled as he ducked under the crime scene tape. "He doubts my magic, doesn't he?"

"It's probably just as well. I'm sure it's better if the two of you don't spend a lot of time together."

We started back toward the mortuary and the Festiva in the parking lot. I was determined to see Gerald Linker before I went home that day. I wanted to do it right away in case a surprise LEP pick up happened. Sometimes it seemed as though Abe forgot that one of his people needed to end their twenty years until the last moment.

"I kept something to myself," Lucas confided as we got into the car.

"Smart." I turned to him. "What was it?"

He rubbed his hands together and then held out his left hand. "I know what the killer looks like."

"Show me."

A pale blue mist formed in the palm of his hand. The mist became more solid, taking on the features of a man. As I watched, the ghost man in Lucas's hand started moving. He leaned against the old brick wall, smoking cigarettes as he waited for his prey.

"I found some gold glittery rings on a few cigarette butts in the alley. They just called to me out of all the other garbage out there. I knew they were important."

"His face is not as well defined as I would like." Lucas and I peered into the tiny blue man's face. "Perhaps I might be able to make it clearer for you."

But the image vanished. Lucas rubbed his hands again, but it didn't return.

"You do still have some magic," I observed, not ever quite sure if this was a good or bad thing.

"It has taken me almost a year to get this far, and still I can't make this what it needs to be. Perhaps there is some control but nothing as powerful as I might like."

"Still, it's something. I wasn't sure if the cigarettes meant anything. I'll go to a smoke shop and see if anyone can ID the wrapper."

"Thank you. I appreciate your enthusiasm."

I smiled and squeezed his hand. At least it was something I could report to Abe to let him know I was working on the case. I didn't have to tell him about the image Lucas had conjured. And I'd have time to check out Gerald Linker.

It was a long drive back to Wanderer's Lake. The weather looked iffy. I didn't want to take Lucas with me to see Gerald, but I didn't want to take a chance that I might have to put it off. If Gerald had any information that could help me with Jacob's death, I was hungry for it.

I started the Festiva—not a bit of trouble. Who knew magic was good for making cars go?

"I need to make another stop," I explained as we left the mortuary.

"The smoke shop?"

"No. This is personal. You don't have to come in with me. You can wait in the car."

"I don't mind going with you. Is there some danger involved?"

"No." I told him about the lead I'd had on Jacob's death. "This man might have some answers."

"Unlikely since you said he couldn't do anything to help his dead wife," he reminded me.

I swerved in and out of traffic as I headed toward the address. "They thought he was crazy. No one would listen to him. I will. That might make a difference."

He looked at me. "Or it could kill you."

"Unlikely since I'm already dead. It will be okay, Lucas. I can handle myself. You wait in the car. Okay?"

I thought the matter was resolved until we came up on the old blue-sided house. Lucas got out of the car at the same time I did.

"You don't have to do this," I said.

"I shall nonetheless." He slammed the door hard enough to let me know that I couldn't change his mind.

"Just don't get in the way. We don't know—you might be able to die."

The front yard of the older house reminded me of what Apple Betty's Inn had looked like before Lucas came to stay. The shrubs, flowers, and trees were overgrown. Weeds grew up through cracks in the sidewalk. The screen door had been taken off the house and set on the porch. The front door was weathered, paint peeling from it.

I took out my Beretta as we approached.

"You said this wasn't dangerous," Lucas said.

"There's no reason to be careless," I told him in a muted voice. "This man has been through a lot in the last few years. I don't want to take any chances."

Lucas nodded, and I pushed myself into the lead ahead of him. It made sense since I had the gun. We went slowly up the stairs. I could feel him scanning the windows and doors as I did. There was no sign that anyone was home, no car in the drive or music coming from the house.

We were at the door. I held the Beretta to the side and down so it wasn't easily visible. I knocked on the shabby wood portal, but there was no response.

"Do you hear anything?" I whispered.

"No." He paused. "Wait—"

Only a breath later, a shotgun shell blew a large hole in the door. I fell to the porch, taking Lucas with me. It seemed someone was home after all.

Chapter Ten

"Gerald Linker!" I called out from my place on the worn porch. "My name is Skye Mertz. My husband died on State Road 3714, just like your wife Julie. I need your help."

There was no response. Maybe it was a good sign. At least he didn't shoot at us again.

"Gerald?" I tried again. "I know everyone has given you a hard time. They don't believe what you saw. They think your wife was killed in the wreck. They think the same thing about my husband, Jacob. Let's work together. We can figure this out."

There was no response again. Feeling hopeful, I raised my head to peer in through the hole in the door. Before I could move, the business end of the shotgun was pushed through it and into my face.

I might have learned the truth about whether or not zombies could die except that Lucas pushed me back and put his body in front of mine. He waved his hand and called out a word that I didn't understand.

Breathing hard, I whispered, "What happened?"

Lucas pushed the door open. The man on the other side of it didn't move. The shotgun was still stuck through the hole. His eyes were transfixed on the door.

I poked him. Gerald still didn't move. "Did you do this?"

"You were in danger." He shrugged and stepped back to look at the frozen man.

"It's the emotional thing, right? You just stopped him with your magic. You've used it twice in one day—actually only about an hour apart."

"It is better than you having a hole in your head, alive or dead."

"You're probably right. And at least you didn't kill him. Do you know how to make him move again?"

He blinked. "I am not certain as yet. Perhaps the answer will come to me."

I sat down on a broken wood chair that was propped up by a kitchen table covered in beer cans and takeout food packaging. "Got any ideas?"

"No. I'm not sure what I did." Lucas circled Gerald the same way he'd circled the spot where Harold had died.

"Maybe we can take the gun away from him before he starts moving again and the whole thing gets ugly." I pried the shotgun from Gerald's stiff hands. He looked exhausted and much older than I expected from the pictures I'd seen of him in the newspaper.

He was pliable though. I took the shells out of the shotgun and put them in my pocket. I put the gun on the table and tucked my Beretta in its holster.

"Now what?" I asked Lucas.

"Now we wait. No magic lasts forever."

"That seems like a broad parameter." I sat in the chair by the table and waited.

It didn't take long. Gerald began to flex his fingers and blink his eyes. The next instant, he was walking and talking. He wasn't sure about what had happened and wasn't happy about it.

"What the hell are you doing in my house?" He glanced around, perplexed.

"Take it easy," I advised, getting to my feet. "I'm Skye Mertz. I want to talk about your wife."

"Go away." He shoved his burly body between me and Lucas to go into the living room. "I don't want to talk about that anymore."

I followed him. The room looked as though it had gone through an earthquake, but I pushed some empty food containers off a chair and sat opposite him.

"I know you've told a lot of people about what happened that night, but I guarantee you'll never find a better audience than me. My husband, Jacob, died the same way. I didn't cause a ruckus like you did because I almost died too."

Lucas raised one brow but didn't say anything.

"I don't know you," Gerald said. "Why should I trust you? You don't know what I've been through."

"Yes, I do. I looked you up. I know what they did to you for telling the truth. I'm sorry that happened, but you and I could still make this right."

Gerald's broad face hadn't seen a razor or soap and water in a while. His clothes were filthy and reeked of food and sweat. There was no air conditioning in the old house, and the scurrying I heard along the walls sounded like his companions were mostly rats.

"Julie is dead. That's what I didn't get when it happened. Nothing can bring her back." He started sobbing and put his head in his hands. "Who cares about the rest of it? She's gone."

I bit my lip, empathizing with what he felt. Hadn't I felt the same way many times since Jacob's death? It was what had kept me from delving any deeper into what had killed him.

"But it does matter, Gerald." I told him the same thing I'd told myself that morning. "It matters because there's more involved than Julie and Jacob. More people are going to die out there. I'm an ex-cop. You're an ex-soldier. No one is better suited to figuring out what happened. It's bred in us to care about more than ourselves."

Gerald was still crying when he looked up at me with terrible anguish in his eyes. "I don't know if I can do this again. So much has happened. I don't believe anymore, you know? I always believed that the system worked for us. It doesn't. There's nothing there but the abyss."

"There's us." I touched his hand. "We can still make a difference. I know you don't have any children, but I have a daughter who asks about her father every day. I want to be able to tell her that I did the best I could to find his killer. Don't you want to be able to say that too?"

He nodded and wiped the tears from his face with the back of his sleeve. "I want to. I really do. I don't know how. There's nothing left of me but memories and anger."

I got to my feet. "Let me help you, and you can help me. Let's do this, Gerald. Let's make Jacob and Julie's deaths mean something."

He got to his feet with more difficulty, but he slowly held out his hand. "Maybe I was just missing a partner. Maybe we can help each other."

I wanted to hug him, but my nose wouldn't let me. The first thing he needed was a shower and clean clothes. I told him as much. He chuckled but quickly went to the bathroom. I searched through a chest I found in the bedroom and got out clean jeans and a plaid, button-down shirt. I couldn't find clean underwear or socks, but I located a pair of sandals that looked as though they would fit him.

"Nice words," Lucas commented. "You have a plan to go with them?"

"First I want to hear his story about the night his wife was killed. We can take a look at the details from both our experiences. Once we compare notes, we can decide what to do next."

"The chances are very good that magic is involved in these deaths." Lucas looked at a picture of Gerald in his uniform that was hanging on the bedroom wall. "They don't sound ordinary to me."

"Not everything involves magic," I said even though my words from yesterday—before I saw snakes coming out of Harold—came back to me. "I know it seems as though there's a lot of magic going around right now. But I worked the streets of Nashville for ten years and never saw anything magical."

"How do you know?"

I was glad there was no time to answer because I didn't have a good response, and it was possible he was right. One thing I did know—I had never encountered a man who was choked to death by a snake. And there were plenty of odd cases, but there was always a rational, non-magical explanation.

Gerald came right out of the shower with a hand towel held in front of his private parts. He must have also forgotten basic rules of society due to his bereavement.

"I'm sorry. My electric razor isn't working, and I'm out of shaving cream." He ran his hand through his shaggy, damp hair. "I really need a cup of coffee."

Lucas smiled but didn't speak.

"I think I could use a cup too." I pointed to the clothes I'd found that were on the bed. "Get dressed, and we'll make some."

Lucas and I ransacked the kitchen while Gerald got dressed. There was no coffee, no food of any kind.

"Not any clean dishes either," Lucas remarked as he opened cabinets and the refrigerator. "I think he lives on food that others make for him."

"Take-out," I corrected automatically. "I don't think he's been out of the house in a long time. We'll have to go get coffee and food. I think he needs to eat too."

"You might not be able to prop him up long enough to get the answers you seek," Lucas said.

"It won't take that long. One good conversation and I'll know what he knows. We just have to get past the crying and get him thinking again."

"He is a warrior? Is my understanding correct?"

"You could say that. At least he was a warrior."

There was pounding on what was left of the front door followed by a brisk voice announcing itself. "Nashville PD, Mr. Linker. Let us in."

Chapter Eleven

"Let me handle this," I said to Lucas. Gerald had come out of the bedroom, still half dressed. "Finish getting ready."

"I have a reputation," Gerald whispered. "I don't know why they're here now, but they've been here before."

"Don't worry about it," I said with more confidence than I felt. "I'll take care of it."

Lucas waited in the kitchen while I pulled open the door with the large hole in it.

"Officers." I nodded to the two young men on the doorstep.

"We need to speak to Mr. Linker, ma'am. Is he here?" The officer closest to the door surveyed the inside of the house that he could see.

"I'm a social worker." The lie rolled off my tongue. "Skye Mertz." I shook his hand. "The department of social services is trying to get Mr. Linker on his feet and involved in a recovery program."

The two young men exchanged glances.

"We had a report of gun fire earlier." He looked pointedly at the hole in the door.

"I'm so sorry." I smiled and straightened my hair a little. "It was careless of me. I was moving the shotgun off the table, and it accidentally discharged. I could never stand to see a gun lying out in the open that way."

"Is Mr. Linker here, ma'am?" The second officer seemed not to believe my story.

"He is, but he's in the shower. Do you have any idea how hard it was to get him in there?" I lowered my voice. "I didn't want to take him anywhere in my car."

Finally the first officer nodded and smiled. "Yes, ma'am. We do. We've had the beat for a while. We know exactly what you mean. I hope you can do him some good. Poor old man."

"Thank you for coming so promptly, officers." I was joking of course. I could have killed Gerald and stolen everything he had before they got there. They had dragged their feet getting here because they knew what to expect. I was probably a pleasant surprise.

"Thank you, ma'am. You take care now." He tapped his cap, and they went back down the stairs.

"Are they gone?" Gerald asked from the bedroom.

"Yes. I've had similar calls myself when I was working. We're fine now."

"What would the law keepers have done if they'd learned Gerald had shot at us?" Lucas asked.

"Taken him in to jail," I answered. "It's illegal to shoot a gun in the city limits."

"Thank you," Gerald said. "It would've been a lot worse than that, Skye. For me, any call to the police is just the beginning of months of harassment. You kept that from happening to me again. Maybe there's something to this partnership idea."

"Let's get out of here," I said. "Your house needs a good cleaning, Gerald, and you need to get some food in here. The police are going to be less likely to harass you if it looks like you're taking care of yourself."

The closest coffee shop was a few blocks away. We headed there first. Lucas didn't really like coffee, but he had a cup of tea. Gerald and I both had large black coffees. I bought him a bagel with cream cheese too. He hadn't eaten in a while, and it was hard for him to get started. But after a small bite or two, he devoured it ravenously.

"What do we do first?" he asked me.

"First we talk. We need to compare experiences. Once we get a sense of what we both went through, we can decide from there."

"But no cops, right?" He scanned the coffee shop with suspicious eyes. "I don't want them involved, at least not until we can prove what happened."

"No police," I assured him. "This is between you and me. I know you liked to talk with the media when this first started—let's not go there either. I work for someone who wouldn't like me to be involved in this. We have to keep it to ourselves."

He nodded. "That works for me. All the TV and newspaper coverage didn't help at all. It might've made things worse. Where do we start?"

"You tell me exactly what happened the night your wife was killed," I said. "Don't leave anything out because you think it might not be important. Everything is important."

Gerald took a swallow of his coffee to wash down the last of his bagel. "We were driving home. It was raining that night. The road was dark, no streetlights. I knew that curve was blind—I'd driven that road plenty of times before. I knew accidents happened there. I glanced at Julie. She was laughing at something on her phone. When I looked up, a big truck was bearing down on us from our side of the road."

His account of Julie's death was so close to what had happened to Jacob and me that it made my chest hurt to hear it. I swallowed hard so I could listen without getting emotional. Lucas grabbed my hand. I knew he understood what I felt.

When Gerald was finished, I could see the emotional strain the story had taken on him too. He wiped his eyes and went up to get another cup of coffee.

"Will you tell him your story as well?" Lucas asked me when we were alone.

"Only if he asks. I think he might be too involved in his story to care whether or not he hears mine."

"Was it what you expected?"

I nodded as Gerald took his seat again with a fresh cup of coffee. He looked at my empty cup and asked if I wanted something else.

"No, thanks. I'm done."

"What about what happened to you?" he asked.

It surprised me that he could get out of his own head that fast. "My story is very similar except that my husband walked away on his own to get help. I couldn't get out of the SUV. He never came back."

"Sounds like you were in bad shape too," Gerald said. "Lucky you didn't die so one of you was left for your daughter."

"Yes."

He was fine just hearing the difference in our tales. I thought over the things he'd told me, about the door being ripped from his pickup, as Tim Rusk had said, and his wife being snatched.

"I know you went over this plenty of times with the police and the highway patrol," I added. "What was their explanation for what happened to Julie?"

Gerald shrugged. "They said I was injured and couldn't tell what really happened. They said she was thrown from the pickup, and the door was busted out in the accident. But I've seen the pictures since then. No way the door just fell off the truck. There was no damage on the passenger side. Besides, she couldn't have been thrown that far from the truck, like your husband. Something is going on out there, Skye. There's an answer, but I can't see it without going all *X-Files* to explain it. I'm not that kind of man."

I wondered what he'd think if I told him the truth about my death, and Lucas being a sorcerer. Would it make a believer out of him?

My phone rang—it was Abe. There was an emergency in the downtown area, near the river.

"I've received a call from one of my people, Skye. I'm not sure what the problem is since our conversation was cut short, but I think you should check on him. Where are you now?"

"I'm headed your way. I can be at Deadly Ink in a few minutes." I was evasive about my answer. I didn't want Abe involved in what I was doing with Gerald.

"I don't want you taking Lucas with you on this assignment. I've already called Debbie. The van is repaired and will be waiting for you at the mortuary."

Funny how the repairs could be done so quickly when we needed the van for Abe's purpose.

I glanced at Lucas. What was I going to do with him while I picked up one of Abe's zombies? He wouldn't be welcome to wait at the tattoo shop. I'd have to think of something.

"Have you learned anything else about the person who killed Harold?" Abe questioned. "I hope you haven't forgotten that I need you to do this for me."

"I haven't forgotten. I have some ideas. I'm checking those out."

"Excellent. I'll see you soon."

Abe hung up, and I put my cell phone away.

"I have to go, Gerald. That was my boss. I'll take you back to your house. I might have a chance to come back later and take you shopping."

"I can take him to buy food," Lucas offered. "If the van is repaired, I can drive the car."

I hadn't thought of that since Lucas had only been driving a short time—illegally since he had no ID to get a license. I hadn't trusted him to drive Kate around Wanderer's Lake, but I supposed driving Gerald would be okay.

"Sounds great. Thanks." I got to my feet and shook Gerald's hand. "You hang in there. We're going to find some answers. Let's make sure your place is set up first. Maybe you should fix the hole in your door too."

Gerald smiled. "I can't tell you how much better I feel just meeting you. It's been a long, lonely road trying to find justice for Julie. Thanks for helping me."

I didn't want to be insulting, but I asked him if he had money for groceries.

"Sure. My pension check goes into the bank every month. I'm fine, thanks."

He started out of the coffee shop. Lucas and I lingered behind.

"Be careful," I warned in a whisper. "Anything could send him crashing off the cliff right now."

"I'll take good care of him. Shall I drive you back to the tattoo shop to get the van and leave immediately?"

"Nope. I'll drive to Deadly Ink, and we can change places."

His green eyes looked hurt. "You don't trust me to drive the car?"

"Not with me in it." I smiled. "Let's get going."

Chapter Twelve

Debbie was waiting at the mortuary with the van. There was still some scrapes and dents in the side that had been hit by the Darcys' car. The passenger side looked even worse where it had hit the wall.

"At least we can get in and out of it," I said when I saw it.

"This thing must be built like a tank," she remarked. "Where are we going? I thought we had the day off?"

"Don't ever waste your time thinking that." I got behind the wheel.

"Oh look! There's Lucas." She waved to him from the window. "Hello! Hi Lucas!" He waved back as he started the Festiva. "Who's that with him?"

I explained about Gerald as we left the mortuary parking lot. "I think he can help me figure out what happened the night Jacob and I died."

She frowned. "I thought you said Abe told you not to investigate Jacob's death."

"He did. Don't say anything." I glanced at her. "I have to know. I found out about Gerald's wife. It's almost the same thing. I passed another wreck in that area. Something is wrong there. You'd want to know if it was Terry too."

"I would." She sighed. "I just don't like to see you antagonize Abe. He could probably kill you with a snap of his fingers. You can't investigate if you're completely dead."

"I know." The van was making an odd clanking noise that it hadn't made before. "I swear, every time I get this back it's in worse shape."

"That's why Abe needs to get you a new one. You deserve it. We do a tough job for him. Speaking of which, who are we picking up?"

"I thought he told you."

"Oh, that's right." She laughed. "He sent it to my cell." Debbie read off the address.

"One of the ritzy condos on the river," I guessed. "I wish I would've asked for more money when I took this job."

"I know. Good thing we have Terry's money. Even so, it's tight. Bowman wants a new cell phone for his birthday. He deserves one—I don't know what I'd do without him. But I don't think we can afford it."

"Sorry. I dread when Kate gets that big." I maneuvered through the heavy uptown traffic, wishing I had the small car again. "I don't think she really understands everything I told her. But by the time she's Bowman's age, she'll know what's going on. I don't want her to hate me for the choices I've made."

"Hate you?" Debbie's voice was full of surprise. "You've given up your humanity to be with her. I think she's gonna love you for being there when you should've been in the grave. I would."

I smiled at her, thinking what a good friend she'd become. I wouldn't have thought it when Abe first partnered us. "There's King's Towers. Yeah, this man has some money. I hope they'll let us in the parking deck with this van."

But there was no problem at the gate that was manned by two security guards. As soon as we'd told them we were there for Ashcroft Benton, they were all smiles. I couldn't believe they let us in without even asking him if it was all right. It had to be something to do with Abe. As I'd learned since becoming an LEP, Abe knew people everywhere. I'd lost count of how many zombies worked for him.

"There's a place over there." Debbie checked her lipstick and put her twenty dollars on the dash. "Well? What do you think? I'm betting he's a runner. He's got everything—I wouldn't want to leave."

I tended to agree with her, but it was no fun betting alone. Besides she always bet on our pickups running. She was bound to be wrong sometimes. I put my twenty down beside hers.

Inside the condominium building it was quiet and cool. There was a fountain next to the elevators and tropical plants growing in the foyer. Debbie pressed the elevator button, and we waited.

"I could live here." She inspected the expensive carpet underfoot and other luxury additions.

"What about your cute little cabin? I love that place."

"I'd give it up. Maybe someday when the kids are grown, Terry and I will live someplace like this. It would be sweet, wouldn't it? I could see you and Lucas living here too."

I laughed at that. "It's all I can do to keep the inn around us. Lucas is a big help, but I don't think they'd let him live here because he offered to trim their grass."

Her pretty brown eyes caught mine. "What about because he's a legendary sorcerer? They'd probably be afraid not to let him live here."

I didn't tell her about the less than perfect state of his magic. We rarely discussed him—there was barely enough time to talk about Debbie's problems with Terry. I didn't want to talk about Lucas or our relationship anyway. Although after the way he'd looked at me that morning, I wished I could confide in her. It threw me to know that he might really care about me. I hadn't planned on it.

But I'd always been a private person. I wouldn't have broached the subject anyway.

The elevator chimed softly, discreetly, and we stepped inside.

"This man is definitely not going to come peacefully." She took out the tranq gun she'd shoved into the pocket of her shorts. "Do you have the Beretta? I know you can't kill him with it, but you could slow him down."

"I have it, but I don't think we'll need it. He's going to come along peacefully because he won't want to embarrass himself in front of his neighbors." I grinned at her. "You'll see."

We got up to the sixth floor and found ourselves in another carefully modulated, softly lit area. We followed the etched numbers on the doors until we came to Benton's condo.

"I'll knock," I told Debbie.

"You knocked last time. Why don't I do it this time? Maybe my voice and my knock will make a difference."

I stepped back from the wood door. "By all means. I'm sure your knock will be more soothing than mine would be."

Debbie smiled and softly knocked on the door. "Excuse me, Mr. Benton. I'm Debbie Hernandez. Abe sent me. I'm sure you know why. Are you having a problem? I'm here to escort you to him if you need help. Please come along peacefully. You don't want to embarrass yourself."

"I can't believe you're trying to convince him not to run. You lose if he goes with us."

"It's true. But if we find out I can talk the runners into just coming along quietly, we'd know we had something—and I'd bet on them not running every time."

I had to laugh at that. Then I heard something from inside the condo. "Did you hear that?"

"Hear what?" Debbie laid her ear against the door. "I don't hear anything. Is that your zombie senses kicking in?"

I heard the same sound again. "I think he's calling for help."

"What do we do if he is?"

"We kick the door in. Excuse me."

I kicked the door, but either my legs weren't what they used to be or the door was granite.

"Probably metal," Debbie said. "You'd have to be the Terminator to get in that way. Maybe you should shoot off the lock."

"Maybe that wouldn't be a good idea if we don't want to go to jail." I pushed at the door. "It doesn't feel like metal to me. If both of us put our shoulders to it, we should be able to get it."

Debbie tucked her tranq gun into her pocket. "Abe should have made you with super zombie strength for this job."

"He didn't make me. Now shut up and push."

We had to hit it with our full body weights a few times before it finally opened. Debbie grabbed her gun and ran inside first. I followed but didn't pull the Beretta.

The inside of the condo was clean and neat. Everything was luxurious and carefully appointed. There was no sign of our LEP in the main room, but I heard him yelling for help from the bedroom.

"Guess you were right," Debbie said.

"In there."

The bedroom was darkened, shades and heavy curtains over the windows. Debbie switched on one of the lamps closest to the bed. We blinked like owls waking up for the night.

"Where is he?" Debbie whispered.

"Up here!"

We both looked up. Ashcroft Benton was on the ceiling.

"Help me, please. I don't know what happened. I was down there one minute and up here the next."

Benton was wearing running shorts and a tank top as though he'd just come from working out. He kept pushing himself down from the ceiling, but he bounced right back up.

"What do we do now?" Debbie wrinkled her nose and folded her arms across her chest.

"I'm not sure. Call Abe. See what he says. I'll try to get him down."

I took a blanket from the bed and tossed a corner of it up to Mr. Benton. He tried to grab it and missed.

"My arms keep going through it," he explained. "What's wrong with me? Is that why you're here? Did Abe do something to me?"

"Calm down, Mr. Benton. No one did anything to you," I told him. "Try to catch the blanket and I'll pull you down."

I tossed the blanket up again and watched carefully. His arms and hands were going right through it—like he was a ghost. I waited after that until Debbie got Abe on the phone.

"I've got him on speaker," Debbie said.

"Hello? What's the problem, Skye?" Abe's voice was deep and solid in the room.

"I can't feel my body," Mr. Benton yelled out when he heard Abe's voice. "I can't hold on to anything. It's like I'm weightless. Help me. Do something."

"That's ridiculous," Abe declared. "You aren't weightless, Ash. Whatever you're doing isn't going to keep you alive past your time. Come along with the ladies. We'll figure this out here."

I turned the speaker off and put the phone to my ear. "Abe—he's like a ghost—really. This isn't something he's doing. There's no way he could control this. He's up by the ceiling, floating in the air."

"Trust me. I've seen many different ruses down through the years. He's not a ghost, Skye. Get some rope and pull him down. Let me know when there's progress."

When Abe was gone, I gave the phone back to Debbie.

"Easy for him to say." She pocketed the phone. "He's not here. What are we going to do?"

"What he says. We can't leave him. Help me strip the bed. We'll tie some sheets together for a rope."

Mr. Benton kept yelling for help. I hoped his ritzy neighbors didn't hear him. I didn't believe we were going to be able to pull him down with the bed sheets or anything else, but Abe's word was law in these things.

Had he really turned into a ghost?

Chapter Thirteen

Once we got the sheets off the bed, we tied them together to make a large rope. I used to do it all the time when I was a kid and wanted to sneak out of a foster home. I'd seen it once on TV, and after that, I always knew I could get away.

But it didn't work with Mr. Benton. Debbie stood on one side of him, and I stood on the other. I tossed the end of the sheet rope to her in an arc that should have gone across him. Instead it went right through him.

I was beginning to get nervous and a little afraid. Was this something new I had to look forward to in my life that Abe had forgotten to mention?

"We need a ladder," Debbie decided. "I'll go down to maintenance and get one. Whatever this is can't be real, right? You've never seen it before. Abe's never seen it."

"At least he's not admitting that he's ever seen it."

"For God's sake, get me down," Mr. Benton yelled. "I'm not trying to get out of my contract."

"Get the ladder," I agreed. "I'll keep an eye on him."

Mr. Benton kept floating along the ceiling. If he was doing this himself, it was a very good trick. I called Brandon—it wouldn't hurt to ask what he thought. But he was as mystified by it as we were.

"So he's like a ghost?" he asked. "And you're sure it's not something he cooked up to get away from honoring his contract?"

"I don't see how." I looked up at Mr. Benton again. "He's floating, and everything goes through him. Are you sure this isn't some zombie virus no one talks about?"

"Not that I've heard about in the last nineteen years. Have we talked about what's going to happen to me next year?"

"You're already at the mortuary, Brandon. I don't think you need a pick up."

"I don't care. I want you and Debbie to bring me in like other people. I can go hang out at the coffee shop up the street, and you can come for me. Make sure both of you wear as little as possible. I'd like to go out with a thrill."

I had to smile. "Whatever you need. I know you must be scared."

"Scared? Nah. Not me. Unless I have to turn into a ghost first. See you, Skye."

I put away my phone. I should've known he wouldn't have any answers—and if he did—he wouldn't share them. I wondered who Abe would find to replace him. The two of them always seemed tight.

"Something is happening," Mr. Benton said in a shaky voice. "Something else is wrong. I can feel it. What's going on?"

As I watched, he went through the ceiling and disappeared. Great. Now what?

Debbie brought the ladder into the condo as I ran out. "Hey. This thing is heavy. Where are you going?"

"Mr. Benton vanished. We have to find him."

We ran into the hall and called for the elevator. The ride to the seventh floor was tense. How were we going to find him? Would he keep going up until he was out of the building?

"This is weird," Debbie said. "It doesn't make any sense. How did he turn into a ghost?"

"I don't know. Abe probably does, but like with the ghouls last year, he doesn't want to talk about it. He's been doing this for more than a hundred years. You know he's seen everything."

Debbie's phone rang. It was Abe.

"Where are you now?" he demanded after Debbie had filled him in.

"We're trying to find Mr. Benton," I explained.

"I'm almost there. Don't do anything until then."

"I guess we'll just track him?" Debbie asked after she put her phone away as Abe hung up.

"I guess so. I'm not sure how we're going to do that. We can't knock on every door on the seventh floor."

But we didn't have to. Two elderly ladies were moving fast toward the elevator as the door opened on that floor.

"There's a ghost in our condo," one of them said as she stepped into the elevator. "I'm not putting up with it. No rats. No roaches. No ghosts. Come on, Martha. Let's go see the superintendent."

"He knows," I said spontaneously. "We're like the Ghostbusters. He sent us up to take care of the problem."

The first woman handed me her key. "Good thing. Can you take care of that kitchen sink clog too while you're in there?"

Debbie said we could as we ran out of the elevator.

Mr. Benton was floating around in the living room this time. He'd turned transparent, appearing more ghostlike than before.

"You two! Get me down from here. I don't feel very well. I don't understand this. Abe didn't say anything about ending up this way. Where is he? Shouldn't he be here?"

"You should go down to the lobby and wait for him," I told Debbie. "One of us should stay with Mr. Benton."

"Why me? I got the ladder. I'll stay with him until you bring Abe."

"Because I'm the senior zombie bounty hunter. Get down there."

She grumbled but left the condo. I hoped Abe was there. If Mr. Benton got any more see-through, we wouldn't be able to find him at all.

He was crying now as he glided across the ceiling. "I wanted to go out with dignity. Why is this happening to me?"

I noticed that his tears weren't water. They didn't fall from his face. It was more like they slid down and froze there.

"Abe will be here soon. Just hold on, Mr. Benton. It's going to be all right."

I wasn't so sure that was true, but it made me feel better to say it. I hoped it made him feel better too.

There was only one more floor in the building. When Mr. Benton disappeared again through the ceiling, I headed up to the floor above me. I called Debbie to let her know where I was. Abe had just arrived with Morris and another man.

"Probably same thing as before," I told her. "I'll try to find him."

This time I wasn't so lucky to catch people running from the ghost as I left the elevator, but I heard screams from the second condo on the floor. I wished it was as easy as taking out my Beretta and shooting something, but a piece of metal meant nothing to this situation as was the case in most of my encounters with other zombies.

I pounded on the door. A man and woman peeked out. Their faces were filled with terror. They immediately took me up on my offer to handle the situation. As the elevator doors parted for them to leave, Debbie, Abe, Morris, and the other man got off.

"Where is he, Skye?" Abe asked.

"In here." I held the door for him. "He changed. He's not solid at all anymore. I could barely see him."

Abe didn't speak as he walked by. Morris and the second man that I recognized as another of Abe's strong arm goons went in immediately after him.

Debbie followed them. "Abe's not happy about this."

"Neither am I."

We walked around the condo, staring up at the ceiling, but now Mr. Benton was hovering in the air between the ceiling and the floor. It seemed that he was losing definition. The outlines of his body were gone. I could see everything on the other side of the room through him.

"Abe." His voice was only a whisper. "I'm glad you're here."

"Don't worry. I'm going to take care of this," Abe assured him.

He reached out to touch Mr. Benton, but his hand went right through him. I saw him bend his head and mutter a few words of magic. Nothing changed.

"What happens now?" Mr. Benton asked him.

"I don't know, my friend. I believe this is the end, though I don't understand it. You will go on now as you would have when our tie was severed. I wish I could help you."

Abe looked sincere as he always did when he spoke to his workers. It felt to me like he thought of us as his children. It was possible that Lucas was right about him being an evil influence, but he at least acted kind and concerned.

"Should you cut the silver cord before he disappears completely?" I asked him.

"I didn't bring it with me," Abe said. "I had no idea this was happening."

"But we told you," Debbie said.

He glared at her, and she was silent.

Our last sight of Mr. Benton was sad. He appeared to be calling out though he made no sound. He reached out to Abe but couldn't touch him. A moment later, he vanished. There was nothing left of him.

Abe immediately collapsed on the floor. Morris and the other man struggled to help him into a chair. They collapsed on the sofa after they got him into it.

"What's wrong with him?" Debbie whispered.

"I think he lost the magic he gave to Mr. Benton to sustain his twenty years. He needed to cut the silver cord to get it back before he was gone."

"Will he be all right?"

"I don't know."

Abe slowly opened his eyes. He'd lost his ever-present dark glasses when he'd fallen. He snapped his fingers, and Morris retrieved them but not before we saw his white eyes.

"I'm fine, Debbie. You don't have to worry. It was but one man—only a small part of my energy and magic. I shall recover."

But I could tell she was thinking what I was thinking. If this continued to happen, Abe would lose all of his energy. What would become of us in that event was anyone's guess.

Chapter Fourteen

Abe had Debbie and me gather up all of Mr. Benton's personal possessions and take them to the tattoo shop. It wasn't a lot, but I worried that he might have relatives who'd like them. I hoped Abe would return them when he was done.

On the other hand, I could see that he needed to find out what had caused Mr. Benton to fade away. I wanted to help in that quest since it had a direct impact on me. I wasn't ready to give up my time with Kate. There had to be some answer for what had happened.

"Abe must be thinking there was a curse or spell on Mr. Benton," Debbie said as we lugged the last of the boxes to the van parked in front of the condo complex. "I'm going home to check all of Terry's things when we get done. I wouldn't want him to become a ghost."

"I wonder if Abe still had a sorcerer if he could have prevented it." I closed the back door to the van and nodded to the doorman who'd been watching us. It was getting late again, but we still had to take the boxes to Abe before we could go home for the day.

"I don't know," Debbie said. "But if that's the case, maybe you could convince Lucas to help him."

"That's not going to happen. I told you how Lucas feels about Abe. He's not going to help no matter what."

"I bet he'd help if something happened to you."

"Maybe. I wouldn't want to bet my life on it."

We drove back to Deadly Ink in the sultry evening weather. Traffic was heavy as usual. The rain still hung above us oppressively, but it hadn't done more than let go of a few drops that splatted on the dusty cars.

Brandon was at the tattoo shop when we got there. We broke up what looked like a deep discussion between him and Abe as they were closeted in Abe's office. As soon as they saw us, they opened the door, Morris and a few others got the boxes out of the van.

"Quite an afternoon," Brandon said, waggling his brows. "Now I have to look forward to going out as a ghost instead of a zombie."

Debbie shuddered at his words. "It was terrible. Don't talk about it. That poor man."

He put his arm around her waist as he stared into her half open tank top at her breasts. "Sorry you had to go through that, honey. I've got just the thing for you over at the mortuary."

"You're so kind." She smiled at him and smoothed a hand down his face. "But I have to get home."

Brandon still didn't move away from her—until Abe stared hard at him.

"Did you find anything unusual in Ash's belongings?" Abe asked me.

"I don't know. There were a lot of clothes, some jewelry, and a few knick-knacks. The super said the condo came furnished. He watched us the whole time to make sure we weren't taking anything that didn't belong to Mr. Benton."

"Perhaps that is an issue we should look into." Abe snapped his fingers and dispatched Morris and another man with the tattoo of a tiger on his face. "Talk to the superintendent. See if he knows something."

When we were alone, I questioned him. Abe was scary, but I tried not to back down from him on important issues. "What caused this? What am I looking for?"

"Magic, of course. Whoever killed my magic user did it for this purpose. Harold's death left me vulnerable to attack." He eased himself into his old chair behind the desk. "My own magic must be guarded by other kinds of magic, such as the type Lucas wields so casually. Without it, all my people will perish and me along with them."

"I can ask Lucas again if he'll work for you."

"No need. I have an interview with another magic user. Continue searching for Harold's killer. That's where we'll find our answers."

Was it me, or did he seem smaller than before? He was weaker, by his own admission. It was terrifying to think that my life and Kate's hung in the balance again. I had no choice but to follow the path I had been set on and hope Abe would be able to maintain his people.

I left his office. The tattoo shop was strangely quiet and empty. Where was everyone?

Debbie was waiting outside as she usually did. She couldn't take the rude remarks from the men who hung around.

"What did he say? Is he okay?" she asked.

"I guess he's okay for right now. We have to find whoever killed Harold." I started walking down the sidewalk. "Let's hit the smoke shop and see if we can find out what kind of cigarettes this butt belongs to."

"Okay, although I have to get home soon."

"Debbie, if Abe disappears like Mr. Benton or dies, so do I. So does Terry. I don't think I can do anything about finding him another magic user, but I can find Harold's killer."

"Lucas cares about you. Tell him he has to protect Abe. He'll do it if you tell him to."

"I'm not his master. I'm not going to tell him to do something he clearly doesn't want to do. Besides, Abe has someone else in mind."

The smoke shop was only a couple blocks up from Deadly Ink and Simon's Mortuary. I thought about stopping and talking to Brandon, but that usually wasted more time than his information was worth.

It was hot and humid on the street. Heat lightning flashed across the dark sky, but it was just a tease. There was no rain in the forecast again, and people were getting worried. The Cumberland River was wide and deep, feeding the water Nashville and the surrounding areas needed to grow, but it wasn't infinite. There was also the threat of fires in the mountains where the woods were tinder dry.

The smells of fried food seemed anchored around us by the lack of rain or even the scarcest breeze. People were sitting out on the curb in plastic chairs, smoking and drinking cold beer. The local drug dealers looked at us and then looked away. They knew who we worked for.

The lights were still on in the smoke shop when we got there, and the open sign was flashing. I took the butts with the gold wrappers from my pocket as we went inside. We were alone with the man behind the counter.

"Good evening." He nodded to us. "How may I assist you?"

I'd seen him at the coffee shop that was close to the mortuary. He was an older Indian man with a red caste mark on his forehead. He always wore the same blue turban.

"I'm looking for the cigarette that goes with this butt." I put it on the glass counter. Hookahs and rolling papers were inside it. "It seems distinctive to me."

He smiled and glanced carefully at the gold wrapped butt. Then he opened the plastic bag it was inside and smelled it. "Oh yes. I know this brand. We sell it here. Would you like a pack?"

"No," Debbie said. "Those things are nasty."

"Yes, please," I contradicted her. "We'd like a pack."

It was a foreign brand, made in Egypt according to the label. I paid him the exorbitant price for it and then put it in my pocket.

"Do a lot of people buy these? They seem unusual."

He shrugged his thin shoulders beneath his white shirt. "Not so many, but enough for me to carry them."

"We're looking for a man." I thought about the image Lucas had raised in the palm of his hand. It was hard to say exactly what he looked like. "Maybe medium height and build."

His dark eyes narrowed. "Are you a cop?"

"No. I work at Deadly Ink."

A look of fear swept over him, and he trembled as he breathed. "Abe."

"That's right." I'd take fear if that helped us.

"Only one man this week was here to buy these." He pointed to the cigarettes. "He was taller than me and didn't say anything. He bought the cigarettes and left. That's all I know."

"Do you have surveillance?" When he looked blank, I pointed to the camera in the corner. "Video of the shop."

"Oh no." He smiled happily about it. "Too expensive. That is a fake I put in myself to fool the robbers."

"Anything else you can tell us about this man?" Debbie demanded.

The man behind the counter glanced away as he tried to think of something else. His face brightened when he said, "He had a tattoo and several piercings. He wasn't old but not young either. He was fair. I don't recall his eyes. He smiled and thanked me when I gave him the cigarettes. I'm afraid that's all."

"Thanks for nothing." Debbie started toward the door. "That could be one of a hundred men who hang out at Deadly Ink. Let's go, Skye."

"Just a minute." I turned to the man behind the counter. "What kind of tattoo? Where was it?"

"He had a tattoo on his arm of a mystical beast—perhaps a dragon of some sort. And another on the back of his neck. I noticed when he turned to leave. It was a sideways figure eight. I believe they call that the sign of eternity."

"Okay. Thank you."

Debbie and I walked out of the smoke shop. We were both sweating since there was no air conditioning in the shop. The proprietor was completely cool or at least appeared that way. Not even perspiration on his brow.

"So one of dozens of men who look the same bought the cigarettes and may have been smoking them in the alley before, during, or after Harold was killed." Debbie summed up what we'd found so far in a critical voice.

"I've solved cases, or seen them solved, with less information."

She yawned. "Is that it? Do we have to go anywhere else?"

"No. We can go home."

Debbie glanced at her watch. "Oh my God, It's almost eight-thirty. We have to hurry."

We got in the van, and I glanced at her. "What's the big deal? Terry might be handicapped, but there's still an adult at the house. And Bowman isn't a little kid anymore."

"You don't understand." She tapped her fingers nervously on the door handle. "I have to be there for Terry. It was okay last night because the kids were out. They can't be there after nine with him by themselves."

Traffic was getting thin going out of the city. I passed a few cars trying to accommodate Debbie's timetable. I could tell from her voice that this wasn't just a random request to get home in time to read a bedtime story.

"What's really happening?" I asked her.

"Terry has started freaking out at nine p.m. each night. I can't explain it. I don't even like to think about it, but I don't want the kids to be there by themselves when it happens. It's scary for me, and I'm an adult. Besides, Bowman has changed so much toward his father. I don't know what he'll do if…"

I didn't understand, but I assumed it had something to do with the changes Terry was going through. "I'll do the best I can. We might make it. It should be close anyway."

We were only a few minutes from Debbie's house when we passed the leaving Nashville sign. Debbie was almost bouncing off the sides of the van. She glanced at her watch every two minutes. When it was nine, she tensed up and let out a short expletive.

"Can't we go any faster? If you're worried about a ticket, I'll pay it. Please, Skye, we have to get to the house."

"Why didn't you tell me you were so worried about leaving the kids with Terry? Maybe we could find someone to take care of them if you have to be out late."

"Like a ghostly mother-in-law or an amnesiac sorcerer?" Her laugh was brittle. "Like I'd leave my kids with Addie or Lucas. If you want to do that with Kate, that's up to you."

Her words put my teeth on edge, but I knew she was upset. I paid attention to the road and getting us to her house safely.

"I'm sorry, Skye. You know I didn't mean it. I'd give anything to have someone responsible like Addie, even if she is a ghost. Things in my life are so far out of control. It's hard to hold it in all the time." She glanced out the window. "I'm thinking about taking Bowman and Raina to stay with their grandparents for a while. I've put it off because they'd have to change schools. I was hoping to finish up the year and let them spend time with my parents. Maybe things will be better by the end of the summer."

"Is this because Terry changes every night?" I knew for Debbie even thinking about taking her kids somewhere else was a move of desperation.

"It's what he's changing into. I...I can't explain it. The kids have already seen too much. I don't want them to hate their father. I don't want anyone to get hurt."

"You're afraid Terry will hurt one of them?"

"No." Her voice was painful. "I'm terrified that Bowman will kill his father."

Chapter Fifteen

We pulled into the driveway. I took the turn a little too fast and gravel spit out from under the tires. There were no lights on at the house. I didn't like it. Someone always left the porch light on for her.

"That's fine. Thanks, Skye. I can handle it from here. I'll see you tomorrow." Her smile in the light from the dash was strained and she was crying.

I parked the van and shut off the engine. "I'm not leaving until I know everything is okay."

Debbie was already out the door and running toward the house. I grabbed the tranq gun and my Beretta before I followed her.

We didn't make it into the pretty log cabin before we both heard screams from the area around the garage to the right side of the cabin. It sounded too high-pitched to come from a man—it was one of the children.

Debbie screamed too and ran toward the garage. I followed her, keeping a close watch around us. I didn't know what Terry had changed into either, and I didn't want to find out as he was ripping at my throat.

In the dim, overhead light next to the garage, I caught a glimpse of something fast that moved along the side wall and disappeared behind the building.

"He's behind the garage," I yelled to Debbie as I tossed the tranq gun to her. "Use it if you need to. Don't let something happen that can't be made right."

She nodded and stuffed it into the pocket of her shorts but kept running.

We heard someone call out again, the voice echoing in the darkness. It was difficult to tell which direction it was coming from. We ran behind the garage, but no one was there. Shadows concealed the back of the garage structure. The light was adjusted to illuminate the front entrance.

There was a large meadow that swept up a hill from Debbie's property. I caught a glimpse of someone running that way and pointed it out to my partner.

"It's Terry." Her breath came hard and fast. "He's got Bowman."

"What do you want to do?"

"Whatever we have to do to get him back." There was no doubt in her tone. If she'd had to kill Terry at that moment to rescue her son, she would've done it.

I nodded and took out my gun. We kept running after them.

It was difficult to track them. The clouds kept even starlight from showing us their passage through the tall weeds and grasses. There was no moon and no other streetlights along the road at that point. We had to rely on Bowman calling for help to continue following them.

We finally reached a ridge on the hill. Lights from a dairy farm that lay on the other side of the sharp ridge helped us see Terry and his son. They stood out as Bowman struggled to get free from his father.

"I'll come around from the other side," I said to Debbie. I was a faster runner with my long legs and lack of bosom. It would also give her time to see if she could handle the situation without force. It was possible she could still talk the pair out of their disagreement.

"Be careful," Debbie pleaded. "Don't hurt Bowman."

I ran along the side of the ridge where I still had the cover of clouds and darkness. Debbie ran straight to the spot where her loved ones were struggling. I hoped seeing her would be enough to calm Terry and end his rampage.

"Why are you here?" the voice was almost a growl—virtually non-human. "Go home. I am taking care of the problem."

That had to be Terry, but it sounded nothing like him. I could see his silhouette in the light behind him. He looked as much like an animal as he sounded.

"Give me Bowman," Debbie implored. "You can run free all night if you want to. Just give me our son."

I sneaked closer to the spot where they were talking.

"Mom! Help me. He wants to kill me." That was Bowman, still high-pitched and filled with terror.

"Let me have him, Terry." Debbie had started crying. "Don't make me hurt you."

Terry roared. "He attacked me. He deserves what he gets."

"He tried to kill Raina." Bowman defended himself. "I hit him with my baseball bat."

"Not a wise decision." Terry shook his son as though he were a rag doll.

Why had Debbie thought Bowman would be the aggressor? She knew Terry was going through these changes. Why had she been so certain he wouldn't hurt their kids?

The answer was obvious—she was afraid all the time that this would happen. She'd hoped things would be all right, but this was why she was so worried about getting home late every day.

"Put him down, Terry." Debbie was still crying, but her voice was steady as she pointed the tranq gun at him. "I don't want to do this, but I will."

I was close enough to get off a shot that would hit him if it came down to it. Terry seemed so engrossed with Debbie and Bowman that he hadn't noticed me. I held the Beretta steady on him and waited to see what happened.

Terry picked Bowman up and slung him across his back like a sack of grain. What he'd lost in height from his transformation, he'd gained in strength. His body was completely covered in stiff, thick hair. His legs were bowed like a goat's, ending in large hooves. He'd grown horns on his head that curved slightly, and when I saw his face, I had to catch my breath.

He looked far more like an animal than a human. The change had taken him over.

Debbie didn't wait another instant for him to run with her son. She fired the dart from the tranq gun that we used to subdue runaway zombies. Usually one did the job.

It had no visible effect on Terry.

She fired again and again. I could see the darts sticking out of his back, but they didn't stop him.

Before Terry could make it any further from us down the hill toward the farm, I aimed the Beretta at him and fired low, catching him in the leg.

He dropped to the grassy hill, moaning and swearing. He and Bowman rolled over and over like a pair of young children having fun. Debbie screamed when she heard me fire and started after them.

Judging the position she was going to be in when they got to the bottom of the hill, I ran back for the van and pressed hard on the gas pedal to be there when she needed me.

I thought about checking on Raina—she could be hurt and alone in the house. But I judged that Debbie was going to need me more. I rounded the curve in the road that led to the farm and drove quickly down the gravel road.

Debbie was on the ground with Bowman and Terry. She was hugging her son and sobbing. I got out of the van and, hoped no one had seen what had gone on.

"We should get him in the van," I said. "Whoever lives here could wonder what's happening."

Debbie pushed to her feet, furious as she charged at me. "You shot him. I can't believe you shot my husband."

She punched at me a few times, but I fended her off.

"He was leaving with Bowman. What else could I do? You said whatever it took. At least I only winged him."

"No, Mom." Bowman got to his feet and wrapped his arms around his mother. "He would've killed me. Thanks, Skye."

Debbie collapsed against her son. "Why is this happening? I don't understand."

I didn't encourage her to ruminate on the problem. "I don't either, but we aren't going to get any answers standing out here, and the farmer might call the police. We have to get Terry in the van and get out of here."

Bowman nodded and helped his mother into the front seat. He came back and stared at his father who was writhing and howling on the ground. "I wish you'd killed him," he said. "Look at him. He wanted to tear Raina apart tonight. I could see it in his eyes. Did Mom tell you that he dragged her down the stairs two nights ago? I tried to kill him then, but he's too strong."

"I know this is hard." I put my hand on his shoulder and stared into his angry face. "But this is all we can do right now. Grab his legs and help me get him in the van. Don't think about anything else. Let's just get this done."

He nodded and squared his narrow shoulders. I got up under Terry's head and neck, but he swiped at me. His long claws caught my arm and the side of my face.

"This isn't going to work. We can't knock him out. We can't reason with him. We'll have to tie him up."

I sent Bowman to the van for plastic restraints that I wasn't convinced were going to hold him, but I didn't know what else to do. His clawed hands kept waving at me, trying to catch me again. I finally sat on top of him and held his arms to the dry ground beneath us.

"Hurry," I urged Bowman. "I can't hold him for long."

Terry was stronger than I'd imagined. Bowman and I probably couldn't have managed him if Debbie hadn't reluctantly left the van and helped us. Together we put double plastic restraints on his wrists and legs. His hooves kicked out at us, but there were no more injuries. We lifted him and pushed him into the back of the van. I slammed the door closed and leaned against it.

"Are you okay, Skye?" Bowman asked when he saw the blood on my face and arm.

"I'm fine. I just need a few bandages."

"We have those and antibiotic ointment at the house," Debbie said in a flat voice. "We can clean you up there."

We got in the van—I was ready to start the engine— when I saw a shotgun sneak up close to my ear. I'd left the window open and a serious-looking farmer had shoved the end of the barrel inside.

"What the hell is going on out here?" he demanded.

I raised my hands and improvised. "We were looking for our lost dog."

"Dog? What kind of dog?"

Great. Now he was going to want to talk about lost dogs he'd found on his property.

"A poodle. Actually, a peek-a-poo. Barely two months old. Very small. Very harmless."

"But we're worried she might have been hurt," Bowman added from the backseat. "Have you seen her, sir? She has little red ribbons in her hair. She just got back from the groomer."

The farmer put down his shotgun. "No, son. I haven't seen your pretty dog out here tonight. Aren't you the boy who lives next door in the log cabin? I think I bought some school raffle tickets from you last fall."

"That's right." Bowman laughed almost hysterically. "You bought twenty dollars' worth. I hope you won something."

"Yeah. My wife got a new blender out of the deal." The farmer spat on the ground. "I'm sorry about your dog, son. I'll keep an eye out for her."

"Thank you." Bowman's voice shook. He was near his breaking point.

"You all haven't seen any sign of a wolf about here, have you?" the farmer asked. "It's been breaking into my hen house pretty regular like. I think it even attacked one of my cows the other night. I put in a call to the wildlife officer. He says we're gonna get a hunting team together and track it down."

"No," I answered. "I sure hope it doesn't get our little peek-a-poo. Thanks for your help."

He stepped back, and I got out of his yard.

"Dad's been coming home every morning covered in blood and chicken feathers," Bowman said in a scared voice. "Will the wildlife officer track him back to our house and kill him?"

"Don't say that," Debbie hissed. "He's still your father. He just needs help."

"Sure, Mom. Whatever you say."

When we got back to the cabin, Raina came running out. She was disheveled and crying but not injured. Debbie and her kids hugged each other. I looked away, wishing I was home with Kate. It was going to be another night where I was out past her bedtime. No doubt Addie would have plenty to say on the subject.

Maybe she was right. Maybe I deserved it. I was leaning too heavily on her and Lucas to fill in the gaps. I knew I needed to be home more—I just didn't know how to make that happen.

"What do you want to do with him?" I asked Debbie, suddenly impatient to leave.

She wiped the tears from her face. "I think we should lock him in the basement. We don't have to go down there much. It would keep him out of the way until we can figure this out."

"I think you should take him to Abe and demand to know what's going on," I argued. "Whatever this is, a doctor can't resolve it. You need help."

"That's my decision," Debbie said. "At least for now. I don't trust Abe to do what's right for him. I know what he wants from me. He might be willing to kill Terry to get it."

Or let him change into something you can't live with.

"Sorry." She glanced away. "I didn't mean to sound like Abe would do anything—I'm just a mess right now."

"Don't worry about it." I squeezed her arm. "Let's get him inside."

Chapter Sixteen

We dragged Terry into the basement with him fighting us the whole way. He slid down the stairs, bumping his head every few seconds. It couldn't be helped. Bowman found some strong rope, and we tied him more securely.

"We need a cage for him," Debbie said. "He needs to be safe until we can fix him. He can't stay this way."

"Any idea who's going to fix him if you don't take him to Abe?" I wiped blood off my face.

"What about Lucas?" She faced me with frantic eyes. "You could ask him, right? Maybe he could help."

"I could ask him," I agreed with a sigh. I couldn't assure her that he'd come running over, but I could ask.

"Good. Thanks, Skye."

When we had Terry settled, he seemed to calm down and even had a more human appearance and disposition. I didn't trust that it would last. This had been slowly creeping up on him since last year. I believed he would eventually transform and never change back again.

I didn't say what I was thinking to Debbie before I left. She'd been sitting at the kitchen table with a blank expression on her face. Bowman had gone up to bed. Raina had followed him. I said goodnight to my partner and left. She didn't respond.

Despite feeling bad leaving her, I really wanted to go home. Even with the idea that Lucas could be an evil sorcerer, home was still the safest place I knew. I wanted to kiss Kate's face even if she was sleeping. I wanted to feel normal for a while. I knew my life would never be normal again, not the way I'd known it before Jacob's death. But at least I could pretend things were normal at Apple Betty's Inn.

This time I didn't take the shortcut past the place where Jacob had died. If there was something else going on there, I didn't want to know. Not tonight. The lights were on outside the inn, and a few windows were lighted inside. The old Festiva was there beside the pickup truck Lucas had repaired. At least he got back all right.

I dropped my shoes in the mudroom, glad to feel the chill of air conditioning as I walked in the door. Maybe I could still feel heat because I was going to hell in seventeen years for cheating my natural death.

The Christian concept I'd been raised with had crossed my mind from time to time in the past three years. But if that was the case, so be it. I didn't care—after all I'd seen since my death. I wasn't even sure I believed in heaven and hell anymore.

Addie wasn't waiting for me. She was around the inn somewhere and didn't want to see me. Probably angry that I was late again. That was fine. I wasn't sure how I'd react to one of her scoldings anyway.

Lucas was in the kitchen. He handed me a glass of whiskey. I sat at the table with him and drank it in one gulp. His dark brows went up.

"Bad day." It wasn't a question.

"Yes." I poured myself another. "You have no idea."

He nodded as he sipped his first glass. "Terry has been acting up again."

I glanced at him. "You knew?"

"I...hear things."

"Great." I drained the second glass. "How long has this been going on?"

"Never mind that. It's not important. You should go up to Kate's room before you can't walk up the stairs and you pass out on the sofa."

The bottle was in my hand. He was right. I had to see Kate.

She was asleep, thankfully. I started crying when I saw her face. I cried for her and the innocence of her childhood that I felt was lost. I cried for Jacob and for me. I struggled to remember why this shell of half-life was important. Most of the time, I'd rather be dead.

I felt better after I'd cried. Jacob used to laugh at me when I cried over silly things like taking Kate to the doctor for shots. He said I was too tenderhearted and then he'd held me his arms.

Lucas was waiting in the bedroom. He'd brought the bottle of whiskey up with him. I bypassed that and an empty glass to settle against him. I closed my eyes as he put his arms around me. He didn't try to tell me that everything was going to be okay, as Jacob used to. He didn't say anything.

We made love in the big bed with the constant fire of the hearth throwing red flames on the walls and ceiling. Usually when we came together, I fell asleep immediately after. It was a blessed stretch of blankness—no thoughts, no dreams.

But not tonight.

I was still restless and got up from bed to wander aimlessly through the dark inn. I didn't see Addie. She was really avoiding me. I only spent a few minutes in Jacob's room. My mind couldn't focus on trying to figure out the puzzle of his death.

I ended up in the kitchen again, at the table. I wanted to cry, but there were no tears left. I tried to marshal my thoughts, but they were wild and beyond my reach.

Deciding that I still might fall asleep if I went back to the turret room and lay down beside Lucas, I put my hand on the old wood table—and my hand went through it.

It was probably going to happen to all of Abe's zombies. Leave it to me to be the last of Abe's legacy. He'd been doing this for over two hundred years, and it had never happened before.

As I thought about it, I felt a curiously light sensation. I looked down at my body. It was becoming transparent. I'd begun to drift away from the table. It was like being in a dream, soft and gentle. I was changing. No need to worry. It wasn't a big deal. I closed my eyes and let it happen.

Suddenly something grabbed me. I was still solid enough that I could be held. I opened my eyes and looked into Addie's frightened face.

"What the hell are you doing? You can't just disappear. Kate needs you." Addie said the words to me quickly and then opened her mouth to let out a horrible, shrill call. "Lucas!"

I was out of my dream state by then and frantically clawing at the ceiling, trying to hold on to something. I grabbed the ceiling light, but my hands passed through it. Addie was trying to pull me down to the floor, but couldn't get a good grip anymore.

"Lucas!" Addie yelled again. "Get your butt down here!"

"Grandma?" Kate was out of bed and scurrying down the stairs. "What's wrong? Why is Mommy on the ceiling?"

"Go back to bed, Kate," I said.

No words came out. My mouth moved, but I had no voice.

She started crying, and I forced myself out of the peaceful dream I'd allowed myself to be lulled into. This couldn't happen to me as it had happened to Mr. Benton. I couldn't leave Kate. Not yet.

I pushed at the ceiling with my feet, but I couldn't get away from it. I tried to wrap my legs around the light—nothing. I grabbed Addie's hand, which was surprisingly strong and real. I kept trying to scream. I couldn't say anything.

Lucas came down the stairs after Kate. He saw me on the ceiling, and his gaze riveted on me. I wondered if he'd know what to do. We'd certainly found no answer for Mr. Benton.

"Addie, you have to meld with Skye," Lucas said.

The expression on my mother-in-law's dour face was almost one of horror.

"Meld with her? What does that mean? Do some magic. Make her solid again."

"I can't. Not like this. You have to put yourself inside her. Because I've been helping you gain your abilities as a ghost, I think I can help Skye—if you are inside her."

"I can't do that." She glanced at me. "I can't go inside another person. That's crazy. Not to mention disgusting. There has to be another way."

"There isn't, and there is no time to argue. Look at her. She's starting to go through the ceiling. If she disappears from the house, there is nothing we can do."

Addie clearly wanted to help, but not at the cost Lucas was requiring of her.

"Please, Grandma," Kate asked. "Please save Mommy. I don't want her to go away like Daddy did."

I knew Addie couldn't resist Kate's plea. Her expression might be something she'd wear as she was contemplating picking up after a dog, but I knew she'd at least give it a try. I wasn't sure it would work and cursed my stupidity for not telling Lucas what was happening to the other LEPs.

Why did I think I'd be immune?

"Okay. Okay. I'll try it," Addie said. "So what do I do? Do I have to go in through her mouth or her ear? Because I'm not going through the other area. I don't care if she floats into space."

"No. It doesn't matter," Lucas explained. "Remember when I showed you how to get inside the refrigerator without opening the door? That's all you have to do. Don't think of her as a person. Just hop inside and stay there for a moment to anchor her."

Addie screwed up her face and did as he said. I could immediately tell the difference. I started coming down from the ceiling, feeling solid again. I wished Kate would go back to bed. I didn't want her to see me this way.

"There." Addie nodded my head. "I'm in her. It's no picnic so whatever you're going to do better be fast, sorcerer."

Lucas smiled as he touched my hand. "That's fine. You did exactly what I needed. You're wonderfully strong now, Addie. You could do anything."

"Quit the BS and get on with it. Have you ever been inside another person? You know I can't take a shower anymore."

"I need to talk to Skye so I can understand why this happened," he said. "You're the dominant spirit in this form. You'll have to release some control for her to speak."

"Sure. The first time I have the edge on her, and you want me to give it up." She shrugged. "All right. If I can figure out how."

"Say something, Skye," Lucas said. "You should be able to speak and be heard."

I tried to say something again, but nothing came out. I was worried about that last phase I'd seen Mr. Benton go through where he was simply not there anymore. I didn't want to go out that way.

"Skye?" Lucas shook us.

"I'm here." I spoke, but my voice was strange and unfamiliar. "I should've told you, but there was so much going on. This happened to one of Abe's people today. He just became invisible and finally disappeared."

"What did Abe do?"

"We all stood there and watched it happen. He didn't know what to do. It's never happened before. Lucky me, huh?"

I wondered if I looked like me or if I looked like Addie. Did I have Addie's face with my nose? I couldn't look down and see myself. I'd thought becoming a zombie was the weirdest thing that could happen to me. I was wrong.

"So he had no idea what was causing this or how to stop it?" Lucas's brows knit together above his green eyes. "It seems to be a curse. It has to be anchored by something all of you share. I may not be able to reverse it. Without knowing the spell, it's very difficult."

He contemplated the problem at length until Addie took over the form we shared again.

"Kate, get up to bed right now. You still have school tomorrow." It was Addie's voice. "And Lucas, is this going to work or not? I can't stay inside Skye forever."

"I don't want to go back to bed until I see what's going to happen," Kate argued.

"Your mother is going to be fine. Now go back to sleep."

They finally agreed that Kate could sleep on the sofa in the family room. I could see her still watching us through the kitchen doorway.

"Well?" Addie addressed herself again to Lucas.

"I think I have the only possible answer," he said.

"I don't care what it is," Addie said. "Can you fix it or not?"

"I believe so, but it will take some risk." Lucas stared into our eyes as though he was trying to see me inside Addie. "Let her speak again. She must make this decision."

It was easier this time trading places with Addie. I found my voice and asked what he could do.

"I think the curse is on Abe's mark upon your foot. If I remove that mark, you should be back to normal."

"Normal? Like dead, but not dead?"

"Yes. But there is a chance that if I remove the mark, you will simply die."

Chapter Seventeen

It wasn't a difficult decision to make. If I stayed in this ghost form, I would definitely be gone. At least I had a chance with Lucas's plan.

"Okay. But how are you going to remove it when I'm not solid. Can you remove a ghost tattoo?"

He shrugged. "If you're asking me how it will work—I'm not sure. Magic put that tattoo on your foot. Magic should take it away."

"Magic and a tattoo artist. He made the mark first and then Abe put the magic in it. Can you do that? Do we need to get someone from Deadly Ink to remake the mark?"

"I don't think we have time for that. I shall create a magic mark that should sustain you. Do you want to try?"

It occurred to me again that Lucas had been practicing magic quite a bit more than he was letting on. He had control over what he was doing, even if it didn't always quite work out the way he wanted.

I was scared, but he was right—I could feel that drifting feeling again even though Addie was inside of me. I didn't have much time. I had to take a chance on his abilities, and hope he could keep me here.

"All right. Let's do this. Can you close the kitchen door? I don't want Kate to see me if it goes bad."

He closed the door and returned, bowing his head to me. "On my honor, Skye Mertz, I will care for your family if this doesn't work. I will not allow your daughter to be alone, hungry, or cold. She will not suffer for your death."

His words were fiercely dramatic and sincere. I knew he was swearing an oath to me in the only way he knew how. I appreciated what he said and tried not to smile at the way he'd said it.

"Thank you, Lucas. I trust you to care for Kate."

He rubbed his hands together. "Addie, you must leave Skye now."

I could feel Addie's fear. Though she'd complained about being inside me, she was worried that I wouldn't survive when she left.

"It's okay," I told her. "It's gonna work. If it doesn't, take care of Kate."

"You don't have to tell me that. I'm not a nincompoop. Just get on with it. If you don't come back, give Jacob a hug for me."

Addie's spirit disengaged from mine. I saw her standing beside Lucas. I wasn't floating away again as I thought I might. There seemed to be a green glow holding me in place. I was still becoming more and more transparent, but I wasn't fighting the ceiling.

Lucas laid his hand on my foot that sported Abe's tattoo. He closed his eyes and spoke a few words that had no meaning to me. My foot began to glow green too. I thought that I should have called Abe to warn him. He might feel the change when Lucas was finished. He could suffer that bout of weakness again as he had when Mr. Benton had disappeared.

But it was too late.

I looked at my feet and legs. They were glowing bright green, and the color was spreading up to my torso and through both my arms and hands. Lucas was staring at me. My mind was unfocused, fearful. I reached out to grab his hand and was able to touch him.

"I hope she's not gonna stay green like that all the time," Kate said from the doorway. "She can't ever come to school again like that."

Lucas took both my hands in his and smiled. "I believe we've been successful. How do you feel?"

The green glow around and through me was gone. I felt good—solid and human again. I reached out to touch the wall behind me. No problem. Kate ran up and jumped into my arms.

"I'm good." I held my daughter tightly. "I think you're right. You did it. Now we know how to reverse the curse. Thank you."

"Abe will have noticed this," Lucas warned. "You are not the same as you were before, but you are still here among us."

"Come on, chicken feet," Addie insisted as she shepherded Kate to bed when I put her down. "I think you've had enough excitement for tonight. I'd better not hear any complaining in the morning when you're tired either."

"Aw, Grandma." But Kate grinned. "Goodnight, Mommy. Goodnight, Lucas. Thank you."

Lucas gallantly bent his dark head to her.

When we were alone in the kitchen, Lucas made coffee as I dropped into a chair.

"You're better at magic than you let on, aren't you?"

"It comes and goes," he answered. No commitment.

"You don't have to lie. It's not like I'm going to kick you out even if you're a full-fledged sorcerer of universal power."

He grinned as he poured coffee into two mugs. "I'm not sure what that is, but I can assure you that I mean no harm to you or Kate. I still have moments when all magic deserts me. I can't make myself remember how I came to be here. But I am stronger."

"Thanks for what you did tonight." I took the mug from him. "And what you've done since you came. Everything looks great. Is that what sorcerers do to regain their power?"

Lucas sat across from me and grimaced as he took a sip of the coffee. "Sometimes to learn is to start from scratch. Plus, this place needed some aid. I was glad to help."

"Well I know Addie appreciates it. I do too. I'm just not as enthusiastic about cleaning and pruning as I should be."

Lucas's gaze turned serious as he sipped his coffee. "Perhaps you shouldn't mention this to Abe."

"I think he'll know."

"But he won't be certain unless you confirm it."

"I'll have to tell him if we're going to help the rest of the zombies. It's not happening just to his people who are finished with their twenty years. He found a new sorcerer, if you're worried about him asking you to help him."

"I know how to say no. I don't know what his response will be to your new status."

"My new status?"

He nodded toward my foot. "You've changed. I don't know how much as yet. Only time will tell that."

I lifted my foot that had the tattoo of a pale blue A in a circle. In place of that was a green mark that was a circle with an L inside it.

It took my breath away at first. Was Lucas's magic keeping me alive now? What would Abe say if he saw this? I hadn't appreciated being branded as one of Abe's people in the first place. I wasn't any happier wearing Lucas's brand.

"Was this necessary?"

"The magic must reside somewhere. At least it isn't on your forehead."

I looked up quickly hearing the amusement in his tone. "It wasn't like I enjoyed feeling as though Abe owned me, Lucas. I don't like feeling that way about you either."

"I can take care of that." He raised his hand, and the mark disappeared.

"But it's still there, right? Just screened by magic."

"It's all I can do for you right now, Skye." He got up from the table and held out his hand. "Will you lie with me for what is left of the night?"

I wanted to sleep and forget about everything that had happened that day. But I couldn't. I had to deal with the change I felt inside me.

"I'm going for a walk. I'll be back before breakfast. Goodnight. And thanks again."

He nodded. "You are most welcome."

Outside, the air was thick and humid. It continued to feel as though rain was hanging just above the tree line, ready to fall, but something was holding it back. There were landscaped walking trails in the woods behind Apple Betty's Inn. They'd been put there by Jacob's father for the guests who were looking for something to do.

Tiny lights had been set in the trees, most not working after being ignored so long. No doubt Lucas would find his way out here at some point and clear away the brush, replacing the fairy lights. There were benches and cute statues of dwarfs and frogs. A nice fountain had long gone dry, and the bridge over the little pond was broken.

I walked the trails, knowing them by heart. When Jacob and I were first married, we'd been out here all the time at night. It had been a place of magic to us then.

A few branches had fallen across the path making some of it inaccessible. It had been three years since I'd been out there, but I could still hear Jacob's laughter as I'd tried to jump the pond and missed.

I scrubbed my hands across my ears. Now wasn't the time to get nostalgic about the past.

Lucas seemed certain that Abe would know what had happened to me. What would he say or do? Was Lucas's magic keeping me alive now, or was it some combination of the two?

What had seemed so simple three years ago when I'd signed Abe's contract was suddenly more complex. I knew about magic—and lived with a sorcerer. I wanted to keep investigating Jacob's death, even though I knew Abe wouldn't like it if he found out. And most important, I knew Abe's magic had limitations. I'd thought it was absolute when he'd told me he could offer me another twenty years with Kate.

Things change.

I walked the paths until my hair was wet with dew and my clothes were saturated. Just before dawn, I went back inside to the room Jacob and I had once shared and took a hot shower. I wrapped a towel around myself and looked at my face in the bathroom mirror.

My face looked the same—wide blue eyes, crazy blond hair, and a stubborn mouth. I wanted to believe that everything was going to turn out okay for the rest of my zombie time, but increasingly, I wasn't sure.

Was it running into Lucas that had changed everything? Or was it just the way things happened?

I hadn't known what happiness or security was since Jacob and I had died. This was as close to it as I imagined I would ever get. I had to remember that I was there for one purpose only in the coming years. That was all that was important. I had to focus on what was important—Kate.

Lucas's vow to care for her had touched me. I believed he was sincere when he'd made it. I thought he would take care of her if it was needed. That made me smile.

After getting dressed, I went downstairs. There was bacon and French toast for breakfast. Lucas was smiling and joking with Kate and Addie. Addie was packing Kate's lunch for school. We were just like any other ordinary family on a school day. Even Addie looked so alive that it might be hard for anyone else to know that she was a ghost.

I poured coffee and orange juice and took my seat at the table.

Kate seemed fine except for the dark smudges under her eyes. Lucas and I took her to school, after I'd explained the situation at Debbie's. He'd agreed to take a look at Terry and see if there was anything he could do. I figured he'd managed to turn ghost-me back into zombie-me. Maybe there was something magical he could do with Terry.

"Are you going to try to be home before bedtime tonight?" Kate asked me in the car line at school. "I haven't heard *Goodnight Moon* in a long time."

"I can't make any promises, but I'm going to try really hard. Why don't you have Grandma read it to you?"

"Because she told me it was stupid, and now I don't feel the same about her reading it." She flashed her sweet brown eyes at me. "And I think you should be home early sometimes. Maybe that wouldn't have happened to you last night if you weren't out late all the time. Grandma says nothing good can come of people being out all night."

"Well, Grandma should know." I smiled and ruffled her hair. "I'll do my best to be home early tonight."

"Okay." She looked back at Lucas. "You heard her, right? You're my witness."

"That's right." He laughed. "If she's not home by bedtime, maybe you and I will go looking for her. Perhaps we could help her do whatever she's doing so she gets done sooner."

I didn't say anything to him until she got out of the van, and he'd moved into the front seat.

"What made you say something like that? I hope you know better."

"Maybe I don't." He shrugged. "Maybe we'll come see you at your job. I'm sure that would be enlightening for Kate."

That made me mad. "You don't get to judge me. I do the best I can."

"Your daughter—the reason you agreed to that blasphemous arrangement with a demon—needs you too, just to spend time with her."

If the van would have had more power, I would have laid down some rubber at the end of the school driveway. "I appreciate everything you've done for us, Lucas. But don't try to make me feel guilty about her. And don't ever say something like that again. She's a kid. She doesn't know you're not serious."

"Perhaps I am serious. I imagine seeing Kate at the tattoo shop would remind you when it's time to come home."

I didn't say anything else about it. I was too angry to speak and keep my eyes on the road. We drove to Debbie's house and got out.

"Let me handle my relationship with Kate. I don't need your help with that. She's my weak spot. We both know that. Don't use her against me. You won't like the result."

He bowed his head. "My apologies. It won't happen again."

I marched into Debbie's house—the door was open. Lucas was behind me. There was no one stirring, which immediately threw me into a panic.

"Debbie? Bowman? Raina? Where are you?" I called, fear gripping my throat.

Chapter Eighteen

"In the basement," Lucas said. "I can hear them."

"That's where we put Terry last night." I pulled the Beretta out of my holster.

I ran down the stairs. Terry was still tied, sleeping on his side in a tight fetal position. He hadn't changed back to anything that looked like a man.

Debbie, Bowman, and Raina were asleep on blankets close to him, but not close enough that he could reach them without breaking his bonds.

Relieved, I put away the gun and shook Debbie. "Time to get up. I brought Lucas with me. Your kids are gonna be late for school."

She flew up like a small bird, raising a fuss until her kids were up and moving too.

"I'm so sorry, Skye. Hello, Lucas. Thanks for coming. Do either of you want breakfast? Coffee?"

"We don't want anything. Just get ready so you can take the kids to school. Leave us down here with Terry for a while."

Debbie glanced at her husband. "Okay. Just don't hurt him. He can't help what's happened to him."

"I swear he will not be harmed," Lucas promised.

"Call me if you need anything." Debbie finally broke herself away from Terry and followed Raina and Bowman upstairs.

Lucas squatted close to Terry. He didn't touch him—just looked at him. Terry woke up and stared back at Lucas the way a dog will sometimes stare at his owner.

"What do you think?" I asked.

"*Shh.* Why don't you go upstairs with your friend and leave me to it? I'll let you know when I have an answer."

"If this is because of what I said to you about Kate—"

He glanced up at me. "The two have nothing to do with each other. Go now. You brought me here to see if I can help. Let me have some time."

I went upstairs, still angry about what he'd said in the van and feeling that he was dragging this out with Terry because of it. It only took him a few seconds to know what to do with me last night. Why was this taking so long?

He still wasn't finished when Debbie was ready to take the kids to school. I went with them rather than sitting and waiting for her. Bowman looked like he'd been in a fight, scratched and bruised. He was also sullen and didn't speak. Raina just stared out the window.

On the way back home, I told her how Lucas had managed to change me back from being a ghost.

"My God, Skye," she said. "You were so close to being gone, again. You were lucky he knew what to do."

"I hope so. If he changed me too much and Abe guesses, I could be dead again in no time."

"Maybe Lucas can help Terry since he helped you." She stopped her minivan in the driveway and ran into the house.

I followed her, but Lucas was upstairs. His news wasn't good.

"I can't help him," he told Debbie, holding her hands as she cried. "This change that has come over him is deep within him. It was part of his nature, perhaps his family curse. It has progressed too far. There is nothing I can do. I'm sorry."

From the basement, Terry began to howl and call Debbie's name.

She sat on the sofa, sobbing. "What should I do? I can't take him to Abe. I'm afraid he'll kill him."

"What makes you so certain Abe visited this affliction on him?" Lucas asked.

"It began happening after he brought Terry back to life. I assume that's why he changed."

Lucas was silent, appearing to consider her words. "I understand from what Skye has told me why you don't trust Abe to help your husband, but I think he might be the last hope Terry has."

Debbie's phone rang. The school was calling. Bowman had collapsed, and they needed her to pick him up.

"I can't go in today, Skye. I'm sorry. I should've kept the kids home. It was too much to think we could all go on like normal after what happened last night. Can you handle it if you have a job?"

"Yes. Don't worry about it. Give yourself some time to recover. I don't think Abe is going to send anyone out on a pick up until he figures out what's going on." I squeezed her hand, and she hugged me. "I'll see you later."

"Let me come with you," Lucas petitioned as we left Debbie's cabin. "I can help."

"You don't want to work for Abe."

"That doesn't mean I don't want to be there for you. I might be able to better explain to him about what I did last night. There may be a way he could imitate it. Take me with you, please."

My mind did a rapid reversal. At first I thought there was no way he was coming with me. Then all the stress I'd shared with Debbie's family, compounded by turning into a ghost, caught up with me.

Why *not* let Lucas explain to Abe what he'd done? If there wasn't a job, I'd go home. What could it hurt?

"All right. I could use the company." I started the van. "And you're probably right about being the best one to explain this to Abe. Just don't expect any applause from him. You're not exactly his favorite person."

"I can deal with that. Perhaps I could help you if you have to pick up a zombie becoming a ghost again?"

"Maybe. But where would we get another ghost to go inside the zombie like Addie did?"

* * *

Deadly Ink was quiet for once. Maybe it was a reflection of Abe's mood. He couldn't have been happy about the situation with Mr. Benton and might know that Lucas had taken his mark off my foot.

I had the complete story of how it had happened set in my mind as I walked through the nearly empty tattoo shop. I could explain exactly why Lucas had done what he had to and saved me.

"He's in the back," Morris said. "I think he wants to see you."

"Thanks."

"He can't go back there." Morris inclined his head toward Lucas. "Abe didn't say anything about him."

"Well he's going anyway. Abe is gonna want to hear what he has to say, and I don't think any of us are in the mood to deal with your crap today."

Morris eyed Lucas and stepped back. "Whatever. It's on your head if Abe kills him."

As Lucas and I walked through the hall toward Abe's office, Lucas muttered, "I would like to see him try."

"Shut up unless you want to wait in the van."

The door to Abe's office was open. I saw Brandon lounging back in a chair with a snarky grin on his face. There was another man in there too. I couldn't see his face until I'd entered the room.

I'd never seen this man. He was dressed in a sharp gray suit and wore a burgundy tie. His shirt was a dazzling white. This was a man who cared about what he looked like. I caught a glimpse of a large ruby ring on his finger. He had very blond hair and bright blue eyes. He was smiling until Lucas and I were fully in the office.

"Abe." I nodded to him. "I brought Lucas this morning because—"

The stranger jumped to his feet and tossed the chair where he'd been sitting against the wall. He held out both his hands toward Lucas, and the ruby ring began to glow.

"Lucas Trevailer! Stand ready. I mean you no harm, but I will defend myself if attacked."

I turned slowly to face Lucas who had adopted a similar pose without the glowing ring as he faced the stranger. "You have me at a disadvantage, sir. I do not know you, but I do not mean you harm."

There was so much tension in the small room between the two men that I could almost hear the electricity snapping. Neither man moved, but each kept a careful eye on the other.

Abe got to his feet and slammed his hands on his desk loud enough that the concussion hurt my ears. "Enough! None of that in my office. Take it in the alley if you must fight."

Sorcerers. *Geez!*

This was exactly what had happened with Jasper, Abe's necromancer. At least this man didn't pull out a sword immediately and come after Lucas. That might've been harder for Abe to stop.

Both men put their hands down, and while their eyes remained on each other, each of them took a seat in the office. It seemed the challenge was over.

Abe sat behind his desk. "This is Artemis Elkheart. I assume you both realize he is a sorcerer of the highest rank. I brought him in to help with our ghost problem."

I gulped, realizing that I hadn't breathed or swallowed while the two sorcerers had faced each other. "I brought Lucas for the same reason."

"I appreciate your offer of aid." Abe smiled at Lucas. "But I believe we have this well in hand now. Perhaps it would be best if you left."

Lucas got up to leave without a word.

"Wait! What about the ghost?" I asked him.

"Abe and his sorcerer have it well in hand." Lucas smiled in a predatory manner.

I looked into his eyes and knew it was best to let him go. "I'll be out in a few minutes."

When Lucas had left the office, Brandon closed the door behind him.

"There was another attack last night, Skye." Abe shuffled through some papers on his desk. "I'm not sure which of my people was destroyed, but I felt it. I know the whole thing is part of a curse, thanks to my new sorcerer."

Artemis got to his feet and shook my hand. "I'm sorry there was no proper introduction. You know my name, but I don't know yours."

"Skye Mertz. Nice to meet you."

It wasn't nice to meet him. He was a threat, just as Jasper had been. Lucas was well-known in magical circles. He might not remember them, but they certainly knew him.

Artemis said he was glad to know me and had heard a lot about me from Abe and then sat back down. Brandon was smiling and shaking his head. I supposed it was funny to him somehow.

"As I was saying, I'm leaving it to Artemis to locate the person who became a ghost last night. Because I don't want this to happen to any more of my people, I have retained him as my sorcerer and tasked him with finding the answers to this problem before it becomes a plague."

I watched Abe as he spoke. He looked older and more tired. The shiny black flesh on his face sagged. Was it me he was talking about? Was Lucas right, and Abe couldn't tell that I was the LEP that had changed last night? He could feel the loss of the magic that had escaped him but didn't know who it was?

"I am honored to be working with Abe on this problem." Artemis got to his feet again. He kept fingering the ruby ring. It wasn't glowing, which I assumed meant he wasn't accessing its power. Was he nervous or worried that Lucas might be waiting for him outside?

"Artemis has already come up with a plan to save my people," Abe said. "We know that not only those returning to me can be infected. Artemis has come up with a way to preserve my people as this curse strikes them."

"I am on the verge of that discovery," Artemis corrected. "In the meantime, since there are too many of Abe's people to keep watch over all of them, I will be going out with you, Skye, when you are required to bring in another worker."

Everyone looked at me. I shrugged. "Okay. Is that it?"

"For now," Abe said. "Once we have a way to locate a problem before it becomes bad, I might need your help going to everyone. Until then, we'll do the best we can."

I got to my feet. "Nice to meet you, Artemis. Give me a call when you need me, Abe. I'll be working on Harold's murder."

"Fine. Thank you, Skye." Abe nodded and smiled. "I'll be in touch."

Brandon waved but didn't move. I left the office and Artemis followed me.

"You look like an intelligent woman, Skye. I must warn you about your companion. Lucas Trevailer is not to be trusted. He is a madman and a murderer."

Chapter Nineteen

I toyed with the idea with telling him to mind his own business. But he was dangerous, and there was no reason to antagonize him. I hoped he and Lucas wouldn't go at it like with Jasper. I didn't want it to become an issue between me and Abe.

"Thank you. I appreciate the warning." I smiled, turned away, and started to leave.

Artemis put his hand—the one with the ruby ring—on my shoulder. Something was coming from it, like prickles after your foot goes to sleep. I knew it must be magic. Was he trying to influence me against Lucas?

"You shouldn't be with him, Skye. He will harm you and those you love. Leave it to me and I shall protect you and your daughter."

His eyes glowed as red as his ring. He was exerting himself into my thoughts and emotions.

I wasn't sure how I knew that so clearly unless it was because I had been around Lucas's magic for a while. Lucas might be as evil as Artemis was trying to convince me, but he had never tried to use his magic to influence me this way.

"I understand. Thank you, Artemis." I smiled again, but my patience was beginning to wear thin. "I have to make those decisions. And I don't appreciate you including my daughter in this. We'll work it out. You concentrate on Abe's problems. I'm sure that will be all you can handle."

He seemed amazed that I didn't heed his advice and that his magic seemed not to affect me. Artemis removed his hand from my shoulder. "I fear for your life. Be careful and call me if you need help. I know Lucas is powerful, but I can defeat him."

I was done smiling and being polite. "Okay. Sure. I guess I'll see you later."

"You doubt my word?" He peered closely into my face. "Do you not know who I am?"

Brandon popped his head out of the doorway to Abe's office. "Sorry you two. Artemis, if you're done with Skye, Abe wants you back in here."

All the glowing and weird side effects were immediately gone. Artemis nodded curtly and went back to Abe's office. I left the tattoo shop like a rabid dog was chasing me.

Lucas was waiting outside the van with the air of an impatient man.

"Well? What happened? Did he actually figure out the answer, or was he just bluffing?"

"I don't know. He didn't give out any details, except for warning me about you." I glanced at my phone and saw that I'd missed a text from Gerald Linker. He wanted to meet with me at the spot on the road where Jacob, and Julie, had died. Maybe this was a good time to meet with him and see what he had to say.

"What did he say about me?"

"That you're evil and you'll kill me and Kate if you get a chance." I got in the driver's side of the van. "There was something odd though. I think he was trying to use his magic to make me believe him. I can't explain it—something just popped into my mind, and I *knew* it. Probably spending too much time with an evil sorcerer, huh?"

Before I could start the van, he put both his hands on my arms. "Yes. I can feel his magic on you. I can almost smell it. He's very strong. I'm surprised you weren't influenced by him."

"Thanks." I started the engine. "I have enough common sense not to trust someone like him. He even brought Kate into it. I guess Abe must've told him I had a daughter. "

"This has nothing to do with common sense, Skye. Power was exerted to control your thoughts. Only someone with magic could deflect it."

"We've already been through this, Lucas. I don't have any magic—that can't be what brought you here or what stopped Artemis from causing me to hate you. It must be something you've forgotten."

He wasn't happy with that answer. I couldn't help it. I explained that we were going to meet Gerald and got the van out into traffic.

"Abe didn't say anything about you being different, did he?" Lucas asked.

"No. I guess you were right. He didn't notice. He knew one of his zombies had become a ghost. I could tell he'd felt the loss of magic from the way he looked though, couldn't you? But he didn't know it was me."

"He appeared weak and fading." He changed the subject. "What will you and Gerald do at the site of Jacob's death?"

"I don't know. I'm assuming he wouldn't have texted me if he hadn't found some other information he wants to share. This is about justice and finding out who killed these people. If Jacob had survived instead of me, he would've done the same."

"Have you considered what you will do when you find this person?"

"I'll make sure he's arrested. What did you think?"

"I believe you'll find that Gerald has other ideas, Skye. He wants to kill whoever killed his wife. He doesn't care about your sense of justice."

"We'll cross that bridge when we get there. This is the closest I've been to understanding it. If we can take it one step further, we could have this person in custody."

Lucas was quiet for a few minutes as we drove out of Nashville. I saw him watching the road ahead of us out of the corner of my eye.

"Artemis Elkheart is very strong," he finally said in a low voice. "The magic contained in his ring is a diversion. He uses it as a distraction to pull your eye away from what he really intends."

"I noticed that he fiddles with it all the time."

His dark brows went up. "Fiddles?"

"Messes with it. Plays with it. I noticed right away. I didn't know why, but thanks for telling me. If we ever get into a sword fight like you and Jasper did, I'll be sure to ignore the ring."

He smiled. "I don't think that would help you."

"Maybe not, but if we get into a sword fight, I'll just shoot him anyway. No distractions." I pulled the van off the side of the main road near the woods where Jacob was killed. "I'm glad you've kept your sense of humor about it. I'm not afraid of Artemis, and his words mean nothing compared to your deeds."

Lucas shook his head. "Don't underestimate him, Skye. His magic is real. It could be deadly."

"Deadly?" I puzzled. "You think he might have killed Harold?"

"It's possible. As you've witnessed—twice. We seem to fight amongst ourselves."

"I noticed." I studied his face. "Didn't you have the urge to kill Artemis back there?"

"No. Perhaps it's something else missing from my past."

"I guess that's just as well. Let's go."

Lucas and I found Gerald wandering through the forest. He was using a metal detector and putting small items he'd found into a cloth bag he had slung over his shoulder.

He jumped when he heard us and pulled a pistol. "Who's there?"

"It's me," I reassured him. "Skye Mertz. You texted me to meet you here. Remember?"

"Oh yeah." He put the pistol into the cloth bag too. His hands were shaking, and his eyes were wild. "Sorry. It makes me nervous being out here, you know? But I don't see any way to avoid it."

"Did you find something new?" I asked.

"I thought of something." He grinned. "That's good for me. I'm looking for evidence to prove it."

Lucas and I walked with him through the woods as he continually stopped and picked up objects. There were parts of vehicles—from broken taillights to bumpers—strewn through the trees. Fragments of human lives were scattered everywhere. Teddy bears. Dolls. Flashlights. Broken cell phones. These things were what had been left behind when accidents were over.

"What exactly are we looking for, Gerald?" I finally asked.

"Proof that your husband and my Julie weren't killed in the car accidents. It's out here somewhere. We just have to keep looking."

"And what of the creature who stalks these woods?" Lucas asked. "Are you seeking proof that it exists?"

Gerald and I both stared at him.

"What do you mean *creature*?" Gerald questioned. "There's not a creature out here stalking victims. It's a man. Right, Skye?"

Lucas smiled grimly. "Smell the air. Does that smell like a man to you?"

We both took a deep sniff.

"So it smells like dogs or wolves." I shrugged and refused to believe it. "We have both around here. They don't rip people from their vehicles. They don't wait here for the next wreck."

Lucas knelt, and lifted a handful of soil. "This creature is neither dog nor wolf. He is not a man. Check your dates against the full moon. I'm sure you'll find more interesting proof than exists here now."

Gerald and I exchanged crazy glances.

"Are you saying a werewolf killed my wife?" Gerald laughed. "Man, you're crazier than me."

But in the execution of my duties for Abe, I had watched a werewolf change back into a man one day before I took him to the mortuary. I knew they existed but had never considered a werewolf had killed Jacob.

"Why would it stalk these woods?" I glanced around as a breeze rustled the leaves, making me shiver in the heat. "It could be anywhere, right?"

"It probably lives within a few miles." Lucas got to his feet and dusted the knees of his jeans. "But I tell you that the werewolf is what you seek. No doubt your loved ones deaths came on the night of its change. Find the wolf, and you find your killer."

Gerald was skeptical. He continued walking through the trees with his metal detector.

I stopped Lucas from going with him. "Why didn't you mention this before?"

"I had my theories, but this is the first time you've brought me here. I can feel the creature. It will hunt here again. It is the way of it. We all look for the tried and true."

"It's hard for me to believe a werewolf waits out here for cars to wreck." Even though I knew it was possible, it was hard to believe. I studied the woods with new eyes, going back over everything in my mind.

"If a cat is stalking a mouse and finds a spot in a barn where mice come to eat corn, the cat returns for plentiful hunting. These woods are, no doubt, safe during the month, except for the full moon. Cars may find catastrophe here at other times. I believe you'll find that the unexplainable deaths happen here when the creature hunts."

My mind couldn't settle on the idea. I'd been so full of conspiracies and theories of how and why Jacob was killed. This seemed too simple, too easy.

Too crazy.

A werewolf had killed Jacob. I couldn't even say it out loud.

"Will you keep an eye on him?" I asked Lucas after realizing that I had left my phone in the van. "I'm going to check the full moon schedule."

"Certainly."

I ran back to the van and pulled out my phone, flipping through the internet until I found a page that had a listing for every full moon for the last hundred years.

There was the date that Jacob was killed. I skipped forward. There was the date that Julie had died.

My breath was strangled in my chest. I'd been so focused on bringing Jacob's killer to justice. Now there was no justice—only a sudden, extreme urge for vengeance.

I could kill a werewolf. That wasn't the same as killing another human being who could go to prison for his crimes.

Another thought occurred to me. Had Abe known about the werewolf? He'd had one in his employ previously. Was that why he hadn't wanted me to look into Jacob's death? Had he known all along and not told me?

I had to force myself to back up.

One theory at a time, even though the question of Abe's possible involvement burned in me. The first thing I had to do was find proof. Even if it was a werewolf, there had to be some way to prove what had happened. And then we'd have to locate the werewolf, if such a thing was possible.

Looking at the moon calendar, I saw that we were in the middle of a full moon cycle. Was it possible to capture a werewolf? If so, we could compare its DNA to blood samples taken from Jacob and Julie.

Was that the wrong approach? Should I be out buying a weapon to kill the beast? If so, what kind of weapon?

I remembered what a tough fight it had been getting Terry into the van last night. He wasn't a werewolf—still not quite sure what he was—but I had to imagine a wolf would be smarter and stronger.

I saw Lucas and Gerald coming out of the woods toward the van and jumped out to see if Gerald had found anything useful.

"Do you believe this werewolf thing?" Gerald was openly skeptical.

"I don't know what to believe," I admitted. "I'm not well-versed in werewolves or vampires. Not much of a supernatural person. What about you?"

He held up the one thing he had found in the trees. "I might have to get some books."

In his hand was a large, dark claw that still had dried blood on it.

Chapter Twenty

"If you think a werewolf killed Julie, I'll meet you back here," he said. "It's gonna take me a while to get drunk enough to deal with it and then get sober again."

"Yeah." I waited until a fast-moving cement truck passed us on the road. "Me too."

"Why are we taking Lucas's word for this?" Gerald whispered. "How does he know?"

"He studies supernatural things." It seemed the best way to interpret it without sounding completely insane.

"Okay." He shrugged. "I'll be here."

We made sure Gerald left the woods before us. I figured I'd probably need his help to pull this off. We both needed to think about it, maybe look things up.

"So how do you kill a werewolf?" I asked Lucas as we left the wooded area.

"You should think about hunting the werewolf first. And that you should do when it is in its human form. Much easier to kill. Your plan to meet Gerald here after the creature would have changed is folly."

"Folly, huh?"

He nodded. "Stupid. Ridiculous. You have to discover who the wolf is."

"And how would we do that? I don't think we can knock on doors in the area and ask."

"No. The creature would be very secretive. Only members of their pack would know their human names. The beast is vulnerable, especially in its human form. You might have to track the beast after it has hunted and fed to learn its human identity."

"I can't let someone else die so we can figure it out." I told him my possible theory about Abe knowing that the werewolf was out here. "But if I tell him, he'll know I was going against his orders not to look for Jacob's killer."

"Abe's opinion of you may not matter any longer, Skye. His magic may not be sustaining your life. You may not be tied to him."

"But you don't know that for sure, right?" I glanced at him. "And I can't ask him without giving the whole thing away. If I'm still tied to him and if he doesn't like your mark on my foot, that could be it for me. He probably doesn't want me to threaten his werewolf either."

Lucas didn't respond. I knew it was because his magic was still uncertain. I had no doubt that he would free me from Abe if he could. And maybe that was exactly what he'd done. But I had no way to verify it. I was still stuck with Abe even though the tattoo on my foot had an L on it now.

We'd reached Apple Betty's Inn when I got a text from Abe. There was another report of a zombie turning into a ghost.

"I have to go. I'll be back as soon as I can."

Lucas got out of the van. "I think I'll trim the trees along the path in the woods today. That will make it easier for you to walk when you are worried."

I watched him go into the inn. He always seemed to know exactly where I was and what I was doing—and that was before he'd put his mark on me. I wondered if it worked the same for Abe.

Debbie wasn't in any condition to go with me. I didn't tell Abe she wouldn't be there until I got to the house in Nashville where the call had come from. I was surprised to see that Abe was there with Morris and another bodyguard. Brandon was there too.

Abe rarely went into the field himself to see what was going on. The personal attack on him, the effects of his magic being drained—those were good reasons to stretch his legs. Maybe he was checking up on his new sorcerer.

I got out of the van and walked over to Abe's shiny Lincoln. Morris hadn't turned off the engine while they waited. Was he worried about making a quick getaway?

"Where is your partner?" Abe asked. "Where is Debbie?"

"At home, resting up after her husband shapeshifted into something that almost killed her and her kids last night. I helped her tie him up and lock him in the basement, but you can imagine that it was a difficult night for them. She needed the day off."

"And you made this decision for her?"

"Yes. I'm sure you would've made the same decision for her benefit if you'd known." I smiled, reminding him that he had to keep his eyes on the prize if he really wanted to be with Debbie.

I didn't think it was going to happen, but as long as he did, he'd probably be generous.

"How long has he been changing?"

"Since last year when Debbie became my partner. She told you once. She's afraid to tell you again."

"Ridiculous. I doubt I could help, but she shouldn't fear me."

I pushed the limit further. "Why can't you help? He's your creation. Your zombie."

Brandon smirked but covered it quickly.

Abe ignored him. "Please, Skye. You know I hate that term. Terry and Debbie are part of my family—just as you are. Sometimes things happen. Difficulties occur. Nothing is ever without its problems."

"So sometimes you give someone an extra twenty years, and they turn into some kind of creature. Is that what you're saying?"

"It happens." Brandon leaned his head around Abe's so I could see him. "Some of them have to be put down."

"Does this ever include werewolves, by any chance?" My heart was racing, but I couldn't stop myself from asking.

Abe removed his sunglasses and stared at me with his dead, white eyes. "I have never seen a werewolf, have you, Skye?"

"There was that one pick up—"

"I know you said you thought he'd changed. But when I saw him at the mortuary, he was a man."

"Oh, come on, Abe. You know what I mean."

He replaced his sunglasses and nodded toward the house behind me. "You and Artemis should go in now. Already I feel my magic waning. My family is in jeopardy."

"Shall we?" Artemis was abruptly standing close to me. I jumped, angry because he saw it.

As we walked toward the house, he told me that he'd found an early warning system that would allow him to know when one of Abe's people was about to become a ghost. "This will enable us to reach the person before the loss."

I saw his smug expression and decided that I wasn't going to tell him how Lucas had managed to save me from being a ghost. He was so smart—let him figure it out.

Artemis stood back while I knocked at the front door. There was no response from within. Recalling how I was unable to speak, I took out my Beretta and shot the lock off the door.

"After you, sorcerer."

He went in slowly, his head swiveling from side to side as he searched for the LEP who lived here. I kept my eyes on the ceiling since that was where Mr. Benton and I had both drifted.

We found her in the kitchen, still wearing a pink fluffy robe and curlers in her dark brown hair.

"Help me," Her voice was barely audible. "Please. What's wrong with me?"

"Calm down, ma'am." I tried to assuage her fear even though I knew what she was going through was terrifying.

"Can you help me? I don't know how much longer I can hang on this way."

Artemis watched her clinging to a small chandelier over the kitchen table that still held the remains of her breakfast. He didn't say anything—just observed her like she was a fly caught in a spider web.

"Can you do something or not?" I hoped that would nudge him into action.

"Of course." He blinked as though he'd been far away in his thoughts and it had surprised him to have me speak to him. "Excuse me. It takes time to get the proper magic together."

By this time, the woman was barely visible. She couldn't hang on to the ceiling fixture any longer and was against the white tiles. Her voice was gone, but I could still see her wide, frightened eyes. I was sorry I hadn't told him about needing a ghost to be inside of her so he could save her. The words almost sprang from my lips as I watched her suffer.

Then Artemis set up a red hazy perimeter around her, the way Lucas had set the green one around me. The woman slowly came back down to the tile floor. He approached her, putting his hand on her head and closing his eyes. She was enveloped in the heavy red mist until he stepped back from her and the mist evaporated.

"Oh my lord!" the woman exclaimed in a normal voice. "You saved me. I don't know how you did it, but you made me whole again."

She dropped to the floor at his feet, thanking him and crying. I couldn't tell what she was saying since she was sobbing so hard. But I noticed that the mark on her foot—the A in a circle—had turned red instead of blue. It had changed slightly too. The circle wasn't complete as it had been. Space under the A was left open.

The same thing had basically happened to me when Lucas changed my tattoo green. The tattoos had changed color and form. A thought flitted through my mind that the woman now belonged to Artemis. But I had no proof of that. I didn't even know if the change in my tattoo meant anything.

Artemis took a deep breath and smiled. "You may summon Abe and tell him that my plan to save his people has triumphed."

I was happy to do it. For some reason, he hadn't needed a ghost inside a ghost to work his magic. Maybe it was because Lucas either wasn't at full power or had forgotten how to do the spell without that extra step.

Abe came into the house, looking larger than life as always. His black silk suit was perfect as was the white scarf he wore around his neck. The woman ran to embrace him and sobbed against him for a few minutes.

"Check her tattoo," Abe instructed Brandon in a soft voice.

Brandon got on the floor and lifted the woman's foot. "Looks fine. The magic is still intact."

Abe grinned at Artemis. "Pay him, Morris. Good work, sorcerer. I know my people are safe now."

As the rejoicing continued and Morris gave Artemis a velvet bag that sounded as though it contained gold coins, I pulled Brandon to the side of the room.

"What does it mean that the tattoo has turned red?" I asked him.

His clear blue eyes looked worried. "What? I didn't see that. Did it change?"

He got back on the floor and checked the woman's heel again.

"It's not red," he told me. "It's what I like to call 'Abe' blue."

I took another look too. The tattoo was still bright red.

"I don't know what's going on," I whispered to him. "But it looks red to me. It turned red after he did his magic. His magic color seems to be red—like Abe's is blue—and Lucas's is green. It's red, Brandon. And it's not quite the same mark. Why can't you see it?"

He dropped to the floor again, but this time the excitement was nearly over and Abe had noticed him looking at the woman's foot again.

"Is something wrong?" Abe's deep voice filled the small room.

Brandon glanced at me. "No. Just looking at it again. Nothing's wrong."

Artemis looked up, too, but didn't say anything. He was busy playing with his ring and counting his money.

Brandon came back and stood beside me. "You're tripping, Skye. The tattoo is as blue as my eyes. You've been through a lot, sweetie. Maybe Debbie isn't the only one who needs a day off."

I didn't understand why we both saw different things. Would my new tattoo look blue to Brandon as well? Was it him? Or was it me? Maybe this was one of those things Lucas had warned would be different about me.

I realized that I wouldn't gain anything by questioning Artemis's magic. If I was right and he was somehow cheating Abe of his power, I had to find a way to expose him before everyone who was part of Abe's *family* became Artemis's property.

My job was done. I told everyone I was leaving and headed out to the van. Maybe Lucas would have some idea about how to stop Artemis, if it came down to it.

Artemis followed me—again. "Leaving so soon, Skye? I'm sure there will be a celebration following this. You'll want to take part."

"I don't think so. I'm glad you were able to solve the problem. Now I'm going home. Abe has my number if he needs me."

He came up close and laid a hand on either side of my face. "You are such a lovely young woman. I'm so sorry this has happened to you."

"You mean this as in being here scraping zombie ghosts off the ceiling?" My heart was pounding furiously. I was afraid he'd give away the fact that I had used Lucas's magic. I figured if Lucas could smell Artemis's magic on me, Artemis could probably smell Lucas's too.

"That is precisely what I mean." He glanced at the house. "He had no right to do this to you."

"Abe? I made the choice. My daughter is worth it."

"There was never a choice you needed to make. Abe is holding this over you, but you are not one of his people. I assure you of that."

I had no idea what he was talking about. Maybe it was a thing with sorcerers. One of the first words that Lucas had spoken was about freeing me from Abe's evil influence. It was probably a territorial thing, the same reason they had to challenge each other as soon as they met.

I stepped back from him, and he dropped his hands from my face.

"I don't see anything right now, except that what you did worked for that woman. I'm sure Abe is extremely grateful. I gotta go."

There was genuine anguish on his face. "I wish we could get to know one another better. There are things you should know."

"I'm sure we will until this ghost curse is over." I laughed as I walked around to the other side of the van. "See you later, Artemis. Don't spend all that in one place."

The engine started quickly, and I was gone. My hands were trembling. It wasn't bad enough that I was Abe's zombie. Now I was afraid he'd find out I wasn't his zombie anymore.

Life was so much less complicated when I was alive.

Chapter Twenty-one

I wanted to stop at Debbie's house on the way home, but I really didn't want to see the mess their lives had become. It was awful of me not to support my partner. I just couldn't handle one more thing.

Instead, I went home and grabbed a scythe out of the garden shed. I could hear Lucas working on the path behind the property. For once, doing something outside sounded good. It was hours before Kate would be home from school. Cutting down small trees and pulling up vines seemed like perfect therapy.

Lucas was surprised to see me—and I was surprised to see Addie on the path.

"I didn't know you could leave the house."

"I can do what I want." She was defensive with me right away. "Lucas taught me how to go other places. It wasn't hard."

"That's amazing. You'll be driving again in no time."

She tossed her head. "What about you? Since when do you work outside, or inside, for that matter? I thought yard work wasn't your thing?"

"It's not. I really wanted to talk to Lucas about some stuff, and he was out here."

"That's what I thought." Addie vanished.

"I guess she went inside." I shook my head. "She and I won't ever get along. I don't know what it is."

Lucas had been snipping vines that were hanging in the path. "It could be that the two of you are very different people who happened to have loved the same man."

I listlessly moved the scythe from side to side across some weeds. "I suppose that's it."

"What did you want to speak about?"

I told him what had happened with Abe's new ghost and the sorcerer. "He took care of the problem really easy. I was surprised. But I think there might be something wrong. I think he changed the mark on the zombie. The tattoo turned bright red. The initial was close to being the same but not quite. And it was red instead of blue. Like you did with mine."

"Basically it was the same process. Why were you so surprised?"

"Because I was the only one who could see the mark was red."

He stopped cutting vines. "You could see Artemis's magic?"

"I guess so. I didn't say anything. I just wanted to get out of there before somebody guessed that you'd changed me."

"That's interesting." He took the scythe from me and handed me the snippers he'd been using. "It's not surprising that the new sorcerer's magic would change Abe's mark, but it should have been visible to everyone. They surely agreed on what was acceptable in the transference."

"Artemis talked to me again privately. He was all about saving me from Abe and how I didn't deserve to be a zombie. I'll have to figure out a way to keep my distance from him. I have a feeling he wants something from me."

"Yes?" He used broad swipes of the blade to hack down tall grass growing in the path. "What do you think he wants?"

"I don't know." I sat on one of the benches. My need to garden was over. "But he should've been able to tell your magic was on me, right? If that was the case, why didn't he say something or tell Abe?"

"I agree that something else is going on with Artemis Elkheart. I'm not a seer, so I can't tell you what it is. But be wary of him, Skye. Whatever game he is playing with Abe could be disastrous if you are caught in the middle."

I watched him work for a few minutes. It was hot and humid again with thick clouds holding water bringing out mosquitos that buzzed by my head. Not a single mosquito ventured near Lucas. He didn't swat or try to evade. They just ignored him. Maybe it was a side benefit to having magic. If so, I wouldn't have minded having some of that too. If Lucas was right and I had some magic, it wasn't anything useful.

"What about the werewolf?" I asked him after a while. "Can it be stopped with magic? Can you do that magic?"

"I'm not sure. It would have its risks. I might be able to stop him, or I could make him stronger so that no human being could kill him."

"That doesn't sound like an option. You have to use a wood stake to the heart, right?"

"That is folklore for a vampire." He looked up and smiled at me. "You really are an innocent, aren't you? Folklore for a werewolf is silver. But that doesn't really work either."

"What about bullets or a grenade? If I blow it up, will the pieces come back together again?"

"That's doubtful, but you would have to get close enough to blow it up. A werewolf moves faster than the human eye can observe. If you are close enough to shoot it, you're already dead."

We talked about all things werewolf, including tracking one. I took in the information like the proverbial sponge. I wanted to know everything about my enemy. When Gerald and I fought it, I wanted to win. When I felt like I'd exhausted the subject with him, I asked about sorcerers— especially Artemis.

"What would it take to kill him, hypothetically? Would I have to use a sword? Could I just shoot him?"

"Why are you asking? Do you fear him enough that you want to kill him?" The look in Lucas's eyes didn't bode well for the other man.

"I'm not asking you to kill Artemis." I hoped I was clear on that. "There's something odd about him. I'm not sure what it is, but he keeps acting like he has some secret interest in me. It makes me uncomfortable. If he gets any worse, I'd like to know what I could do to keep my distance."

He sat beside me. "Your best bet is to ignore him. He may sense my magic about you. He may even sense your magic, untrained as it is."

I swatted a mosquito feasting on my neck. "He must be desperate if he wants my help with something."

"Is that what you sense about him? That he wants your help?"

"I don't know. There's just something about him. I can't describe it, but it bothers me."

"Trust your instincts, Skye. As you were able to ignore his magic, you may be able to sense other things about him"

"And you know that how, since you don't remember being a sorcerer?"

"Call it intuition and common sense."

The whole conversation made me more than a little uncomfortable. "I don't like this whole belonging to other people. We outlawed slavery in this country a long time ago."

"What do you think Abe is doing with his workers?"

"Giving them an extra twenty years of life. And he still pays us a decent wage."

"So you're saying you'd be all right belonging to me if I pay you?" He was angry and skeptical.

"No! That's not what I'm saying." I stood quickly and glanced at my watch. "I'm going to get Kate early from school. We're going to hang out and eat ice cream. I'll see you later."

He nodded and started working again. I didn't extend an invitation for him to join us. I needed some alone time for me and Kate.

She was thrilled when I picked her up. It was always exciting not riding the bus home. I got to hear all about what she did at school that day and all the latest kid gossip.

"Mary is submitting a poem to the school writing contest," Kate confided over huge root beer floats at the ice cream parlor. We sat outside and looked at the lake across the road.

"What about you? You like to write."

She shrugged. "I've been working on a short story. It's about my life."

That struck me like a death knell. "What are you writing about your life?"

"You know—you and daddy died—but you came back. Grandma died, but she came back. Lucas moved in with us until he can figure out what happened to his magic. That kind of thing. I think it would be interesting, don't you? I might even win."

"You might," I said carefully. "But maybe you could write fiction instead. Or you could say your story about us is fiction."

She wrinkled her nose. "I'm not sure what that is."

"Fiction is like superheroes and cartoons. Those things aren't real. Non-fiction is writing about things that really happen."

"Why would I write about superheroes when I could write about Grandma learning to use her magic ghost powers?"

I tried to think of a way to explain why her story, and what she told other people about us, needed to be less than truthful. "People don't like strange things they don't understand."

She slurped ice cream from her spoon. "You mean like ghosts?"

"That's what I mean. People like to think that everyone lives like they do. They don't like the idea of little girls being raised by ghosts and mothers who are already dead."

Kate swung her feet under her chair as she considered the matter. "I understand. It's why I can't have friends come to the house, right? I know you said I'd be a grownup before you really died and went away with Abe, but are you sure? You could get into another car accident or another sorcerer could come that Lucas can't cut his head off. What then?"

How could I answer those questions? I didn't have the answers, but I could see the trusting look in her face as she waited for me to respond.

"Lucas won't let another sorcerer come to the house. I promise. And I can't die until you're a grownup."

"Even if you turn into a ghost again?"

"You see too much." I kissed her soft cheek. "Things happen, Kate. None of us know when they're going to happen. We do the best we can. Some day when you're a grown up, you can write all about your unusual childhood. It will have to be fiction because no one will believe it could be real. But maybe you'll make a million dollars and be on all the talk shows."

"Okay. I like that idea." She seemed to consider the challenge. "Maybe I'll write about Daddy instead for the contest. There's nothing weird about him, right? He was a hero."

"You're right." I swallowed hard over the lump in my throat. "Daddy was a hero. He died trying to save my life. I think that would be a great thing to write about."

We went home, and Kate did her math and reading. She worked on her short story after that until dinner was ready. Lucas had made spaghetti. Addie made toasted garlic bread and even banana pudding. Kate and I set the table and poured sweet tea into tall glasses filled with ice.

Addie sat at the table with us, somehow holding herself in a chair. After my experience being in that shapeless form, I appreciated how difficult it was. I could see the determination written on her plain, worn face. I noticed how clearly defined her features had become. No more wavering lines or blank spaces. She was learning a lot from Lucas.

After supper, Kate and I did the dishes and then watched *The Princess Bride* on DVD. It was one of our favorite movies. Lucas watched too. I wondered what he thought of the humorous romantic comedy.

It was great being home at bedtime. I brushed Kate's hair as we talked about the story she was writing. We took turns reading a book of nursery rhymes that Jacob used to read to her. I'd taped a picture of them together reading the book on the inside flap so she'd remember him.

The evening was a lovely end to a day that had been troubled and scary. I knew it wouldn't last, but I was happy not to get a call from Abe until after Kate was asleep.

"I have an emergency pick up, Skye. Artemis says this person is going to become a ghost next. Please see to it. He'll meet you there."

As always, he never waited for me to answer or even acknowledge that I'd heard him. His end of the conversation was over.

"Are you going out?" Lucas asked. "Is it another ghost problem?"

"Yes and yes." I pulled on jeans and planned to wear boots. I never knew where the pickup would take me until I was there.

"Artemis will be there?"

"Yes. That's the way this works. "

"I could go with you."

"I'm fine." I stuffed my wallet into my pocket and pulled on my holster. "I can handle him."

"Shooting him isn't the answer."

"And I don't plan on doing it unless things get really bad. Don't worry. I've dealt with worse things than this sorcerer."

He stood close to me. "Careful. You know nothing about him."

I smiled. "I knew nothing about you either when we met. Whatever it is with him, I can take care of it. See you later."

I had to stop for gas as I was going into Nashville. The address that Abe sent as a text was back in the city again. It was a good place to stop anyway. Gas was cheaper here.

As I was pumping, Tim Rusk pulled up in his highway patrol car. He got out, carefully scanning the area around him. He didn't put on his flat-brimmed hat as he would normally have done if he'd been working.

"Hey there," he said with a slight smile. "Where are you off to this time of night?"

"Part of my job. It happens at all times. You know how it is."

"What was it you said you do now, Skye?"

"I'm kind of a bounty hunter. I work for a private firm in the city." I hoped he wouldn't ask for more details. I could think of answers, but I didn't want to lie to him.

"I hear you met up with Gerald Linker." He glanced at a red pickup as it pulled into the station.

I was finished pumping and put back the hose. "That's right. It was interesting. I guess news travels fast."

"You could say that—especially since he was arrested a few hours ago for breaking and entering. I asked a buddy of mine who was there at the scene. He said Gerald told him he was looking for evidence to prove werewolves had killed his wife. Know anything about that?"

Chapter Twenty-two

So much for not lying to Tim.

"No. Werewolves, huh? Where did he break into? Is there a werewolf institute or museum that I don't know about?"

Tim chuckled. "Nah. He broke into a psychic place over near the river. There was something on the sign about being able to help with supernatural events that bother people. He seemed to take the owner at her word. They had a meeting a few hours before he broke in. It seems he waited until she left and then picked the lock on the front door."

Gerald. I sighed, hating that he'd gone overboard. I'd hoped he'd be able to handle it. I guess he was still too fragile. I could blame this breakdown on myself.

"Sorry to hear that. I wouldn't have gone to see him if I'd known it could cause a problem for him."

"I'm sure it wasn't your fault. He's not right in the head anymore, you know? Anything could've put him over the edge. But I wonder why werewolves?"

"Maybe it was the way his wife was killed. I've seen the pictures. She was ripped apart, even worse than Jacob. I couldn't blame him for thinking something supernatural did it since no one has come up with an answer that makes sense."

"I guess that's true. Given his background, mental problems and all, werewolves could be something he'd think of."

"I suppose so." I watched the traffic moving by on the main road. "Thanks for telling me. I have to go to work. Have a good one."

As I was turning on the engine in the van, Tim put his hand on the open window ledge next to me.

"You're not thinking anything weird like that, are you, Skye?" His brown eyes were steady on mine.

"No. Cops don't have that much imagination, right?" I smiled and waved.

He gave me a friendly salute and moved his hand. I took off. My brain hummed with ways to get Gerald out of jail before the system began to work on him again. I didn't want him to go back to the hospital. I didn't think he was crazy. He'd just leaped on the idea too soon and panicked. I might have done the same thing if I didn't have Lucas to talk to.

But I had to meet Artemis first before I could do anything that might help sort out Gerald.

Was it me, or were the werewolf questions Tim was asking more pointed than I would've expected from someone in law enforcement? I couldn't imagine having a straight-faced conversation with someone about werewolves when I was a cop.

I was still mulling that over when I found the address Abe had texted me. The houses were middle-class family styles with small driveways and no garages, which meant there were cars parked everywhere on the street.

Abe's Lincoln wasn't there, so he really trusted Artemis after last night. I had to keep myself out of it, at least until I had better answers or had a way to prove to Abe that Artemis was cheating him.

I scanned the block, no idea what kind of vehicle Artemis drove. He answered my question when he dramatically appeared in front of me, directly in the headlights.

"I guess I didn't have to worry about finding you, did I?" I said as I got out of the van.

Dressed completely in black this time with a black, red-lined cape theatrically spreading out behind him, he looked more like a magician than Harold ever had. I had to admit that he was a handsome man with his aquiline features and thick blond hair.

His arms were raised, pushing the cape back from his shoulders. I caught a glimpse of a large tattoo on his arm, but I couldn't be sure the design was.

Could it be the dragon the man at the smoke shop had talked about? How would I ever make Abe believe Artemis had killed Harold, if I found it to be true? He already trusted the sorcerer so much.

"It's lovely to see you again, Skye. I wish the circumstances were different. Perhaps after we have mastered this problem, you and I could step out for a drink."

"My daughter is waiting for me at home." It wasn't exactly a lie, Kate was at home. "Let's get this over with."

I wished he stop flirting with me or whatever it was. I didn't appreciate his interest but had to tread carefully if I wanted to prove my suspicions about him.

We went up to the small house with yellow aluminum siding on the outside. There were lights on inside all the windows. I hoped one of Abe's workers had turned them all on and we weren't going to have to explain all of this to a loved one.

Not a chance.

A young woman, maybe in her early twenties, answered the door with frantic eyes. "Thank God you're here. I assume Abe sent you. My brother is disappearing. Is this part of the contract he signed? Because he's supposed to have another eight years left. If his contract was going to change, someone could've told us."

Artemis passed by her as though she was a bug. "Let me through. I shall handle the problem."

The young woman had been crying. She wiped her eyes quickly as he went by her.

"Don't worry," I assured her. "This is something like a virus. We'll clear it up, and he'll have his eight years."

"Oh, thank goodness." She sagged in relief. "I didn't know what to think. We wouldn't have done something like this except that I was sick at the time—cancer—and he saw me through it. I don't think I would've survived without him."

Out of curiosity I asked, "What does he do for a living? Not that it matters. I'm always interested."

"He works for the government. It's not a big deal. We were surprised when Abe asked him to work for him."

I heard Artemis with our zombie in the bedroom and cut the conversation short. I wanted to see how he handled the problem this time. I told the sister to wait for us in the living room and went back to see what was going on.

In the bedroom, the quickly fading man was face down on the bed. He was groaning but still able to be heard. Artemis had his tattooed foot in his hand. His eyes, and the ring on his hand, glowed red.

An instant later, so did the tattoo on the man's foot.

As soon as the color changed, the man started looking human again. The tattoo on his foot remained red as it had on the previous LEP—at least to my eyes. I wondered if anyone else could see it this time.

I was at the doorway when the man's sister joined us. She started crying again but this time tears of joy.

"You saved him. You were right." She hugged me. "Thank you."

"You're welcome," I said even though I hadn't done anything except show up.

"Why did the tattoo change color on his foot?" the woman asked.

"You mean you could see it?"

"Yes. It was blue before. It's been blue since that day at the hospital when we met Abe. Is that part of getting rid of the virus?"

"Absolutely." I was secretly thrilled that I wasn't the only one to see the tattoo change color. Why hadn't Brandon seen it?

The woman ran to her brother. I noticed that Artemis laid his hand on both of their heads in a gesture that reminded me of what Lucas had done after he'd saved me from being a ghost. They both hugged him, and Artemis immediately left the room.

"I'll meet you outside," he muttered as he swept by me with a wave of his cape.

I didn't acknowledge him. The man was up, off the bed. He and his sister were thanking me.

"I don't know what came over me," the zombie man said. "Does this happen often?"

"No. Not often at all." I smiled. "You should be fine now. You'll just have to find new matching shoes for your red tattoo."

I was joking, of course. A little zombie humor.

He looked puzzled. "What do you mean?" And lifted his foot. "It's blue, just like always."

His sister glanced at it too. "Yes. It's still that nice shade of blue."

"But you just agreed with me that it was red," I reminded her.

I took another look myself. The A on his heel was bright red and not a complete circle.

"Well, thanks for your help," The young woman smiled and quickly led me to the front door. "We appreciate you coming out so late. You have a wonderful rest of your night."

I felt a little kicked to the curb as I found myself on the porch. Why had the woman changed her mind about the color of the tattoo? Was it something Artemis had done to make them see it differently?

The hand on the head.

It felt crazy to even consider that he could put his hand on their heads and make them see what he wanted. But I knew it was exactly what he'd been trying to do to me at Abe's office. He thought he could make me see and feel what he wanted.

Outside in the humid darkness, I hesitated to confront Artemis alone. Even if Brandon was there, I wouldn't be as scared. What if he put his hand on my head and I forgot everything he wanted me to?

That hadn't happened with Abe or Lucas. I died so there could've been a detail or two I'd forgotten. But not something big like that.

Nothing had happened last time Artemis had tried his magic on me, but since I didn't know why I'd been protected, I couldn't risk it again.

I was sure—or at least I thought I was sure—that Lucas hadn't changed me at all besides the color of my tattoo. But what if I was wrong? He kept saying I was different. Maybe I was seeing the world now the way he wanted me to see it.

Shaking my head, I knew I had to focus if I wanted to have any chance at all to get through all this crazy stuff and still be me.

Artemis was waiting for me at the van. "What about that drink, lovely lady? You and I have a lot to talk about."

His bravado was staggering. He was changing—perhaps stealing—Abe's people right out from under his nose. For some reason, I could see it, but Abe couldn't. No one else could except Artemis.

"Thanks, but like I said, my daughter is at home. That's where I'm going. I guess I'll see you later." I put my hand on the door handle to make my escape.

Artemis came up behind me and put his big hand on my head in the same manner that Lucas had—the same thing he'd done tonight to the man in the house.

He whispered a few weird magic words near my ear. I couldn't see anything around his big paw, and I couldn't move. A terrible dread that I was about to forget everything important in my life raced through me. I knew I had to fight back.

I held Kate's image in the forefront of my thoughts. I even imagined Addie and Lucas. I saw Jacob's smiling face and our room at Apple Betty's Inn. I kept those pictures in my brain and refused to let them go.

He took his hand away, a swaggering grin on his face. "You are surprisingly strong! Come with me, Skye. You and I belong together."

I smiled back at him and raised my hands toward him. In one of them was my Beretta.

"If you ever touch me again or try to do magic on me, I'm going to shoot a big hole right through your head and all your spells are going to fall out. Do we understand each other?"

He actually took a step back. I thought it was my threat but that didn't seem to bother him.

"How is it possible you avoided my magic?" His face and tone was filled with disbelief.

"I guess I'm better than that." I nudged him aside and opened the door.

"But you don't have the training or resources, not yet." He sniffed. "Wait. Something is different about you, isn't it? You've been fooling around with Lucas. Deny it if you will."

While he'd been babbling, I was already in the van with the engine started. If he'd jumped in front of me again, I would've run him down and dealt with the consequences Abe would bring later.

"Leave me alone. I don't know what you're doing yet, but when I find out, I'm going to tell Abe and he'll take care of it."

He laughed. "He's only a puppet master. Not even a real sorcerer. Say whatever you want to him. He won't believe or understand you."

I put my foot down hard on the accelerator, but the van didn't move. The wheels spun, and the engine revved. But that was it.

"You're making a mistake, Skye. But don't worry. It's one that will be corrected."

He released his hold on the van, and I went careening down the street between parked cars before I could slow down. Even then I didn't stop until I was miles away. I pulled over, panting as though I'd run a race.

"Traitor," I said to the van. "How could you let him possess you that way?"

The engine clunked along like it always did. Eventually I was able to put Artemis's threat behind me and drove home as quickly as possible. I could swear I felt him coming after me the whole way. I didn't feel safe until I was inside the inn.

"What's wrong?" Lucas met me at the door.

"I need a drink. And how *do* you kill a sorcerer?"

Chapter Twenty-three

Later, when we were alone in bed, everything that had happened spilled out of me.

Lucas listened silently until I'd been quiet for a few minutes. "What do you think Artemis has in mind?"

"I think he wants to own me, for whatever reason, like he's taking over Abe's people one at a time. Maybe he's the one who created this crazy curse in the first place. He's getting bolder every time I see him. Why doesn't his magic work on me? I mean, I'm glad it doesn't. He made that brother and sister see what he wanted them to see."

"Has he made romantic overtures to you?"

I smiled at his prim words. "No. I could handle that. It's something else. He mentioned you and that I've changed."

"If you shielded your mind from him, it was reinforced by your magic."

"But wouldn't Abe have known I had magic when he turned me into one of his people?"

"Yes. He knew. He took advantage of your grief and weakness in that moment. You didn't need him to stay alive. You must acknowledge that you have a gift. Once you understand and begin to develop that gift, you'll be stronger than Abe."

It was too hard for me to grasp. Maybe I had magic, but I didn't feel like it. I couldn't make my van stop moving with a nod of my head like Artemis had.

"What should I do? If Artemis takes over all the zombies, Abe will die."

"You won't die. Trust me on this. Whatever happens to Abe won't affect you."

Lucas was only interested in my welfare. What happened to Debbie and Terry and all the others meant nothing to him. How could I explain that I cared about them too?

And it didn't seem that my 'magic' would have kept me alive that night after Jacob had died. It was Abe who brought me back. I couldn't help feeling that I owed him.

I wasn't able to sleep again that night, wandering the house aimlessly. I finally ran into Addie in Jacob's old room. Sometimes I'd find her there, resting a foot above the blankets.

"Are you working in here now?" she asked in a cranky voice.

"No." I took a deep breath. "Addie, have I been different? Do I act like someone else is controlling me?"

She sat up. "If you're talking about Lucas, I don't know what to tell you. It's hard to see my son's wife with another man in my own house. Yes, you've been happier since he came here—we all have. I wouldn't say he's controlling you. It seems to me that you're making the stupid decisions on your own."

"Thanks."

"Why are you asking? Worried that betraying Jacob's trust is wrong?"

"Go back to sleep." I smiled at her, but it was more in relief that she knew me well enough to see if I'd changed—and enjoyed telling me when I was wrong. It had to be that Lucas's magic hadn't made me his zombie. She would've had a field day with that.

I knew by morning what I needed to do. I joined Lucas in the shower and told him what I thought. "Artemis killed Harold the Magician so he'd have access to Abe's people. All I have to do is find a way to prove it."

He dumped shampoo on my head and spread it around with his hand.

"Watch it." I put my hand on his. "I'm getting a little sensitive about people touching my head—especially sorcerers."

"A good sorcerer doesn't need hand gestures. They are only for show, as is Artemis's ring, so that people he wants to impress know something is happening."

"You put your hand on my head too," I reminded him as I worked the shampoo into my hair. He always used too much.

"Exactly. I wanted you to be impressed too." He grinned and shoved my head under the shower spray.

I came up for air, blustering and spitting. "I know you like showers, but you're getting carried away. Addie told me you're taking four or five a day. We pay for the water, you know. It's not free."

"I adore hot running water. In my day, there was no such thing. Not even for sorcerers."

"In your day? Have you remembered something of your past?"

"I remember bathing in a tub of hot water that several other people shared. It wasn't this hot rain that you have. It is a wonder."

"What else do you remember?"

"Bits and pieces." He closed his eyes. "There was a castle. And great wealth. But also great poverty. I remember riding on the wind at night, and a terrible war that scorched the earth."

"Were you part of the war?" I poured shampoo on his head. "Riding the wind, huh? Sounds exciting. Have you tried it here yet?"

It was his turn to have his head under the super hot water. The action didn't seem to bother him. He opened his eyes and let the water sluice over him.

"I don't know about the war. I haven't tried riding the wind because I can't recall how I did it. Perhaps it's only a dream."

"How about other spells—like taking away a sorcerer's power? If we could do that, everyone would be safe. I have a feeling that might be what it takes to get rid of Artemis."

"Really, it would make no sense for me to tell you how to render one of my kind powerless. I believe it would be a secret no sorcerer would share."

"Are you scared I might use it against you?"

"Not you—but someone you might give the information to."

"Thanks! I can keep a secret, you know. I don't want anyone to hurt you."

"It might not be something you could control." He smoothed a hand down the side of my face. "Not that it matters. I don't know how to do it."

"It might come to you at the last minute like it did with Jasper."

"Artemis is a much better, stronger sorcerer than Jasper or Harold." He turned off the water and got out of the shower. "I'm not certain I could defeat him if I challenged him."

"Like he knows how to ride the wind, right?"

"Yes." He tossed me a towel. "You needn't fear that I can't protect you and Kate. That is a different matter. A sorcerer must be sure of his magic to challenge another."

I dried myself and then his back. "I guess I better not outright challenge him either then. I'll have to sneak around and try to find ways to make him look bad until I can prove to Abe what he's doing."

"A realistic goal. What is your plan? Perhaps I may be of assistance."

I raked my fingers through his dark hair until it was out of his face. "I think it might be better if we don't use your magic. That might be a challenge to him. I can figure this out and impress Abe with it. I don't know how yet, but it will come to me."

"I have every confidence in you, Skye. But I could help in non-magical ways if you need me."

"Knowing that you're here keeping Kate safe is the best thing you can do for me. I don't want a repeat of the ghoul in the kitchen."

"I can do that." He folded his arms around me. "But be careful. If Artemis meant to kill you, or have his way with you, he would have done so already. What he wants from you might be worse."

"And on that piece of advice, I'm going to get dressed. I think I figured out a way to get Gerald back on track. After I check in with Debbie, I'm going to sort him out too."

It was still early. I went to help Kate get ready for school. We talked about things she could do over the summer while she was out of school. I remembered how exciting the thought of summer vacation was when I was her age every time I looked at her face.

"Macy and her parents are going to Canada over the summer." She peeked at me as she pulled her T-shirt over her head. "You think we might be able to do something like that?"

"I don't know. Would you like to go to Canada?"

She shrugged. "I don't know. I'd like to go to Disney World. I bet Lucas would like Harry Potter Land since it's all about witches and magic."

"I'm sure you're right. I'll see what I can do about that." Yeah, when the power company stopped charging for electricity.

"What about Lucas taking us there with his magic?" she asked as she pulled the blanket up on her bed and arranged her stuffed animals the way she liked them. "He could do that, couldn't he?"

"I don't know. He's not exactly Harry Potter."

"But he's not Voldemort either, is he?"

"No. He's not evil and faceless, and he would certainly never kill a unicorn." I kissed her cheek. "Let's get through these last few days of school, and we'll think about it then. Okay?"

"Okay."

We had breakfast—biscuits that Addie had taught Lucas how to make. They were delicious. Addie actually blushed as we complimented her. I took Kate to school and called a friend of mine as I drove to Debbie's house.

Colin Lister had been a street lawyer and confidential informant when I'd first graduated from the police academy. He was ambitious even then. His parents were poor, and he had a brother who was a drug addict. But Colin had moved from his tiny law office in an old neighborhood to a Nashville assistant district attorney in record time. He'd been leveraging to become the next Nashville DA for a while.

He was a good man who was glad to help me with my Gerald problem.

"I'll get your friend out, Skye. I know his case. I followed it because of what happened to you and Jacob. What's up? Are you helping Gerald out now for the same reason?"

"I feel bad for him for the same reason," I admitted. "It's easy to slide over the edge."

"But hanging around with this guy isn't the answer. You should go back to work with the police department. Jacob wouldn't have wanted you to quit because of him."

"I know. I'm doing the best I can. Thanks for your help. I'll pick Gerald up."

"You know I'm here for you. Don't be a stranger. Come over for dinner one night. Pattie and the kids would love to see you and Kate."

"I'll do that," I promised, knowing it would never happen. We had nothing in common anymore. I couldn't tell him about my new life. I could only imagine his response.

I felt responsible for Gerald's breakdown. I had to find a way to get him to back off while we worked together to try to figure out if a werewolf was really killing people.

With Gerald's situation in hand, I pulled into Debbie's driveway. She was tired and frustrated when I knocked at her door. She invited me in for a round of loud snarling and growling coming from the basement.

"You should've called, Skye." Her hands went to her hair and dirty clothes. "Does Abe have a pickup?"

"No. Not as far as I know." I told her what had happened last night with the brother and sister and Artemis. "I just stopped by to see how you were doing and to see if I could help."

Terry stopped growling and began howling. I could see every nerve in Debbie's body reacting to the sound.

"That's how I'm doing." She started pacing the floor. "All day and all night, he snarls and growls and howls. When he's not making animal noises, he gets angry and yells threats. Then he starts pleading for us to let him go. I don't know how long we can do this. I haven't slept since we put him down there. I bought ear plugs for Bowman and Raina, but I'm afraid to wear them. What if he gets out, and I don't know it?"

"Are the kids at school?"

"Yes, of course. It's going to be a lot worse when school is out for the summer. I'll have to send them away."

"Never mind that now. Take a shower and change clothes. Come with me to Nashville, and we'll talk to Abe. Maybe the new sorcerer can help."

"But you said he's probably evil," she argued.

"Maybe he is, but he still works for Abe. Just get dressed, and let's get out of here."

Debbie finally agreed and went upstairs. I walked into the basement and took a look at Terry. He hadn't changed since we'd brought him home. He was caught somewhere between a man and a beast.

I took his picture with my camera phone, and he growled at me.

"Skye," he pleaded in a harsh, guttural voice. "Help me. Tell Debbie she can trust me to leave the basement. I have to get out of here. It's driving me crazy."

"I don't think that's a good idea, Terry. I'm sorry you have to go through this."

He lunged at me, reaching the length of the rope that had him tied to one of the house supports. "Let me out. I'll kill you all. First I'll run my tongue over your body and nip off those extra tasty parts."

I'd heard enough. I took another picture of him with my phone, hoping they might help identify the problem. Even though Lucas didn't know what to do, Abe would, and he could send Artemis to work some magic.

I was waiting at the door for Debbie when she finally came downstairs. She was clean, her hair was brushed, and she seemed composed, even though there were still dark shadows under her eyes.

"Let's get going. I've got a few things to do in town," I told her. "We're going to find a way to fix this. Try to stay positive."

She was crying as we went out to the van. "I wish I'd let him die, Skye. What's the point of him being alive like this? I've ruined my life and the kids' lives too."

"Hang in there a little while longer. There's got to be an answer. Abe knows why this is happening—he did it even though it was an accident. He admitted it. He must know a way to stop it."

Debbie wasn't so sure, but she didn't argue. She fell asleep in the van on the way to the city. We stopped at Deadly Ink first.

"You shouldn't have let me sleep." She fussed with her hair and pretty blue top.

"You needed some rest," I told her. "Let's go in and talk to Abe."

"But what are we going to say? I don't even know what Terry is turning into. How can I explain?"

"I have a picture. Maybe it will be worth the thousand words we need."

We were lucky. The tattoo shop was crowded, but Morris told us on the way in that Artemis hadn't arrived yet.

I hurried in, not wanting to let this opportunity go by without trying to explain to Abe about Artemis. Debbie might be upset if I led with my knowledge about the sorcerer, but we could always tell Abe about Terry when Artemis was there.

Brandon was in Abe's office, but I wasn't worried about him. I immediately plunged into my account of the ghost zombie from last night. I knew before I'd finished that Abe was skeptical.

He made a pyramid of his fingers in front of his sallow face as he considered the matter. "I have seen no sign of the treachery you are accusing Artemis of, Skye. In fact, he warned me that you might say something like this after you tried to disrupt his work on my behalf last night."

"What? I didn't try to disrupt anything. He went in there—*on your behalf*—and changed the man's tattoo. I think he's making his own marks on them while he's claiming to get rid of the curse. He may have killed Harold and put the curse on us in the first place."

Abe slowly sat forward. "I believe we begin to see the real issue here. Artemis told me that Lucas may be using you to cause havoc in my organization. He believes Lucas killed Harold, as I thought, for his own benefit."

"That's stupid," I retorted sharply, forgetting my vow not to challenge Artemis openly. "You can't see what's happening because Artemis has you in his power too."

"Let's determine if that's true." Abe calmly suggested. "Remove your shoe please, Skye. Let me see your tattoo."

Chapter Twenty-four

Artemis must have worked it out. He knew what Lucas had done. He knew my weak spot and had already gone to Abe with the information he needed to turn him against me.

"Skye?" Brandon asked. "Show him. I know you haven't done anything. Prove it. I don't like that guy anyway."

I didn't know if I should run and take my chances or plead my case. I looked at Abe and Brandon. There was no way they weren't going to see the change in my tattoo.

I was sitting closest to the door. I'd decided to run when Debbie reached down and flipped the sandal off my foot.

"There," she said with a triumphant smile. "That's over now. Can we talk about *my* problem?"

Brandon lifted my foot. "See, Abe? There it is. I told you Artemis was wrong. He was trying to cause trouble for Skye. Maybe what she's telling you is true."

Abe got up and walked around the desk. He bent down low to look at the heel of my foot. His observation was met by a low grunt and a return to the other side of his desk.

Couldn't they see? Had Artemis's magic kept them from seeing the change Lucas had made in me too?

Or was it Lucas's magic covering it up?

When I looked at my heel, the green tattoo of the letter L was still there. But then I could see the red tattoos Artemis was leaving behind too. I wasn't in the position to question what they could see or not see. I slipped my foot back in my sandal and glared at Debbie.

"I was only trying to help," she said. "You didn't tell me you were going to talk about all this other stuff before I could ask for help with Terry."

I didn't argue with her. Whatever magic was keeping them from seeing Lucas's mark on me had worked in my favor. I was clear, as far as Abe was concerned. That gave me the push to add one last thing to my description of the sorcerer trying to take over Abe's zombie empire.

"I can prove it," I told him. "I can prove that he killed Harold to take his position and steal your people."

Abe's brows went up in his smooth face. "Yes? I have only heard theories so far, no proof. Bring me that, and we'll see what happens from there."

My conversation time seemed to be over as Abe reached across the desk to take Debbie's hand.

"Tell me about your dear Terry," he invited. "Skye told me you two are having difficulties. What can I do to help?"

I gave Debbie my phone so she could show Abe what Terry was changing into, as soon as she stopped crying. Brandon and I walked out of the office and left the tattoo shop.

"I don't know how you're going to prove any of what you were saying to Abe," he said, lighting up a cigarette. "Abe is sold on the man because he's keeping the zombies from turning into ghosts. It's gonna be tough—I assume you don't really have anything on him."

I looked at the cigarette he was smoking. It was the plain, filter-less kind you could get at any convenience store. I thought about the cigarette butts I'd found in the alley with the gold wrapper. Maybe there was still some way to use that to prove Artemis had killed Harold.

But if the sorcerer smoked, I hadn't seen any sign of it. I had to come up with a way to get him to smoke in front of me. Maybe then I could get one of the butts from the cigarette. It sounded weak and desperate. Maybe Artemis had a snake tattoo. Maybe he smoked these unusual cigarettes in the alley while he was waiting for Harold.

He was definitely changing Abe's life. And I couldn't prove that either.

Not knowing how far Artemis's control went over Brandon, I didn't share my thoughts with him. He wished me luck and offered to help if he could before he went back to the mortuary.

I went back inside to wait for Debbie.

A group of young men were watching a tattoo artist create an amazing image on another man's back. I'd learned that watching tattoos being done was almost as good for enthusiasts as having one done on themselves.

In this case, the subject of the art was what caught my eye. It was a man with snakes coming out of his mouth, ears, eyes, and nose. It looked exactly as Harold had in the alley. Even the kinds of snakes were the same as I remembered.

I'd noticed the man doing tattoos around the shop many times. I didn't know his name, but I was sure he'd seen Harold before Morris had time to cover the magician's body. The detail was too accurate to ignore. If there was a witness to Harold's death—that would be sweet!

Debbie was still in Abe's office. I hung around in the tattoo shop watching as the young, long-haired artist worked on the tattoo he'd begun. He kept pushing back his glasses as he concentrated on the image.

"That's all I can do today, Simon." The man under the needle got to his feet slowly and took a good look in the mirror at the creation that was appearing on his back. "That is awesome, man! I can't wait until it's done."

The man thanked Simon and tipped him before going to counter to pay Morris for the work.

I watched as Simon cleaned his tools and put them away. He was so used to having an audience that he didn't even notice me. He seemed very intent on everything he did, each movement carefully considered.

I followed him out of the shop and into the alley where he lit up a cigarette and leaned back against the old brick building.

"That was some amazing art," I said.

He looked up, startled to see me there. "Thanks." He pushed his glasses back again and took another puff.

"Where do you get your ideas? I mean, why a man with snakes coming out of him?"

He cleared his throat, and glanced around the alley nervously. "I don't know. It's something about a man biting off more than he can chew."

"But don't snakes mean rebirth? Is it supposed to be about rebirth?"

"No. It's supposed to be about death. Death is cruel sometimes, and we never know when it's going to happen."

His voice revealed his distress as much as his narrowed eyes and nervous movements.

"That's interesting." I looked at the spot on the pavement where Harold's body had been. "You know, a man died right *here*, exactly the way you pictured him in your art. Weird, right?"

"I don't know anything about that," he denied. "I didn't see anything."

"I know you didn't." I smiled at him. "Because if you had, Abe probably wouldn't like it. He tried really hard to keep anyone from seeing it."

"I couldn't help it," he muttered. "I didn't mean to be out here. I fell asleep on the other side of the alley. I woke up, and it was happening, okay? I know I wasn't supposed to see it. Don't tell him. I'll give you any art you want."

"I appreciate the offer, but I'm more interested in what you actually saw, Simon. Was someone else out here too?"

He stubbed out his cigarette and wrapped his arms protectively across his narrow chest. "There was another man. I've seen him around the shop. I don't know who he is. He doesn't do tattoos. I think he might work for Abe."

"Can you describe him?"

"Sure." He shrugged. "Tall. Thin. Blond hair. Weird clothes. He didn't try to help while the snakes crawled around on the other man. He was dead, I think. Still, he didn't even try to help him. I mean, I didn't either, but I think the man standing there was getting a kick out of it, you know?"

"I know." He'd described Artemis pretty well. I didn't know if his word would have any impact on Abe, but it told me that I was right. Artemis had killed Harold and enjoyed watching it.

But again, how was I going to prove it?

I let Simon go—with a warning that he should stay home for a few days. I got his cell number. Making a fuss over him would only bring Artemis down on him, and there would be another death by snakes. It would be best to keep Simon in my back pocket until I had more evidence against the sorcerer.

Simon left Deadly Ink on a nice motorcycle and didn't look back. I realized that he might be gone for good. I would be, if I were him. He was close to something he didn't want to be part of. I hoped his cell number would still be good, but no matter what, I didn't want to be responsible for his death.

Debbie was finally finished talking to Abe. I met her as I started back into Deadly Ink. Her eyes were so puffy she could hardly see. Morris was kindly helping her out the door, with his hand on her backside.

"Thanks," I said to him. "I can handle it from here."

He grinned and leered at me. "Anytime, sweetie. Morris is always here for the ladies."

We reached the door to the van, and Debbie asked if he was gone.

I told her he'd gone back inside. "Yeah. I thought we could manage without him. What happened with Abe?"

"He was wonderfully sympathetic and even called Artemis in to discuss it with him. Artemis is going to come over tonight and take a look at Terry. It was more than I'd hoped for."

I helped her sit down and put a box of tissues on her lap. "That's good, I guess. Maybe Abe can take care of his screw-ups."

"I'm praying so." Debbie blew her nose repeatedly. "Do you have any eye drops? My eyes feel like someone rubbed salt in them."

"Sorry. We could stop and get some on the way over to the county lockup. I have a friend who needs a hand, but we should be back at your house in plenty of time for Raina and Bowman."

"We can't be late." She grabbed my hand. "The kids are getting off the bus at the house. I don't want them there alone."

"Not a problem," I assured her. "It'll be okay."

"Skye, I was just trying to help in there when I took off your sandal. I hope you aren't angry. It got me all flustered for them to think you'd done something wrong."

"It's okay." I didn't feel like I could trust her any more than I could trust Brandon. I was going to have to keep her in the dark until I could make sense of Harold's death and the magic Artemis had been doing. "Why don't you close your eyes for a while again? You'll feel better."

"Thanks," she said with a watery smile. "I just hope Artemis can really help Terry."

The last was on a sigh as she immediately fell asleep. I glanced at her exhausted face and hoped Artemis could help Terry too. Somehow I doubted it, though he might do something to take them both over. I really didn't think Artemis was there to help Abe.

I got to the county lockup and exchanged greetings with people I still knew who worked there. But Colin had already released Gerald, and he was long gone. I thanked everyone and promised to keep in touch before I headed to Gerald's house.

Debbie slept through the whole thing. I didn't see any reason to wake her. Besides, the less she knew about my quest to find Jacob's killer, the better. This way Abe wouldn't be mad at her too.

Gerald's door had been repaired with a piece of cardboard where he'd shot through it. I was careful that I stood to the left side instead of where he could accidentally shoot me.

But he'd been watching for me—Colin had told him why he was being released. "Come on in, Skye. I've been waiting for you."

"I wish you would've waited before you tried to tell the world that a werewolf killed your wife." I closed the door behind me. "Now the werewolf knows we're on to him. He's going to be twice as dangerous."

He scratched his head. "Yeah. I know. Sorry about that. I just couldn't handle it at first. Now I'm ready."

He was dressed in a complete camo uniform including a hat. Guns, knives, grenades, and various other weapons were strewed across the table in the kitchen.

"We can't do anything until the moon is full."

"That's tonight." He pulled out a funeral home calendar and showed me.

I glanced at my phone again. He was right.

"We have to get ready. I've been studying werewolves. They come out right when the moon comes up. They're strongest at the apex and get weaker or go to sleep as the moon wanes. We have to be there in the woods, waiting for the bastard. It will be next month before we get another chance. He could run or decide to change his killing area. We can't let that happen."

"I agree, but I don't know if we're really prepared. Lucas said they move faster than we can see and a gun won't do us any good."

"Okay." Gerald knocked the guns from the table to the floor. "No guns. What did he suggest?"

"Magic. But I'm not sure he's up to the task. Lucas suggested doing surveillance on the area and waiting until the wolf is human again."

"Come on, Skye. Are you going to kill him when he's human? I sure as hell am not taking him to the police. Believe me. No one wants to hear about supernatural enemies."

I didn't know what to say. I hated whoever had done this to Jacob, but the werewolf had no choice. It wasn't like he woke up one day and wanted to kill people. He was cursed. I'd considered that if we could catch him as we had Terry, something might come to Lucas, and he could remove the werewolf curse. It wasn't any different in my mind than a person with a mental illness who wasn't responsible for their actions.

"We could catch it when it's human," I suggested.

He slammed his fist on the table. "No! We want this thing that murdered the people we loved to be dead. That's it. There has to be a weapon that will work on him. If it's nothing I have on the table, we'll regroup and find something else. Don't go soft on me."

"That's the problem, Gerald. There is no regrouping. If we don't get him the first time, we're dead, just like Julie and Jacob. If we capture it, we might have a chance."

He started loading shells into an M16 military rifle. "I'm not waiting. And I'm not catching it. Come with me or not. I'm killing this thing tonight."

This was not going the way I'd hoped. I didn't know what I'd expected since Gerald had driven himself crazy with trying to figure out what had happened to his wife. But I couldn't let him down at this point. We were here because I had sought him out and given him these ideas. I had to go through with it.

"I'm in. I'll meet you there tonight. What time is moonrise?"

"Seven-fifteen. I'll be in the front like we were before. Remember—this isn't a person anymore, Skye. This is a monster that will keep killing if we don't stop him."

I nodded and started toward the door.

"We'll get him. We can do this. Then we'll share a drink in honor of our loved ones. Thank you for saving me. I was all but dead when you found me."

"I'm sorry this happened to you. I hope it turns out okay."

He laughed heartily. "It's gonna work. You should've been a soldier, Skye. We would've been quite a team."

I left him loading his rifle and went quickly down the front stairs. Debbie had awakened and was crossing the street. She had a million questions that I didn't have answers for. I gave her a general kind of explanation about an old friend hunting a werewolf and left it at that.

It was no surprise that she easily accepted what I told her.

Chapter Twenty-five

That was the only reprieve I was granted.

When we reached Debbie's cabin, Artemis showed up in a bright patch of gold sparkles. He was dramatic enough.

"I'm here to take a look at your husband, my dear." He bent over Debbie's hand as he kissed it. "You have my sympathies on this terrible state of affairs. I will do my best to change these circumstances for you."

Debbie giggled and held the hand he'd kissed in her other hand as she blushed. "Thank you so much for coming so quickly. You don't know what this means to me."

His smile was oily, but she didn't seem to notice as she let him tuck her hand into the crook of his arm.

I argued with myself about not going inside. I didn't have to stay. This was Debbie's affair and had nothing to do with me. I could go home, help Lucas in the garden. Watch TV. Anything would be better than watching Artemis at work.

But Debbie turned her head and asked me to stay. "You will, won't you, Skye?"

How could I leave her there with the man I believed had murdered Harold? I knew he was only doing Abe's bidding, but what if killing or using his magic on Debbie and Terry was part of his plot?

"Sure." I looked for some sign that Artemis was uncomfortable with the idea of me being there. There was none. He was as cool as ever, even remarking that he was glad I'd be there for Debbie in case things went bad. Nothing seemed to bother him.

Terry's howling filled the house as we stepped inside. Debbie started crying again. Artemis asked where Terry was. Debbie said she couldn't go down there yet and asked me to take the sorcerer to the basement.

"I hope you have a better plan for helping Terry," I said between clenched teeth.

"You have no faith in me." Artemis nodded. "I understand, child. I am a stranger to you, but it is not of my own doing."

"I don't want to hear any more of your BS. Just fix Terry and get out of here."

The basement was beginning to smell really bad. I didn't know how Debbie thought she could keep someone down here and not clean up. I supposed she hadn't really considered that yet. She was still living the dream that Terry would go back to being normal.

"This is a complicated procedure." Artemis slowly walked around Terry as the transformed man tried to claw at him.

I remembered how sharp and fast those claws were. Part of me hoped Terry might kill Artemis. I knew it would be bad for Debbie—the only thing worse than your husband changing into a beast was knowing he'd killed someone.

But I couldn't help it. I had a feeling things were going to get worse with Artemis. His death would take care of that problem.

"Okay. I'll bite. What's complicated about it?"

"First, this man is not one of Abe's people. He used his magic to save him, but your friend upstairs is actually the one I'm looking for."

"Are you going to stand there and confess that you've been taking advantage of Abe and stealing his people?"

"Yes." He glanced around the empty basement. "Who is there to hear but you? And you aren't going to give me away, are you? After all, it would be simple for me to allow Abe to see the real mark on your foot. I can smell Lucas's magic on you. Abe can't because I've blocked his senses."

"So the cards are on the table." I nodded as I looked for a weapon. I had the Beretta, but from what I'd seen of sorcerers and magic users, bullets meant nothing. A nice, sharp, metal stake might be better. "Why are you telling me this now?"

The answer was obvious, of course. He meant to kill me in Debbie's basement. He'd probably make it look like Terry had done it, and then he'd be rid of me. I was the only one asking questions and making waves. Killing me would solve his problems as much as killing him would solve mine.

"I know you fear me." He had to raise his voice for me to hear him over Terry's snarls. He waved a hand, and Terry fell back, unconscious, to the dirty concrete floor.

"There. That's better. As I said, I know you fear me. But there is no reason. You and I have so much in common. It's almost humorous that you think I would harm you. I would rather cut off my own arm than hurt you."

I didn't believe him, though I thought it was an over the top speech to make before he killed me. I wished I had that magic Lucas was always insisting was mine. I'd make Artemis fall on the floor and not move, at least until he could be killed. The least I could have done was to record what he was saying to me so there would be some witness to my death.

I goaded him, hoping to distract him, as I slowly slipped my cell phone from my pocket. "Don't bother making excuses. We both know I can't die by conventional means, but I'm sure you have a magic spell up your sleeve that could do the trick, right?"

It's hard to find the right button when you're trying to sneak pictures from your camera. It was always difficult to capture those super cute moments with Kate. It wasn't any easier to get a sorcerer to confess and record it.

I glanced at my phone out of the corner of my eye. He raised his hand—and Debbie called out from upstairs—a perfect distraction.

"Is everything okay down there? Do you need me?"

Artemis turned his head toward her voice, and I managed to push the button to record.

"Everything is well, dear lady," he called back without a touch of tension in his voice. "We shall be up momentarily. Never fear."

He looked back at me. I wondered if this would crack his smooth mask.

"You better get it over with if you want to kill me like you killed Harold. I won't go down without a fight. And I won't let you take over Abe's people.

He kicked a soccer ball out of the way with his highly-polished dress shoe. "What can I say that will assure you that I have no plans to harm you, Skye? Would it help if you knew that I am your father?"

I wasn't expecting that—and I didn't believe it. But neither did Luke Skywalker, even though it was horribly true.

Artemis the sorcerer couldn't be my father. I was an orphan. I didn't have a father.

"That's the weirdest thing anyone has ever said to me," I told him. "If you think I'm letting my guard down because you claim to be my father, think again. I know you want me out of the way. Just get on with it and stop talking."

He reached his hands out to me, an imploring look in his eyes. "I know you've been alone. You don't even know your real name. You were taken from me and your mother when you were just a child and abandoned here in this wretched place. I have come to help you claim your birthright. You will be a powerful magic user one day. Abe and these people will mean nothing to you. As for that sorcerer you value so highly, you won't feel the same about him once you know who you are."

His words had a terrible ring of truth to them. Maybe it was because he knew I'd been abandoned. Maybe it was because Lucas kept telling me that I had magic I had never used.

Whatever the reason, I was more scared of the relationship he was claiming between us than any werewolf or sorcerer. I couldn't be his daughter. I didn't want to believe it was true.

I pulled out my Beretta, even though we both knew it wouldn't have much impact on him. I needed something in my hands that felt safe and familiar.

Facing him with it, I said, "Get out of here. Everything you've admitted has been recorded on my phone. I'm taking it to Abe. He'll hunt you down if I can't figure out how to kill you."

But my hand was trembling. We both knew it.

Artemis smiled slowly at me. "Take it in. Let it fill you. You and I have a future together. Stealing Abe's magic is only the beginning. Every time he loses one of his people, I am stronger. We can rule this little kingdom he has created until we are ready to seek something larger."

Debbie screamed upstairs. I glanced that way, and when I looked back, Artemis was gone. Terry had begun snarling and jumping around again. I ignored him and ran upstairs.

Debbie was floating toward the ceiling, her hands desperately trying to grab on to anything that could stop her from disappearing.

"What's happening? I'm not dead."

"No, but you're still marked with Abe's tattoo. Anyone with the mark is affected. Artemis just chose this as an opportune moment to get away."

"Do something, Skye." She kicked her legs and flailed her arms as she slowly became more transparent.

"I don't know what to do. Lucas kept me from disappearing. Artemis kept the others from vanishing. I can't replace your tattoo. I could call Lucas, if he'd pick up the phone."

"What about Abe? He says he loves me. Call him. I'm sure he doesn't want me to float into space."

"He'd say he was going to send Artemis. He won't help you since he caused this in the first place. You aren't getting it."

Debbie screamed again and clutched at the lamp on the ceiling. "Something has to keep this from happening. I can't leave my children with Terry. Help me."

I called my house, hoping that Lucas or Addie would pick up the phone. I knew Lucas had been teaching Addie how to use the phone again so her hands wouldn't just slide through it. He'd also coached her so her voice would project over the device.

"Pick up," I urged, staring up at Debbie. "Please pick up."

"Hello. This is the Mertz residence. Please leave a message."

We didn't have an answering machine.

"Addie, I know it's you. This is Skye. Don't hang up. Get Lucas. Tell him to come to Debbie's house right away. She's disappearing. Artemis won't help her."

"*Beep.*"

"Seriously," I argued with the gravelly voice. "Tell him, Addie. And quit pretending you're an answering machine."

There was no response. The line went dead. I had to hope she would give Lucas my message. But what was I going to do with Debbie?

As far as I knew, Lucas couldn't appear and disappear at will like Artemis. He hadn't mastered that skill, if he ever had it in the first place. That meant he had to get in the old pickup and drive here. That could take twenty minutes to half an hour. And that was saying he got my message. Addie wasn't very good with messages even when she was alive.

"Skye, my hand is going through the ceiling tile. I'm not going to last much longer. You've tried calling Lucas. Try calling Abe. I know he can save me."

For her sake, I called Abe's cell phone. "Debbie is disappearing. We need help right away."

"I'll send Artemis immediately," he reacted.

"He won't come. He confessed to killing Harold to steal your magic. He put this curse on your zombies. He made this happen to Debbie so he could get away before I could shoot him."

In his usual cool manner, Abe chuckled. "Forgive me. Shooting a sorcerer with the power that Artemis has would be next to nothing. I'm sure you misunderstood. I'll put in a call to him right now. Don't lose Debbie."

He was gone, and I was still left with no way to help Debbie and uncertain that help would come in time.

Terry was howling in the basement. I could hear him throwing himself against the walls. Tools and other items close to him became projectiles that flew across the room. Was it my imagination, or did he seem louder and more upset than he had before? Maybe he understood that something bad was happening even though he was trapped in his animal brain.

I heard a loud popping sound that was quickly followed by his galloping footsteps on the stairs. He'd escaped from the ropes. No doubt they would need chains to hold him.

I didn't want to hurt him, but I knew he was going to hurt other people if I let him go. There wasn't anything I could do for Debbie, but I could stop Terry.

He came through the wood door, splintering it with his body. He snarled at me as I pulled the Beretta on him, and I took a step back.

Debbie was crying, her tears dropping down from the ceiling. Half of her body was through the tiles, the other half barely visible.

Was nothing going to go right today? I felt stupid and powerless in the situation.

The unexpected happened as Terry made a leap for Debbie, ignoring me completely. I tried to make him leave her alone by throwing pillows and other household items at him. He barely acknowledged they'd hit him.

He finally got his mouth on Debbie's dangling foot, and wrapped his claws around it to hold it steady. Debbie looked like she was screaming, but no sound came from her. I watched as Terry hung on to her, and she slowly began to fall to the floor.

At the same time, a change was coming over Terry. He was becoming less hairy and deformed. His legs grew straight and more like human legs. He was naked but had lost all aspects of the beast by the time they were both on the carpet.

Debbie was slightly more visible. She wrapped her arms around her husband and rested her head against his chest. "Terry. What happened? I had this terrible dream. You were a monster."

Terry was a muscular, good-looking man. His handsome face was turned to hers. "I am a monster, Debbie. I don't know why I'm changing back right now, but I know it won't last. I have to get out of here. You have to let me go before I hurt one of you."

"No," she cried as she held him to her. "You saved me. You're not a monster. Abe can fix you. Just stay here with me. I won't let you go. Maybe if we hold on to each other like this, you'll be human again."

"It won't work. I want to stay and see my kids grow up more than anything. I want to be with you." He kissed her. "I don't know why I've changed right now, except that I wanted so badly to help you. But I know it can't last. I can feel it inside me."

It was the most heart-wrenching thing I've ever seen. I was crying when I saw Lucas walk through the front door. I ran to him and told him what had happened.

"He's probably drawing the curse from her temporarily as she's absorbing the magic from him." Lucas shook his head. "He's right, Skye. It won't last. It's only because of their love that it happened at all."

Terry stared at Lucas as though he recognized him for what he was. "Hurry. I can't hold on much longer."

Lucas went to Debbie, closed his eyes, and muttered the same words he'd used to bring me back. Her foot with Abe's tattoo on it turned green, as mine had. She became more solid.

"Help him," Debbie pleaded. "You helped me, Lucas. You can help him too. Don't let him go back to being that way. Please!"

Lucas put his hand on her head—the move he said was only for show. Debbie fell back on the floor, her eyes closed, not moving.

"I would help you if I could." Lucas stared into Terry's eyes. "Perhaps someday if Abe refuses to make this right, I may be able to help you stay human. Do you understand?"

Terry nodded, but he was already changing back into the beast. He ground out a harsh version of *I love you* close to Debbie's head and licked her ear.

The change came on him faster after that. The human version of him was completely gone, leaving only the satyr-type animal that snarled at Lucas before bounding over Debbie and running out the front door.

Chapter Twenty-six

I was almost too stunned to deal with Debbie as she regained consciousness. She was completely back to her normal self, and she was furious with Lucas.

"How could you let him go that way?" She pounded on his chest. "He'll kill someone or someone will kill him. We have to find him and bring him back. If you can't fix him, Abe will, or some other sorcerer who can actually do magic. You're useless, Lucas. I don't know why Skye keeps you around."

She stared at him and then ran out the door after Terry.

"I'm sorry. She doesn't understand. I know you did what you could. You saved her."

"No need for apologies. Her heart was torn. I expected nothing less." He put his arms around me. "I'm very happy that you are unharmed."

"Thanks." I took my phone out of my pocket and held it up. "I have all the proof I need right here to make sure Artemis doesn't mess with Abe anymore."

I pushed play on the phone, but there was nothing except static. None of Artemis's words had recorded. Full of anger and too much emotion, I threw the phone against the wall.

Lucas looked at the smashed phone on the floor. "I thought you said that was a costly apparatus."

"I did."

"Then why—?"

"Shut up, Lucas." I started toward the door. There was nothing more I could do there. "I'll meet you at home."

I saw him gather up the parts of the phone but left anyway. If he wanted to play with it, that was his thing.

Addie wasn't around when I got back. I'd have to find her and thank her for what she did, but that would have to be later. I poured myself a glass of Tennessee whiskey and brooded at the kitchen table. I still had a couple of hours before Kate got home.

"I've done some research on werewolves while you were away." Lucas made tea for himself and sat with me. "I'm not sure how much of what is on your computer is accurate, but many of the ways they show to kill the beast are wrong."

"Yeah." I sipped the whiskey, feeling it race through my body.

"You do still want to kill the wolf, I assume?"

"I'm meeting Gerald there tonight at moonrise." I glanced up at him. "I don't really want to kill it—there's a man or woman in that wolf skin. I'd rather catch it and turn it over to the police for trial. But I guess that's just old habits dying hard. One way or another, we should be sure it never kills again."

"I think I may have devised a plan, although I still strongly urge you not to attempt it. I understand your need for vengeance, but it's more likely that the wolf will kill you."

"Can I be killed by it? I'm a zombie, right? I can't be killed by conventional means."

"I wouldn't call death by the hand of a werewolf conventional, Skye."

"So it could kill me." I thought about it, emotionless. "What's your plan?"

The house phone rang, and Addie was quick to answer it. She did her answering machine routine and turned to smile at Lucas. "What are you doing here, Skye?"

The voice on the phone was Tim Rusk. He must have looked up my home number when my cell phone didn't work.

"Skye, this is Tim. Can you meet me at that little bar off the highway where we met last time? I've got some information for you. Whatever you do, don't bring Gerald Linker. I'll be there in about an hour."

Addie hung up the phone.

"You did very well." Lucas commended her with a smile. "I don't understand the message followed by the 'beep'. Wouldn't it be simpler to answer the phone as yourself?"

"Simpler maybe, except everyone knows I'm dead."

"Oh yes. There's that."

"Thank you for answering today and for giving Lucas my message," I broke into their conversation. "You saved Debbie's life. But you don't have to try to sound like an answering machine. You don't have to say who you are. Just answer and tell them you can take a message. They'll think you're the housekeeper or something."

She pursed her lips, said, "I guess nothing is ever good enough, is it?" and vanished.

"Never mind." I finished my whiskey and glared at the table.

"There was nothing either of us could do for Terry," Lucas reminded me. "Not all magic is reversible. If that is Abe's spell on him or if it truly is a mistake as he claimed, he may be the only one who can change it."

"And since Terry not being there anymore will probably get him Debbie, I think it's unlikely that he'll change it."

"That may be so."

I wanted to tell Lucas what Artemis had told me about him being my father. I didn't believe it, but it bothered me. I couldn't find the words, and part of me was afraid if I said it out loud, it would be real.

We talked about possible ways to kill the werewolf. Most of them involved enchanted bullets, spears, or knives. I could tell his heart wasn't in it. He was willing to attempt the enchantments on those weapons if there was no way he could talk me out of it.

Feeling a little abused by magic, I was glad that he still felt the need to discuss the options with me instead of using his magic to make me go one way or another.

I left to meet Tim at the bar. Lucas said he'd practice spelling several items to find out if he was capable of it before Gerald and I went against the werewolf. I wasn't sure how he'd figure that out until I saw him in the rearview mirror as I was leaving. It looked like he was trying to get the garden shears to cut one of the bushes near the house by themselves.

If that was the case, it was a miserable failure. The garden shears danced around on top of the bush and then went after him. The last glimpse of him—the ancient, feared sorcerer from the past—was running into the house and slamming the door behind him.

"God help us, Gerald. I hope Tim has something better." I pulled the van onto the main road.

Tim was waiting for me at the bar. It took me longer to get there because I had to stop for gas. The bartender nodded when he saw me and got me a beer. I thanked him, surprised at his memory, and sat opposite Tim at the table.

He glanced at his watch. "I was about to leave. Where were you?"

"I had some errands." I wondered why he was so edgy. I hoped he hadn't paid Gerald a visit and found him stocking up on werewolf-killing weapons. "What's up?"

He was in his uniform but must have been off-duty since he was drinking too. Not beer this time but scotch. Not the best scotch either by the smell of it.

"You got Linker out of jail, didn't you?"

I nodded. "I don't think he belongs in jail. Do you?"

"Where else would he be ranting about werewolves killing his wife?"

"Maybe a mental hospital—if it wasn't true."

"Don't tell me a level-headed woman like yourself is getting dragged into his crazy fantasies." He shook his head and polished off his scotch, pointing to the glass when he caught the bartender's eye.

"How do you know it's crazy?" I leaned forward and whispered the question. "I might've thought that too a few years ago. But I've seen stuff that doesn't have a rational explanation. Open your eyes, Tim. It's out there."

I thought he might get up and walk out. This wasn't a conversation most rational people would get involved in. If I hadn't been so upset by everything that had happened that day, I might not have said anything. I didn't really think I could convince him that I'd been dead for three years and had a sorcerer living with me.

"There's something I have to show you." He took a wrinkled sheet of paper from his pocket and smoothed it out on the table. "This is a map of this area and about fifty miles around it."

That wasn't the response I'd been expecting. "What's with all the red X's on it? What do they represent?"

"People who were killed just like your husband and Gerald's wife." He took a deep, ragged breath as the bartender brought his new glass of scotch.

I looked at all the X's on the map. There had to be two hundred of them.

"Some of these deaths are attributable to wild animal attacks, no vehicles involved. But too many of them are accounts of people being ripped from their vehicles after accidents and breakdowns. After each event, the victim was mauled and dragged too far away from the vehicle for them to have crawled or been thrown."

I searched his face. His eyes were filled with terror and questions.

"What do you make of it, Tim?"

"It's impossible. The wild population isn't there for that number of animal attacks, much less the incidents with the vehicles. I don't know what to make of it. But now that I know your reasoning, Skye, I like it even less."

"I don't like it either." I glanced toward the bar where the bartender was drying glasses. There were a few other men that were drinking beer and watching sports on TV. "I don't like thinking that there are werewolves out there killing people. I don't like that there is anything out there I can't kill with my Beretta."

"How do you deal with it? I couldn't sleep last night thinking about it. It feels like the whole world has gone insane."

I agreed as I sipped my beer.

He finished his new glass of scotch and called for more. "So what do we do about it? What do you and Gerald have planned?"

His question rolled around in my head. I wasn't sure if I should tell him the truth even though he seemed to be a new believer in the supernatural. It had been thrust on me at the same time that I'd found out I was dying. I had to make a decision immediately, and I had chosen to go on.

But I didn't think he was ready for that kind of commitment.

"Whatever is killing people out in those woods at the top of the hill—we're going to kill it. I don't know if it's a werewolf. I don't know what it is, but I don't think it's human. Gerald won't be at peace until it's dead, and I owe him that after bringing him into this. I'd like to catch it, but neither one of us can do it alone. I'm siding with him."

Tim let my words sink in. "You know, it's been an age since I went hunting. When are you gonna to do it? Maybe you could use another hand."

"Are you sure?" I searched his face. "I don't know what we'll find out there, and I have it on good authority that we may not survive the experience."

"If all this is true, I plan to retire anyway." His grin was crooked. "My wife always told me I'd go out with a gun in my hand. She may be right."

"Okay. We're meeting at the woods at seven p.m. Bring whatever you've got. We aren't sure what can kill it. I hope between the three of us that we have whatever it is."

He nodded. "I'll be there."

I put my hand on his. "Don't let me down on this, Tim. If you think it's crazy, just don't show up. I don't want to see a group of law enforcement up there waiting for us."

"That's not what I'm about." He glanced at the map and the X's on it. "My little girl is twenty-three now. She travels those roads to school and back in Nashville every day. Her car broke down on the side of the road last week. If it wasn't for a farmer who picked her up and brought her home, she could've been one of those X's. That's what *I'm* about."

I finished my beer and got up to leave. "I'll see you at seven."

Chapter Twenty-seven

I stopped by the school and surprised Kate by getting her off the bus. We went to the convenience store in Wanderer's Lake and each got junk food snacks and sodas. We sat on the shore and picked up empty clam shells. Each of us tried our hand at skipping stones across the water.

Being with her, watching her laugh and run down the shore, almost made me back out of helping Gerald.

I was supposed to be here to watch her grow up, not hunt for Jacob's killer. Maybe that was why Abe had told me not to investigate his death. Looking back was never a good thing. No matter what I did, I couldn't bring Kate's daddy back to life.

But I was pretty sure there was no such wisdom behind Abe's request.

It was more likely that he'd created werewolves with his zombie magic, by accident of course, like the creature Terry had become. Abe might even know that Jacob was killed by one of his creations. I wouldn't go so far as to think he'd set up Jacob's death, but I felt like anything was possible.

Maybe he knew I'd end my twenty year service to him if I went against the werewolf. That would mean the tiresome ordeal of looking for someone else to pick up his people when it was time for them to go.

But as much as I loved Kate, I was also determined to find out what had happened to Jacob. My heart still ached when I thought about him being gone. A part of me hoped we were right about a werewolf killer. Taking an unruly, murderous beast's life would be a satisfying end to the ordeal.

If I was killed while doing it, I had at least given my daughter a few years to grow up. Addie was much stronger now, and Lucas had sworn to protect her. I believed that he would. They wouldn't be me. I had to hope Kate would understand if the worst happened.

"Why are you so sad and quiet?" she asked, holding a quartz rock in her hand.

"I don't know. Just thinking, I guess." I smiled for her benefit.

"You're thinking about Daddy, aren't you?" She sat on my lap. "I know because I look like that when I think about him too."

I hugged her close. "Yes. I was thinking about Daddy."

"Grandma says it's good to remember him but bad to be sad. She says he's in a better place now and that he loves us very much."

"She's right." I smoothed her fine hair that the lake breeze had ruffled. "But sometimes I get sad anyway. Do you?"

"Yes. I miss him. And sometimes, I worry that you're going away too."

I wished I could promise her that it wouldn't happen, but that would be unfair. It could happen, if not tonight then some other time.

"Everyone dies, Kate. We have to love people as much as we can while they're alive."

"I love you, Mommy." She looked off at the lake. "If you're still alive next week, can we go on a boat ride? Mary's family just got a new boat. It made me wish we could go on a boat ride. I remember doing that with Daddy once."

"Yes. If we're both alive next week, we'll go on a boat ride. We'll take Lucas with us because he might not have ever been on a boat ride."

"Really? Is that because sorcerers don't like boats?"

"I don't know." I glanced at my watch. "Let's ask him when we get home. We'd better go get cleaned up for supper. Grandma won't like it if we're late."

She skipped along beside me to the van. "Can ghosts go on boat rides too?"

I laughed as I opened the door for her. "I don't know. We'll have to ask Grandma about that."

I didn't know if it was right to encourage an eight year old to think about death and dying, much less sorcery, but this was Kate's life. She wasn't going to grow up to be a normal adult. But I hoped she'd grow up happy anyway.

And that she wasn't the granddaughter of an evil sorcerer.

The last thought was uninvited. I tried to banish it as we drove back to Apple Betty's Inn. It seemed like the more I tried not to think about it, the more it took hold of my mind. It couldn't be true, and yet it was so weird and strange that I couldn't imagine why Artemis would say it if it wasn't.

Debbie's minivan was in the drive as we got back. I sent Kate up to get washed as I searched my partner's grim face. Bowman and Raina were watching TV.

"You didn't find him." I guessed.

"No. I looked everywhere, but I had to be back for the kids."

Lucas was at the stove with Addie. They were making corn fritters—he had a thing for pancakes.

"I'm sorry," Debbie called out to him. "I didn't mean the things I said. You saved my life, Lucas. I'd be gone like those others if you hadn't been there."

He nodded but didn't speak.

"What now?" I asked her.

"I'm sending the kids away to my parents. I went to the school this afternoon and let them know Bowman and Raina were taking a few extra days for summer break. It's the only way I know to protect them, and this way I can look for Terry."

"I can attempt a spell that could help you locate him," Lucas volunteered. "He has an unusual vibration that you might be able to follow."

"Thank you." Debbie blinked the tears from her eyes and faced me again. "I went to see Abe again. You were right, Skye. He's not going to do anything for Terry. He made it clear that I still belong to him, and he expects me to honor my commitment. He won't release me."

"I'm sorry. We've both known for a while what he wanted from you. I don't know if what happened with Terry was on purpose, but—"

"It doesn't matter. I've decided that I'm going to find my husband and a way to get us both out of Abe's grasp. I don't know how yet, but I'm going to do it."

I invited her to stay for supper, but she had to go home and pack for the kids. They were leaving that night. Debbie wasn't willing to take any chance on Terry coming back.

"At least I know that he's still inside that thing." She smiled. "As long as there's a chance I can get him back, I'm going to keep looking for him."

"I don't blame you. I think he still loves you. I could see it was driving him crazy not to help you. You're lucky to have him."

"I know. I'll be back as soon as I can. If we get called on a pickup, can you cover for me?"

"Sure. Abe might be a little put out, but we know he's not going to do anything about it. We've got him there."

"Thanks." She waved to Lucas and Addie. "I'll see you later."

I said goodbye to her, Bowman, and Raina. Like Kate, Debbie's kids had a glimpse into an unexplained world that they shouldn't have been able to see. It was going to impact them the rest of their lives. There was no way to take it back.

"The longer the man goes as the beast," Lucas said when she was gone. "The harder it will be for him to recall ever being a man."

"I'd do the same thing if it was Jacob." I set the table for supper. "She has to try. How could she ever love someone else knowing he's out there suffering?"

Addie did her ghost version of clearing her throat. "I don't know. You fell into another man's arms pretty quickly. It didn't seem to bother *you.*"

"Jacob is dead," I harshly reminded her. "There is nothing I can do for him. And I'm tired of you making cracks about Lucas and me all the time. It won't be long, and Kate will notice. Cut it out."

"This is still my house. I can say what I like." She glanced at Lucas. "I'm sorry. I don't mean any disrespect to you, and you've been a big help to all of us. But it's just not right."

She disappeared, and I sighed as I put the beans she'd been cooking into a bowl.

"It's hard for her," Lucas said as he put the giant mound of corn fritters on a platter. "Her son is gone. She wants everyone to know her despair."

"I think we all know it. There's no reason for her to drive it into the ground."

I had no sympathy for her that night as I was about to put my life, such as it was, on the line to avenge her son. I would have told her, but I knew she'd never believe a werewolf had killed Jacob. Unless I came back with its head on a platter, like the corn fritters, it was unlikely she would ever believe it.

I called Kate for supper. Lucas poured sweet tea into glasses filled with ice.

Kate put one corn fritter on her plate with a spoonful of beans.

"We're never going to eat all these fritters," I said as I took one for myself.

Lucas put at least a dozen on his plate. "I believe we can put a sizable dent in these fritters. Kate, eat another one. Let's show your mother that one cannot make too many fritters."

After supper, we put dozens of leftover fritters in the refrigerator while Kate did her homework at the kitchen table. Lucas and I washed and dried the dishes. Addie still hadn't put in an appearance. I had to look for her upstairs so she could be with Kate when Lucas and I left to join Gerald and Tim.

I wasn't surprised to find her in Jacob's bedroom. "I have to go out. I need you to watch TV or something with Kate."

"I know something is up," she remarked without looking at me. "Lucas is going with you, isn't he? Does it have something to do with Debbie's husband?"

I frowned.

"I can't help it. I hear everything in this house. It's part of me." She patted one of Jacob's old stuffed animals. "You might want to consider that when you're in bed with Lucas."

I sat at the old desk. "I don't want to hurt you. You're one of the few things I have left from when my life was normal. I don't want to fight with you. Can't we get along for Jacob's sake if nothing else?"

"Why? We never did when he was alive."

"I'm going out tonight to find his killer," I confessed. "We both know he didn't die in the crash, Addie. I have a chance to prove that he didn't and do something about what killed him."

"Do something like what? What do you think killed him?"

I took a deep breath. "A werewolf. We think a werewolf killed him and some other people in those woods." I told her about Tim and Gerald. "We're going to kill it."

Her dark eyes for once looked happy. "Good. That would make me feel a lot better than all these newspaper clippings on the wall. I guess you'll need Lucas's magic."

"Probably."

"That makes sense."

"Why do you believe me? I thought for sure you'd laugh me off."

"I'm a ghost, Skye. You're dead. My husband was dead for twenty years before he went away. Lucas does magic. It's not too much of a stretch for me to believe there are werewolves and that one of them killed my son."

I was completely amazed. I hadn't given her enough credit.

She sniffed. "You know he's a good man—Lucas. He's not my son, mind you. But he's a good man. You could do worse, I suppose."

"Thanks, Addie." I smiled as I got up to go.

"But keep it down in the bedroom. There's a child here, for God's sake."

She disappeared before I could leave the room.

It would've been nice to have that ability as a zombie.

I looked around at all the evidence I'd collected for the past three years as I'd haphazardly looked into Jacob's death. It had brought me to this moment where there was no way to go back. All I could do was plunge ahead and hope I was doing the right thing.

"I love you, Jacob," I whispered to the empty room before I went downstairs.

Chapter Twenty-eight

Kate barely noticed when I left. She was so engrossed in a BBC show that was also a favorite of Addie's. For all of my mother-in-law's rough charm, she was a hopeless Anglophile.

It was just as well, I told myself as I walked out to the van. I'd rather Kate not worry about what I was doing. I could do that well enough for both of us.

Lucas was waiting outside. The full moon caught his profile as he stared up at it.

"Ready?" I asked. "Is there a special chant or something."

"I am ready." He turned to me. "I hope you're as ready as you think."

"I already saw one man change into an animal and try to kill people." I hopped up on the seat. "What's one more?"

He sat on the passenger side. "The difference is in the details. Terry was clumsy, slow, and weak compared to your adversary this evening. I hope the enchanted bullets and the spell on your gun hold. I also enchanted my crossbow and arrows."

I started the van and pulled out of the drive. "Crossbow and arrows? Where did that come from?"

"I may not remember everything about my past, but I do remember that we hunted with a bow. A crossbow is best."

"But where did you get it?"

"I bartered a few services with the local hunting store. The man assured me the arrows are strong enough to penetrate a large animal such as a bear."

"You did magic for him?" I could only imagine *that* phone call if the magic didn't work.

"Of course not. I clipped his hedges. They were unsightly. It was a good trade."

"It sounds like a good trade. But if my bullets can't kill it, how would an arrow?"

"Neither will work in that case. It's not the weapon but the enchantment that will guide it to your foe. Without the enchantment, we are no doubt dead. I hope you explained that to your friends."

"They know the risks."

I kept my eyes on the ribbon of road ahead of us. In the twilight, the trees and houses took on a burnished hue with the sun setting behind them.

Lucas and I didn't speak again until we reached the woods at the top of the highway. There was very little traffic. I saw a new Chevy pickup that I assumed had to be Tim's. He had brought Gerald with him from Nashville. Both of them were waiting beside the vehicle.

We parked behind them. I nervously checked my Beretta and extra clips. This was it. If I was going to turn back, this was my last chance. I closed my eyes and said a prayer I remembered one of my foster parents teaching me when I was very young. *Angel of God, my guardian dear.* I got out of the van and joined my partners.

Lucas was already with them. He was enchanting an array of weapons that were in the back of the pickup. There was everything from small handguns to the assault rifle and an AK47 that had to belong to Tim. There was even a handheld missile launcher.

It made me smile, despite the circumstances, to see Lucas appear to be praying over them. I knew that wasn't it, and I could see the faint green glow when he was finished. My gun and his crossbow were also tinged with green. His enchantment seemed to work, as far as that went. The question was—would it hold, and was it strong enough to kill the werewolf?

"You're really losing it here, Mertz," I whispered to myself a fair distance away from the enchantment. "You're in the woods with three strangers getting ready to fight something that shouldn't exist. It's time to wake up, girl."

I wished it was that easy.

Lucas turned to me when he'd finished spelling the weapons. Gerald and Tim nodded as they pulled out all the weapons, finding holsters and other places to store them for the fight.

"He's out here somewhere," Gerald said as though he could feel the beast.

"Let's go get him," Tim snarled. "It's a good night for hunting."

Lucas took up his quiver of arrows and slung it across his back. He held the crossbow in his arms as we advanced toward the trees.

In some ways, I agreed with him.

It would be nice to put this behind me. In other ways, my conscience was beginning to bother me. Would it help to kill this thing? Should I have worked harder at tracking it, as Lucas had suggested? I'd let myself be swept up with Gerald's need for blood—my need too, if I was honest.

Lucas touched my arm. Nerves frayed, I jumped.

"The wolf is out here. I can smell it. It's too late to worry about your choices, Skye. It's important to stay focused on our quarry."

"Quit reading my mind. I have enough trouble keeping my thoughts to myself."

"I don't have to use magic to know what you're thinking. I know you quite well by now. Allow that a man can understand a woman without tricks or subterfuge."

"I'll allow for that. Just don't broadcast it, okay?"

"Shut up back there you two," Tim harshly barked at us. "Hunters don't talk while they're hunting."

I could argue that fact but didn't. He was right. Our supernatural prey probably already knew we were here. Gerald was in front of me. His death grip on the rifle told its own story. Everyone was afraid.

As the sky darkened and the stars came out, it only got worse.

Lucas stopped walking. He put his hand on my arm to stop me too. He didn't speak, just stood there staring ahead. I couldn't say anything to Gerald—he was out of reach. Tim was in front of him following what seemed like a trail through the trees.

Everything was quiet. No birds called out. There was no rustling between the leaves on the trees or on the ground. I understood why Lucas had stopped. It was clear the other animals in the woods tonight were terrified of the thing we hunted, and it was close to us.

I started to speak, to call Gerald and Tim back. Lucas put his fingers against my mouth. The moonlight picked out hints of green fire in his eyes as he looked at me.

Gerald's terrified cry was sudden in the night. I could barely make him out in front of me. I couldn't see Tim at all.

Lucas grabbed my hand, and we ducked down behind a large, moss-covered rock.

At first I was too scared to act, but this wasn't being part of a team. I broke away from him and ran after Gerald. The M16 fired several times in the darkness. I found Tim, but there was no sign of Gerald.

When we heard a gurgling scream, Tim reacted. "Over there. Follow me."

I glanced back for Lucas, but it seemed he had stayed in hiding behind the rock. Maybe that was how sorcerers survived. He wasn't a military man or a warrior. Sorcerers were probably more into stealth and strategy. I hoped he survived because of it.

Tim and I ran through the woods, jumping over splits in the dry ground which were probably small streams when it rained. Branches scratched my face and arms as we ignored everything to reach Gerald while the werewolf was still there.

Breathless, we finally reached a clearing where some trees had fallen. I could hear the traffic going by on the road close by. Tim had his AK47 in his hands. He strafed the area in a circle to clear it.

Gerald wasn't there. Neither was the wolf. But a few pieces of bloody clothes, Gerald's rifle, and a single shoe were right in front of us.

"Do you hear anything?" Tim asked in a ragged voice. "I think it got him, Skye. I can smell that it was here, can you?"

"Yes." I wished I had a big searchlight to get rid of the shadows around us created by the moon and trees. Gerald could have been a few steps away, and we wouldn't have known it.

"I don't know." Tim lowered his weapon to wipe sweat from his face. "What do we do now? It's probably laughing at us. Where's the damn magic man?"

My reply was on my lips when the werewolf jumped out and caught Tim with its claws.

The wolf was bigger than a man—taller and broader. His body structure was long and angular. His head was too large to fit on his torso, or so it seemed. I could smell the fetid stench of blood on him as he moved.

Lucas had been right. The creature's movements were efficient and devastatingly faster than a normal wolf or bear would've been. I could make out his extended claws in the moonlight as they tore Tim's flesh from his body. The sound was nightmarish. It was all I could do not to vomit.

I fired the Beretta again and again as I heard the sounds of the beast tearing him apart. Either the enchantment wasn't working on my gun and bullets, or they had no effect. I grabbed the M16 from the ground and braced myself to fire it at the wolf.

The big bullets struck the wolf's body. It growled when it was hit and glanced my way as though it hadn't noticed I was there before. I knew once it had seen me it would come for me when it had finished Tim. We'd been fools to think we could even hurt this thing.

Lucas grabbed my hand again. "You can't stop it this way. Come with me."

"But why?" I forced the words out as we ran in the opposite direction. "Why didn't it work? The wolf barely grunted when I hit it."

"I wish I could tell you. My magic is unreliable. I thought it was working. It should have worked. But the wolf is more powerful in ways I can't define. Perhaps because it was created by a mistake in Abe's magic, it is stronger than most. I don't know if it can be killed."

"Where are we going? We should've stayed and helped Tim."

"Your friends are dead," he said flatly. "You will be as well unless we take an extreme measure. Don't falter. The wolf won't let you live now that it has your scent. He will follow."

We ran until we found another clearing in the woods. This one was bathed in bright moonlight, the trees around it probably felled from storms.

Lucas stopped abruptly. "Stand over there. Have you bullets left in that weapon?"

"Yes. What are we going to do? The bullets didn't work against it. Shouldn't we go back to the van?"

"Do you think your vehicle would provide defense against such a creature?"

"So...what? We just stand here and die? Is that your strategy?"

His voice was deep and resonant as he put his hands on my arms and stared into my eyes. "You shall stand here and shoot the beast *through* me."

I took a step back. "No. That's crazy. You'll die, and it still won't stop the wolf. That's a stupid plan. Is that the best you could come up with?"

"Listen to me. If you fire that weapon so that the bullet passes through me and into the wolf on the other side, my blood will kill it. I may not recall everything I should, but I know a sorcerer's blood will kill this thing."

"And you too." I caught his hand and tugged at it. "Let's go. Maybe we can still outrun it."

"We couldn't outrun it from the moment we stepped into the woods. This is the only way."

"What if you're wrong? Then I would've killed you for nothing. The enchanted weapons didn't work. This may not work either."

"I shall not die."

"Yeah? I don't think Abe will take you on as a zombie. If I shoot you with this thing, you're going to die. Let's go. We have to come up with a better plan."

He smiled and kissed me. It broke my heart, knowing how he felt about me.

"There is no better plan, Skye. If I perish in your service, I die gladly. But no matter what, the wolf will die with me."

Tears slid down my face. I felt like I could hear the wolf coming toward us although I knew it had to be my imagination. I didn't hear a thing when it attacked Gerald or Tim. Still I knew Lucas was right. It wouldn't let us go.

"I can't kill you. Don't ask me to. You're the first good thing that has happened to me since Jacob died. There has to be another way."

The wolf howled, low and throaty, ending in a terrible growl that made my skin prickle with fear.

Lucas moved my hands from his chest and stepped a few paces back from me. At that distance, the M16's bullet would blow him apart. But it would probably pass through him and hit the wolf on the other side, if the timing was just right.

What was I thinking? We couldn't do this. I couldn't shoot Lucas, not even to save myself. There had to be another way.

"He's coming, Skye. Get ready. You have to shoot before he pushes me to the ground. Do you understand? The bullet must pass through me first. You have to do this."

I got the rifle ready, but my hands were almost too unsteady to hold it. I tried to focus. Tears blinded me.

How can I shoot him? He probably wasn't even certain the plan would work. He was doing what he could to save me, buying me time. The wolf would go down. I could escape.

It was wrong. So wrong.

I should have been patient and stalked the wolf. I should have ignored Gerald and done this the way I knew was right. The way Lucas had suggested in the first place.

The wolf was running toward us in the open area. I could see it clearly in the moonlight. It was still ravenous, carrying the smell of blood and death. He was loping quickly across the fallen trees and rocks. It would only be a moment before it sprang on Lucas.

I knew I was dead—for good probably this time. Abe wasn't around to bring me back. I doubted that Lucas's magic was going to save either of us. But since I was sorry I hadn't followed his original plan, I decided to stand my ground and follow this one.

"Please don't die," I called out to him. "I love you."

He didn't say anything. His eyes were closed, and his arms were held slightly out from his sides. I thought his lips were moving though I couldn't hear the spell he was whispering. I thought about how he'd saved me from being a ghost, how he'd helped Addie, and made all our lives more bearable.

The werewolf sprang, its long claws extended, teeth glistening with saliva. He was sated but still ready to tear out Lucas's throat and then mine.

As he hit the ground directly behind Lucas, the beast stared at me and growled. His eyes glowed with a fierce golden light. He knew that I was waiting.

I steadied the rifle in my hands. The shot had to be at exactly the right moment.

"For you, Jacob," I whispered. "And for you too, Lucas."

Chapter Twenty-nine

I squeezed off the round and heard the retort of the rifle.

The sound echoed through the woods, along with the sickening thud of the bullet hitting Lucas in the chest. He fell forward, but not before the bullet passed through him and into the wolf.

The creature let out a wild, high-pitched whine that was followed by a loud growl as he leaped in my direction over Lucas's body.

I shot again and again until there were no bullets left. I felt for my holster and fumbled with the Beretta, but there was no need.

The werewolf finally groaned and dropped at my feet.

I fell on the hard, dry ground, pushing backward until I put some distance between us. Then I scrambled to my feet, gun in hand, ready to shoot again if necessary.

The wolf didn't move.

With a cry of my own, I ran around it to Lucas. He wasn't moving either. I knelt beside him and got him on his back even though I knew there was no way he could have survived the shot.

His T-shirt was covered in blood. I felt around on his chest. There was a large gaping hole where the bullet had entered him and another on his back where it had exited. I tried to feel a pulse but couldn't find one.

"Lucas!" I shook him, wanting to believe, despite myself, that he was still alive. I knew no one could live with a hole through their chest, not even a crazy sorcerer.

I bent my head against him, and my arms went around him. "I think it worked, but you're dead, just like I told you. It was the worst plan ever. I thought sorcerers were smart. That's what they say in all the books. But not you, huh? You lied to me. You saved my life, but not your own."

"What are you babbling about?" He coughed as he tried to sit up.

"You're alive? Wait!" I pushed him back, wiping tears from my face. "You're really alive? Don't move. I'll call an ambulance. Maybe they can still piece you together."

He groaned. "Is the creature dead?"

"Yes. It worked." I reached for my phone and realized that I'd destroyed it. I couldn't call anyone until I got to the van and drove to the bar, the closest place to the woods.

Lucas would never make it.

"Good. I'm glad something I recalled from the past was correct. Did the creature change?"

"No." I shook my head. "I don't know. I left it there so I could see if you were dead. Keep still. You're alive, but you won't make it out of here. I knew this was a bad idea."

"It might be best to check it now. I'm not dead, but I am feeling as though one of your large bullets passed through me."

"You've lost a lot of blood." I pushed against his chest where the bullet had passed through. "I can't stop that kind of bleeding out here. Just lie still. I won't leave you."

He took a deep breath. "You needn't worry. My blood went into the wolf with the bullet. Being a supernatural creature as well, the magic in my blood killed it."

"Okay. Sure." I tried to keep myself from crying, but I couldn't stop. "I'm not leaving you here. Even if your blood went into the wolf and it died. That's still too much blood for you to lose and survive."

"Thank you for your care." His smile was slow and painful in the pale light. "But will you please make sure the wolf is dead? I'll be fine until you return."

I put a new clip into the Beretta and went back to check the wolf.

It was gone.

"I shot it at least a dozen times. It's not here."

"We'll have to track it to its lair." Lucas struggled to get to his feet.

I put my arm around him and helped him up. He wasn't dead—maybe not even dying, but he was weak.

"How is this possible? How can you still be alive?" It had to be shock. I'd seen men take a dozen bullets and keep coming. Sometimes it took a minute or two for them to fall. But they always went down.

I put both my arms around him and laid my head against his chest. His heart was still beating, loud and strong. He was breathing.

"How is this possible?"

"Have some faith in me, Skye." He winced as he tried to stand upright. "You wound my pride."

"Faith?" I laughed. "I saw the hedge clippers chasing you. Admit it. You didn't know if this would work."

"I was mostly certain that it would kill the beast."

"But not entirely certain it wouldn't kill you too." I hugged him tightly. "I have faith in you, Lucas. Maybe not in your magic, but in you."

He put his arms around me. They were strong and warm. He was alive, not another victim to the wolf and these woods. If I had money, I would have burned those woods to the ground.

"Can you walk?"

"Yes, of course, albeit very slowly, please. It will take me some time to recover."

"How are we going to find the wolf?"

"I can see its blood trail. Look—on the ground in the moonlight—this should take us to it."

I saw drops of blood in places, large pools of it in others. It had a faint greenish tinge to it from Lucas's blood. I knew he had normal red blood like everyone else. What I was seeing, mixed with the wolf's blood, was the magic.

"What made you think about such a stupid plan?" I asked as he leaned against me. "*Shoot the wolf through me, Skye. It will die, but I won't.*"

"I admit that sometimes thoughts of what I should do buzz around in my head like flies, driving me mad. I try to grab them, but they sometimes get away from me. This thought was that a sorcerer's blood can break through even the strongest magic. You can imagine that a sorcerer would be reluctant to take this course of action."

"I guess it worked anyway." I finally took a deep, shuddering breath. "I hope the enchantment on my gun and bullets will be enough to finish it off when we find it. We've come this far. I'm not letting it go after it killed Gerald and Tim."

We trudged along, following the blood as the moon rose higher in the sky. The trail was leading out on the other side of the woods, away from where we'd first come in.

"You were right. We should've searched for it instead of assuming we could take it on like a normal wolf. It was stupid. I'm sorry you have to suffer for it."

"Sometimes patience is the best answer." He leaned his head against mine. "Speaking of patience, did I hear you declare your love for me before you fired a bullet through my heart?"

"Now?" I asked incredulously. "You want to talk about this *now*?"

"What better time?" He tried to lift his arm and point to the moon, but he couldn't quite get it up that high. "Regardless. Should we be unable to kill the beast and he kills us instead, I would know the truth. I have heard you declare your love for your dead husband dozens of times in the still of the night."

"You and Addie need to wear earplugs." I grimaced, feeling ridiculous.

"Come along. I know you said it. Addie says 'fess up to it. I believe it is appropriate at this time."

We'd reached the main road. I could see the lights still on at the bar down the hill. The blood trail went in that direction too. I urged Lucas across the street while there was no traffic, and we resumed our hunt.

"Well?"

"Yes. I think I love you. I didn't want to say so. I like our relationship not having strings to it."

"In other words, you want to bed me because it helps you sleep, but you don't want to be in love with me."

"It's not quite that simple." I gathered my thoughts. "It's only been a few years since the only man I ever loved died. I don't want to forget him, and I don't want Kate to forget him. I can't move on with my life. I'm dead. I have to give up everything in another seventeen years."

"Excellent. So you view our relationship as long term." He smiled and kissed my forehead. He grunted doing it so I knew it was too hard for him to reach my lips.

"If you're happy with that, I am too." How could I say no to a man who was willing to die for me? "I like having you around. I wonder sometimes—if you remember who you are—will still want to stay here with us? With all the magic of the universe at your command, would cutting shrubs at Apple Betty's Inn near Nashville, Tennessee be where you'd choose to be?"

"If you and Kate are with me, I would still want to be there too. I believe you have sorcerers confused with faithless magic users who have no loyalty to their loved ones."

"And what if there's someone else in your life that you left behind and can't remember? You might be married. You might be engaged, and the love of your life may be left behind wherever and whenever you come from."

"I don't believe that's true. I have given it thought, knowing how I feel about you and your...insecurity."

"Insecure? Me? I'm not insecure. I'm just saying that she might be out there. What makes you think I'm insecure?"

We had reached the bar's parking lot. There were no vehicles waiting there. The blood trail led up to a back door near a garbage can.

"I hope this doesn't mean—"

"I knew the wolf would be close by."

Matt? Was he the werewolf?

"Jacob and I met here all the time when we were working. I just met Tim here recently. We talked about what was going on in the woods."

"He was probably listening." He nodded toward the door. "It's open, and there is blood on the handle. Let's hope he's not waiting for us to arrive."

Lucas didn't like it, but I left him sitting behind a small storage building. He still couldn't stand upright without me. If the wolf was going to attack, it would be better for me to have both my hands ready to fight him.

"And this way, at least one of us will survive." I smiled and kissed his forehead.

He agreed and reluctantly stayed where I left him. "Do not believe anything he tells you, Skye. Don't get too near him. Stay aware. He may still be able to fight."

"I'll be careful."

"I love you."

I stared down into his face, my fingers still tangled with his. "I guess I love you too."

He raised his dark brows. "I believe we shall have to do something about that reluctant tone I hear in your voice, my lady."

"Not magic," I warned.

"Not magic." He kissed my hand and released me.

I cautiously walked into the bar. I wished again that I had my cell phone—this time to use as a flashlight. The interior of the bar was dark. There was no moonlight to show the blood trail that we'd followed here. I kept the Beretta out in front of me, carefully peeking through the shadows.

There was no sign of the wolf.

I walked through another door into the main part of the bar. Here at least there were small neon beer signs advertising various brands. They helped me pick up on the blood again. The trail led behind the old bar.

That was where I found Matt, the bartender.

He was still partially in wolf form as he lay on the dirty floor that was covered in peanuts and ripped paper napkins. He was moaning and thrashing from side to side. It seemed as though he couldn't go back to being human again. He was dying.

"Skye." The wolf's voice was guttural, almost not understandable. He fixed me with his glowing yellow eyes, lips pulled back from his huge teeth.

"Why?" I asked. "Why were you up there killing people? Did you know you'd killed Jacob?"

"Too hard to fight. It's what we crave—the blood. Didn't mean to hurt anyone. Life is precious to me too."

He barely had enough breath to speak. I didn't feel as though I had to end him to prevent his suffering. I felt sorry for him, like Terry.

But he'd killed Jacob, Tim, and Gerald. I knew there were dozens of other people who wouldn't get this closure of knowing what had killed their loved one. I didn't hate him, but I felt it was justice.

He'd started to change. His face was looking more human as the seconds went by. His hands were reshaping themselves into human hands.

"They'll come for you. I can't help you."

"Who?"

"My pack. Retribution. An eye for an eye. They'll want blood."

"I didn't want it to end this way. But I didn't want Jacob dead either. If your pack comes, I'll deal with it."

"No." He tried to sit up and reach for a red scarf that was folded on the bar. "Give them this. They'll know what it means. You'll be safe. I'm sorry, Skye."

I took the red scarf and shoved it in my pocket. Maybe it wouldn't mean anything to the other wolves in his pack, but I could give it a try.

His breathing was more labored as the change continued. His legs got straight, and his head lost the wolf shape. He looked as he always had serving beer—except bloody and naked.

"You should go." We both heard a wolf howl in the distance. "Don't let them find you here."

I didn't want to leave him. I was responsible for his death. But I'd already pushed my luck tonight, and we still had a long walk back to the van with Lucas not in the best of shape.

When I touched his hand, it was cold. I got closer to his face and realized he was dead. There was a gaping hole in his chest—and one of Abe's blue tattoos on his heel.

Angry and bitter, I gazed at it. This could have been prevented if Abe had told the truth about his magic and its consequences. Jacob, and so many others, would still be alive.

Another good reason to get out of here. How long until Abe felt this and came to see what was wrong?

I didn't want to explain it to the police either, even though my first instinct was to pick up the phone and tell them about Matt. It was hard, but I had to put aside my police training and get out of there without touching anything.

Lucas was where I'd left him, leaning against the side of the building. I helped him up, and we started back the way we'd come.

"It's over?" he asked.

"It is." I didn't tell him about the red scarf or the threat from the bartender. I could tell him later when we got home. "We'd better stick to the shadows, or we could be more popular than we want tonight."

Several black SUVs pulled in front of us, blocking our way out. A group of men with guns jumped out of the vehicle and threatened us. They weren't cops.

It could only be Abe.

Chapter Thirty

Morris, and another man I'd never seen, led us to the back of one of the SUVs.

Abe was lying down with blankets packed around him. He'd lost so much weight that his skin sagged on him, gray and dull. It made him look like a man who was almost two-hundred years old. His vitality was vanishing with the magic stolen from him by Artemis.

He was still wearing his sunglasses but having a hard time keeping them on his face. There had been more stolen zombies from the look of him. Artemis must have decided that he didn't need me to be present to do his dirty work anymore.

"I can't believe it's you, Skye." Abe's breath was shallow, his voice weak, hardly sounding like him. "I trusted you. I thought you understood. Yet you teamed up with this sorcerer to destroy me." He glared at Lucas, no breath left to condemn him.

"Me?" I glanced at Lucas who still couldn't stand on his own. "I'm not sure if I understand what you're doing with your army of dead workers, but I'm not the one destroying you. I told you before that it's Artemis."

"He wouldn't dare," Abe returned with some of his old fire but ruined the effect when he began coughing. "I tried to warn you about this…this sorcerer that you've befriended. He'll be the death of you."

"I think you have your sorcerers confused. Artemis has been stealing your people when he changes them back from being ghosts. You've felt it each time, but he hit you with some kind of spell so you can't see the changes. I've seen them. The marks on their feet turn red, and the circle around the A doesn't quite meet. It's his brand on them as he claims them for himself. I don't know why I can see it—unless it's because he's my father."

Lucas turned an incredulous face to me, hurt and a trace of anger in his green eyes.

Abe was surprised but gave me the impression that Lucas had been right about him. He'd known there was some kind of crazy magic in me. That was probably why he'd offered me another twenty years. Maybe he thought I'd end up being his magic user at some point.

He seemed more amazed that I'd figured it out than anything else.

"You didn't tell me that Artemis is your father," Lucas finally said. "How long have you known?"

"He told me at Debbie's house. He admitted to everything he'd done with Abe too, but my phone decided not to work, remember? He said he wanted me to help him take over Abe's magic and we could share the power."

"You should have told me." Lucas straightened his shoulders and swayed as he pushed away from me to stand on his own. "Why didn't you?"

I was about to answer him when Abe reminded us that he was there.

"Why didn't you tell *me*?" he asked. "You say you've known this was happening. Were you afraid I'd abandon you because he's your father?"

"Really, I didn't say anything to anyone because I was hoping it wasn't true," I answered both of them at once. "It's not every day a dead woman finds out that her father is an evil sorcerer. It's especially a novelty for me since I've been alone for as long as I can remember. If Artemis can be believed, he said I was taken from him and my mother. We didn't get into who might do something like that. Debbie's husband was a distraction with his snarling and howling."

Abe glanced down at the ever-present cell phone in his hand. "Yes. An unfortunate state of affairs. Where is Debbie, by the way? And what are you two doing out here, covered in blood and smelling of wolf?"

I briefly recapped. "Debbie is out looking for Terry who managed to change back to being a human long enough to save her from being a ghost. As far as what Lucas and I are doing out here, we're cleaning up another one of *your* messes. The bartender here, Matt, was a werewolf. You know him, Abe. He was one of your people—another unexpected loss for you. We killed him. He killed Jacob, and no telling how many other people."

"As I said, sometimes things happen that we don't plan for." Abe's words were deliberate. "Werewolves—and other creatures—can be a terrible byproduct of magic. I don't like it any more than you do. But if I never attempted to save anyone—" He drew in a ragged breath. "We're getting off topic. I'd like to believe you about Artemis, Skye, but realizing that he is your father doesn't make you any less culpable for the losses I've suffered."

"Seriously? I'm here telling you the truth about what happened, half of which you already know. Let's go back to the tattoo shop and talk to Simon. He saw what happened in the alley. Take a look at his new snake tattoo. I think that says it all. He knows Artemis killed Harold. I know Artemis did it to take over your power. What more do you want?"

"Proof would be nice, instead of gossip. You don't have any real proof, I assume, since this is what you offer me after your investigation."

"No. You're right. But I can prove it to you."

"How?" He stared at me. "How can you prove something you aren't sure of yourself?"

"In my previous profession, we called it a trap. That's what I'm proposing. We set a trap for Artemis, and when he takes the bait, we'll both know the truth."

He considered it. "All right. What do you have in mind?"

I glanced at Lucas. "We were just working out those details after dealing with your werewolf."

Lucas didn't say anything, but I could see the questions in his eyes. I wasn't looking forward to answering them.

"How can I trust your sorcerer to help me when I believe he's behind your latest rebellion and my demise?"

I had no idea. The brainstorm about trapping Artemis was as far as my plan had gone along that path. But I couldn't let *him* know.

"There must be some magic that could allow you to know what's going on. Something like a listening device—a wire—like the police use for investigations. We could use a real wire, I suppose, but after trying to record him on my phone, I don't think that would work."

Abe nodded slowly. "I may have just the thing back at Deadly Ink. But I warn you, Skye, there will be consequences if you are lying to me."

"I'm not worried about that. Let me show you what a rat Artemis really is. Then you can decide for yourself." I wasn't worried about the men with guns standing around us either. I'd just killed a werewolf. How much worse could anything be?

"You have a day to get this set up. Let me know when you're ready, and I'll give you the charm you require." Abe gave the word to his people. They bundled him up in the back of the SUV again and left us at the bar.

"Would it be terrible to go inside and have a drink with a dead werewolf?" I asked Lucas. "I don't think Matt will miss it."

There was a long, keening response from somewhere in the distant darkness.

"Did he mention companions?" Lucas asked as we started back up the road to where we'd left the van. "Werewolves always travel in packs. It might be better to have a drink at home."

"I was afraid you'd say that." I kicked at an empty beer can in the parking lot as I started walking. "Abe could've given us a ride back. And what did he mean by rebellion? He and I need to have a talk when this is over."

It took a while, but we eventually made it back to where we'd started.

Tomorrow, everyone would be looking for Tim Rusk in the woods where they'd find his abandoned truck. They'd find what was left of him and Gerald. With no car wreck to blame their deaths on, I guessed they'd try to say it was a hunting accident.

Tomorrow, someone would find Matt the bartender, and his wolf friends would know he was dead. They'd probably know magic was involved, might even be able to follow our scent, even though Lucas carefully tried to conceal that we had been there.

I had the red scarf from Matt and hoped that would be enough to settle everything peacefully between us. But before then, I had to come up with a plan to trap my evil father so that Abe would know exactly where my loyalties lay.

Lucas and I had finally made it home. I realized it might be easier to confront a bunch of angry werewolves than figure out how to get Artemis to reveal his true intentions.

And that didn't begin to cover Lucas being angry that I hadn't told him about Artemis being my father.

"Why didn't you tell me?" he asked after taking a hot shower and changing clothes. "What did you fear from me?"

"Honestly, I didn't fear anything." I stripped down to get in the shower after choosing not to shower together with so much blood on both of us. "I was worried that it was true. I guess I hoped if I didn't tell anyone, it would go away."

"He could have extraordinary power over you."

"Which he obviously doesn't since he couldn't make me see things his way."

He followed me into the bathroom. "Blood magic is the strongest magic. Even if you do not see things his way now, it could win out."

"I'll deal with that when I have to. Besides, we only have his word that he's my father, Lucas. Maybe a normal person can't lie to a sorcerer, but I'm sure sorcerers lie all the time. Maybe he was just hoping to convince me that we're related. Abe probably told him my history. It was easy."

I hopped in the shower, glad for the distraction, but he was still there waiting when I got out. "What else can I say?"

"You may be correct," he admitted. "I thought he wanted to bed you. Sexual magic is very strong too. He could have influenced you that way."

"Probably not." I pulled a towel around me. "I can only handle one sorcerer at a time in my bed."

He smiled as he handed me the cotton nightie I liked to wear at night. "I would prefer to think that he might be your father. It would explain the magic in you, Skye. The story could be true about you being taken from him. He had no time to teach, or corrupt, you."

"But you understand why I didn't tell you?"

"I understand, although succumbing to his will might have been a more unpleasant experience for you than my anger."

"You probably couldn't have stopped whatever he wanted to do anyway." I shrugged on the nightie that grazed my thighs. "Not that I don't have faith in your magic."

"Yes, of course."

I touched his face, glad he was still here with me. "Can we put this aside now and talk about what I should do with Artemis tomorrow?"

"Yes." He kissed my hand. "But no more lies between us."

"I didn't lie—"

"Or sins of omission!"

"Cross my heart." I made the X over my heart. "Can we go to bed now?"

* * *

We stayed up the rest of the night in the silent house working on the plan. I sat on the bed in the turret room while Lucas built a roaring fire in the hearth and then stalked from one end of the room to the other.

At least he was walking on his own.

His skin under the shirt he wore was smooth and unblemished—though white as a baby's. It was amazing, knowing that I'd shot him at such close range. He seemed to take it for granted that he had healed. We were fortunate that his plan had worked in the woods.

All we needed was one more brilliant idea.

"I'll just find him and tell him I want in on his plan. We'll do another pickup with a zombie changing into a ghost. Abe will see what I'm talking about with his magic wire thing, and that's that. We're back where we were before, except that Jacob's killer is dead."

"It won't be that easy." He'd already poured both of us a double whiskey and gulped his down. "Artemis will know that you're lying to him. I can tell when people lie to me. We have to assume he has similar magic."

"I'll avoid obvious lies." I was still sipping my drink. "And I'm a good liar."

"Really?" He stopped pacing. "Tell me a lie. It has to be something I don't know."

"Okay. It's not like you know everything about my life."

"Just most of it. But find something."

I searched my brain. There were lots of small details he couldn't know about me. We didn't talk much about those little things most lovers discuss—your favorite color, your favorite food, your favorite music. I didn't know any of those things about him either.

"What about this? I didn't want to be a cop when I got out of school. I wanted to be a dancer."

He paused. "No. I knew you were lying."

"What? No. How? I wasn't lying. I wanted to be a dancer. I only became a police officer because Jacob was going to be one. I didn't want to let him out of my sight."

"You were lying to yourself then," he remarked. "Try again."

"If I tell you it's a lie, how is that going to help?"

"Because I can tell if you're lying, just like Artemis will. Tell me another lie."

"This is stupid and doesn't make any sense. Wouldn't we be better off going outside and doing some kind of magic moon spell for success?"

"Now *that* was the truth." He held his hands behind his back as he began pacing again. "Your only hope is to be very tricky. Don't lie or tell him the truth. Sneak around him. Avoid absolutes."

"Sure. Kind of like I don't necessarily doubt that he's my father."

"Exactly."

"But you believe he is, don't you?"

"I don't doubt the possibility. It makes no sense to tell you of your relationship otherwise. He was hoping his words would enhance your feelings toward him."

"That's what I thought too." I took another sip of whiskey, beginning to feel better despite thinking about werewolves coming to kill me.

"There *is* something else," he said. "He's going to want proof of your allegiance to him."

"I can do that. Just tell him I think he's the greatest thing since cable TV, right?"

"It won't be that easy. He's going to insist on removing the mark on your heel. He'll want to replace it with his own."

"But that's not a good idea, is it? If he does that, he'll control me like the other zombies he's stolen from Abe."

"We may be able to figure a way around that."

"Like what?"

"I'm not sure yet. But you need to be aware that the moment will come. If I truly wanted to believe that you were mine, I would demand it. It's the only way you can show him that you're not part of Abe's army anymore—and that I haven't demanded such fealty from you myself."

I thought about the situation as he described it. "Won't that mean he'll find out I'm tricking him? He'll release me, and I'll be really dead."

"No. Absolutely not. We have to think smarter than him. We have to hide the truth from him, as he has hidden it from Abe."

"So a magic moon spell after all. That's the only way, isn't it?"

"Let's not be too hasty."

"You mean like me shooting a large caliber bullet into your chest to kill a werewolf?"

"As I said, I'm still working on that aspect." He poured himself another glass of whiskey.

"Okay then. Anything else I should think about?"

"You may be actually tempted to join him." He stared at me. "His blood runs in your veins. What he says may be emotionally appealing to you."

"That didn't happen at Debbie's house," I reminded him. "I think I can handle that part."

"Yet perhaps he wasn't trying to influence you as much as he could. Perhaps he was just testing the waters. He may have wanted to know how you would react when he revealed himself. A sorcerer understands how to manipulate emotions to get what he wants."

"Really? More than anyone else?"

Lucas sat beside me on the bed after putting his glass on the side table. "A sorcerer could have the love and loyalty of anyone he set his mind to obtain."

I put my glass on the table too. "You mean like you could have charmed me into loving you anytime you wanted. Then why didn't you?"

He put his arms around me. "Because I wanted your honest emotion, Skye. I was drawn to you from across time and space. I knew we were meant to love one another. There could be no other way."

I kissed him. "That's right. Sorcerers are incredibly patient too, right?"

He smiled as he fell back against the bed, taking me with him. "That's right. Because we know that all will come to us in good time."

"I guess I never had a chance, huh?" I kissed the side of his neck.

"Never."

His kiss lingered, deepening, and making me stop thinking about werewolves and evil sorcerers.

"It's six-thirty," Addie announced from the doorway. "Time to quit fooling around up here, and get Kate off to school."

Chapter Thirty-one

Our day started like most days when Kate was in school. I got her up and helped her dress. We talked about what she was doing. Since it was so close to summer vacation, they were watching movies. We talked about the boat trip we had planned.

We went downstairs together and ate breakfast, oatmeal with raisins. Lucas had started adding brown sugar to Kate's oatmeal. I ate mine with salt and pepper. Addie hung around, smiling at Kate. Lucas ate a mouthful of oatmeal. I had coffee. He had tea.

I took Kate to school and then went back to Apple Betty's Inn.

That's where the day took a turn for the weird. Although how I could think of it that way, I wasn't sure. Weird was every day, a shadow that stretched over the normal things. I didn't know what was normal or weird anymore.

But this day might be the day I was going to foil an evil sorcerer. I somehow was going to convince him that I was on his side because he was my father. Talk about weird.

After that was anybody's guess.

Lucas had worked on a spell that would protect me from Artemis during the supposed changeover between Lucas's magic tattoo and Artemis's. Lucas was convinced this would happen and wanted to make sure I was ready for it. I wished I had more faith in my lover's magic. I wasn't sure it would work when it came down to the crunch.

Though, he had been right about shooting him to kill the werewolf.

"This is going to hurt a little." Lucas stared at the bottom of my foot. "I would normally feel quite bad about it, but perhaps it may be your comeuppance for not telling me that Artemis is your father."

"Thanks. That makes me feel a lot better."

"What did you think I would say? I would hardly turn my back on you."

"Every child without parents that I've ever known always dreams that one day their mother and father will suddenly swoop down and claim them. Everyone wants to hear that they were kidnapped, and their parents have been looking for them."

Lucas glanced up at me. "Which rarely happens, and thus your skepticism. I understand that much." He zapped my foot with a green spark from his finger.

"Ouch! You did that on purpose. It didn't hurt last time."

"Last time, as you say, I was simply trying to turn you back into a being of flesh and blood. This time, we need Artemis to think he's removed my protection. That requires something more."

He smiled slightly, and I kicked him with my other foot. The *ooph* that came out of him was satisfying.

"I think that should work." He examined his magic, still holding my foot. "We have to assume he knows that Abe's magic isn't on you. He'll be looking for my magic. What he won't know is that there is a protection under my mark."

"Or at least we hope he won't know." I took my foot back and sat up on the sofa. "What do I do if he realizes it?"

"Nothing. It's unlikely that he'll tell you, and if he puts the full strength of his magic into you, you won't know anything but what he tells you."

"But I can see his other magic. I'll be able to tell about this too, right?"

He sat beside me. "If he takes you, rest assured that I shall find you. I won't allow you to stay with him as his slave."

"Don't worry about me. Just remember your promise about Kate. I'll get myself away from him."

"You say that only because you don't fear him. That is a mistake. He is a master sorcerer. He will take you if he can, and you won't be able to fight him with your gun."

"Thanks for the pep talk." I put my sandals back on. "I guess I'm ready to go. Anything else I should know?"

He stood up and kissed me. "I love you. Come back to me."

"I will."

I started for the door. We'd been brainstorming this most of the night. I was ready to get it over with.

Addie popped up in front of me in the mud room. "I never meant any of this to happen to you, Skye. How do you always get in such a mess? My husband's twenty-year service to Abe was nothing—no sorcerers, no werewolves, no ghosts. I don't understand why this time is so different."

"It's just me, I guess. Don't worry. I'll be fine. And at least now I probably know who my father is."

"A murdering scumbag? I hope you haven't mentioned this to Kate. This man doesn't seem like grandfather material to me."

"I haven't told her. I don't plan to tell her. Take care of her, Addie."

"Go on. Try not to get killed again."

She disappeared, and I let myself out the back door. Lucas seemed to think that I could call Artemis from wherever I was and he'd show up. I wasn't so sure after our last meeting, but I didn't know how else to contact him.

First I had to get the magic gizmo Abe had for me. Two secret magic things on one dead girl seemed like a lot to get away with. If I could keep that concealed from Artemis, the rest should be a snap.

I walked into Deadly Ink. Simon was there, working on his snake tattoo. He flinched when he saw me. I didn't know if it was because Abe had talked to him or because he was worried that Abe *would* talk to him.

I nodded to him as I walked by. Either way worked for me.

Abe and Brandon were in the office. I could tell by Brandon's face that he knew what was going on. I closed the office door and waited.

"You still want to go through with this?" Abe asked.

"I don't see any other way, do you?"

"You're not taking Lucas with you?"

I thought about the sharp stab of pain in my foot. In a way, he was with me. "I'll be fine."

"All right." Abe took out a black velvet-covered box that looked like a jewelry case. He opened it and then sat back in his chair, breathing hard. "This is a witch stone. Wear it around your neck. I'll hear and see everything you do."

The chain was made of heavy gold. The stone was purple with what looked like light blue glitter inside. The whole thing was big and gaudy. There was no way to hide this under my tank top as I'd hoped.

"I think Artemis is going to see this coming, don't you? It might be better if I don't wear it."

"It's the only way." Abe feebly waved his hand toward Brandon.

Brandon got up on cue and picked up the necklace. He put it around my throat and made sure it was secure.

"Isn't he going to know what this is?" I asked. "I don't think he'll spill his secrets when he sees it."

"It's actually disguised from its normal form. He won't suspect a thing." Abe seemed very certain of his plan. Looking at him made me wonder if he was going to last through his next breath.

"Okay. I'll go see if I can find him." Yet another secret magic charm that Artemis was expected to overlook. I felt like I was going to a gun fight with a switchblade.

"Be careful, Skye," Brandon warned. "Artemis is pretty powerful by now. If he thinks you're trying to trick him, he might kill you."

His words of warning in this situation were funny. I had to keep myself from laughing. How would Artemis miss the fact that we were all trying to trick him? It seemed like I was doomed.

The one thing I had going for me was the feeling Artemis gave me when he'd offered to share Abe's power with me. It was that feeling that had finally convinced me late last night that he was telling the truth about being my father. I was reluctant to admit it to Lucas, again, a little embarrassed to have an evil sorcerer as a parent. But I really believed he wanted me to share his life.

Maybe that was the most naive part of the whole plan. He was my father. Would he kill me the way everyone was predicting? The way Lucas told it, Artemis could have killed me before if that was what he wanted.

I thought about Harold's gruesome death and shuddered.

"How do you plan to find him?" Abe asked. His words were followed by a five minute coughing spasm.

"I haven't had any problem with that since we met. I don't think that will be an issue now."

Abe removed his sunglasses and stared hard at me with his white eyes. "Yes. I see the layers of magic Lucas has tried to use to protect you. I wish I had something to add to those layers. I'm afraid if you're not successful, today will be my last day on earth."

No pressure. "I'll take care of it. Just hold on."

I nodded to Brandon who leapt to his feet and hugged me. I returned his embrace, and he gave me a cell phone. "A little birdie told me that you needed one."

"Thanks." I left the room, closing the door behind me. As the door was nearly closed, I heard Abe say, "She's never going to make it."

It was nice to know that no one felt like I was up to the task. "Come on. I've been through some tough things," I argued with myself. "Give me some credit."

Glad that Debbie wasn't with me, I got in the van and started driving. I had no idea where I was going. The van was headed for downtown. I went with the flow.

"Looking for me?" Artemis was suddenly there in the passenger seat. "Good morning, Skye."

"Yes." There was no point in pretending that he didn't know what I was trying to do. As Lucas had told me, don't lie to a sorcerer.

He smiled. "Thank you. That might be the first honest answer I've received from you. I'm waiting for you at this warehouse."

The older abandoned warehouse near the heart of Nashville suddenly flashed into my brain.

"I'll see you there," he said. "I have a surprise for you."

And he was gone.

I had no doubt that we were playing his game now—maybe we had been from the start. I still had to go through with this. There was nothing left if I didn't.

Following the street map in my mind, it was a short trip to the warehouse where my surprise waited. I wondered if everything Abe and Lucas had told me would be of any use. It felt like I was on my own. I had to deal with my father by myself.

I parked the van behind the building. There were Enter and Exit signs on the doors. Broken bottles littered the parking lot. I guessed the building had been empty for a while.

As I got out of the van, the Enter door opened wide for me. I knew the Beretta was useless against Artemis's magic. I started to take it out of the holster and leave it. But when I lifted it, I knew that I wanted it with me anyway. It was something from my past life—my normal life.

"It's you and me kid," I whispered. "Let's do this thing."

I marched into the empty building thinking about Kate, Jacob, Addie, and Lucas. I tried to stay focused. One thing I knew about sorcerers—they wanted people to be distracted. They didn't want them to see what they were really doing. Watch what the left hand is doing while the right hand is doing something else.

Clearing my mind of everything except being there, I walked inside. I was surprised to see hundreds of people. They formed a circle around Artemis, who was on a raised platform.

Abe's zombies. I recognized some of them. But they didn't belong to Abe anymore. Each of them had a faint red glow about them.

No wonder Abe was so weak. That was a lot of magic to lose. I knew he depended on each person returning their life force to him when their twenty years was over. I had no idea how many people Abe had brought back from the dead.

"Welcome, Skye!" Artemis called out. "Come in. Come right up here."

The people surrounding him moved apart so that they'd cleared a path for me to reach him. Each of them had a blank stare. They were completely under his control. It was different than what Abe expected of them. He allowed them to live their lives for the twenty years he'd given them. Artemis had taken their will.

I stepped up on the platform where he was standing. It was some sort of machinery that had been abandoned when the building was left empty. I faced him, and he stared at me for a moment before laughing.

"Did they really think I wouldn't notice this?" He peered closely at the stone on the gold chain around my neck. "Really? Do they think me some hack apprentice sorcerer? I am insulted that this was the best they could do."

I started to speak but recalled Lucas's warning about lying. "Abe is nearly dead, but he still doesn't think you're responsible for it. He thinks Lucas and I have taken his magic. I was trying to prove to him that it isn't true."

His bright blue eyes widened as though my honest answer astonished him.

"It's only a minor problem, my dear." He snatched the chain and stone from my neck and threw it to the floor. "That's better. Now let's get that pathetic sorcerer's magic off you."

He walked around me several times, his eyes carefully scanning me. I kept my mind empty. I thought about him, about him being my father. His eyes met mine, and I knew without a doubt that he'd told me the truth about who he was.

"My little girl—all grown up. What they have done to you? It makes me very unhappy to see you this way. But don't worry. Soon all of the trappings of the life you've led so far will be gone. It will be the beginning of a new awareness for you. The two of us shall do marvelous things together."

"And my daughter, Kate?"

"Of course we'll take her with us—after I've had a look at her. Sometimes breeding with humans doesn't leave behind magic for the child. You'll understand that we can't take her with us if she doesn't measure up."

I bit my lip to remind myself that I had to stay in the present. I couldn't get angry or lash out. "It's difficult for me to imagine my life without her."

"That's only for this moment. When we're finished here and we've absorbed all of Abe's power, we'll take what we can from Lucas. He may not understand the difference since he has forgotten who he is. Then we'll decide about Kate."

"Okay. What do you need me to do?"

"Nothing. Just stand right there, and I'll take care of the rest. When the other magic has been stripped from you, I'll tell you your real name. It is an ancient, powerful name that has been associated with magic in our family for a thousand years."

I did as he said, just stood there as he used his magic to cover me in a red haze. I could feel something different happening to me. It felt itchy and hot. I took off my sandals. Both Abe and Lucas's marks were gone. There was no mark left behind by Artemis either.

Did that mean I was free from all magic bonds that had been placed on me?

Artemis sagged a little when he was finished. "I didn't realize Lucas had put so many protections on you. I'm surprised and not pleased. Never fear. They are all gone now. It only remains for me to place my charm on you. Once it is there, no one will be able to remove it because you are of my blood."

I watched him cut his arm and take some of the blood that dripped from it into his hand. He rubbed his hands together so that both of them were coated in his life force, and then he came toward me.

Something surged through me at that moment. I don't know what it was. But I knew I couldn't allow him to put his blood on me. I was desperate—he was only a heartbeat away. I had to do something.

Without thinking about it, I drew the Beretta from the holster and whispered the spell I'd heard Lucas repeat several times while he was enchanting the weapons for the werewolf hunt. I steadied my hand and stared into my father's eyes.

Then I pulled the trigger.

Chapter Thirty-two

The shot was loud in the large, empty space. It echoed around us until it was all I could hear. Artemis's elated expression faded as his hands dropped to his side. The bullet had pierced his chest, blood gushing from the wound.

"No!" He yelled as he stepped away from me. "No. This can't be. I've taken your protections. I've given you no magic of your own yet. You can't hurt me, girl. What were you thinking?"

But he crumpled to the metal platform beneath us, his blood soaking his gray suit and pristine white shirt. I realized it was over and put the Beretta back in the holster.

From around us, Abe's people began to awake as though they'd been in a dream. Some of them cried, while others screamed and ran out of the building. A few became hysterical and began to tear at their clothes and hair. I tried to talk to them, to calm them, but it was as if they couldn't hear me.

What had just happened?

Dozens of zombies sat on the dirty concrete floor and didn't move. The rest ran out the door and into the street. The cell phone Brandon had given me rang.

"You did it, Skye!" Abe's voice was jubilant. "You've given them back to me."

"How do you know? He took the necklace away."

"I didn't need it. I knew I'd feel the return of my people when it happened. That was just subterfuge for Artemis's sake. Is he dead?"

I looked down at the metal platform. Artemis was gone. A part of me felt bad about that, and a part of me was glad. How would I ever know who I was or what my real name was without him?

We weren't ready for each other, it seemed. He had underestimated me—I had surprised myself.

And I knew we'd meet again.

"No. Artemis escaped."

"But you weakened him. It will take him some time to rebuild his power, and I'll be ready for him. Thank you, Skye. I'm sorry I thought you had done this. It's Lucas. You have to get rid of him."

"I don't think so, Abe." I smiled as I thought about telling Lucas what had happened. "I'm going home."

"Not so fast. I'll need you to round up my people and bring them here to me. They'll need to be reconnected."

Why wasn't I surprised? "I'll get as many as I can."

"Fine job."

The connection went dead in my hand.

I gathered up all the zombies who were readily available in the old building. It was as much as the van could hold anyway. The others had disappeared and would have to wait until I dropped these off at the mortuary.

It wasn't going to happen today though. After my load of people was Brandon's problem, I went home. I ignored Abe's dozen or so texts and voice mails. I wanted to know how it had happened. I wanted to tell Lucas everything and hope he could put my mind at ease.

I was excited about having used his spell against Artemis—and it working. Did that mean I had magic of my own, as Lucas had told me, even though my father hadn't believed it? I had so many questions.

Besides, it was the last day of school. I was going to pick Kate up to celebrate. I hoped Lucas would join us on our boat trip around the lake.

I got Kate and headed toward Apple Betty's Inn. She was out of the van and in the house before I could even get my door open. I smiled as I took her book bag and posters with me.

Lucas and Addie greeted me at the back door, wanting to know what was going on. I filled them in with the basic details as Kate bounced around the kitchen, eager to go.

It wasn't difficult to convince Lucas to come with us. It seemed he had as many questions about what had happened as I did. Between Kate's excited comments about her school day, we spoke is short whispers about my meeting with Artemis

We drove to the marina and bought tickets for the ride around the lake. We'd be stopping for lunch during the trip and wouldn't be back until dinner.

Kate was in the pilot house with a group of other children, listening to the captain tell them everything about the boat and the lake. Lucas and I stood near the front of the boat, staring at the water, trying to get out the last of the details about Artemis and Abe.

"I can't explain what happened today." He wrapped his arms around me. "But I'm glad you came back safely. I told you that you have magic."

"Maybe you're right," I admitted. "Can a person have magic and not know it?"

"I would say Artemis found that to be true today."

My phone rang again. I looked at the number. It wasn't Abe, so I answered it.

"Hello? Is this Skye Mertz?" A pleasant female voice asked.

Probably wanted to sell me something. "Yes. But whatever you're selling, I'm not interested."

I was about to hang up when the pleasant voice continued. "I'm so glad I can finally speak to you. This is your mother, Skye. We have so much to discuss."

About the Authors

Joyce and Jim Lavene write award-winning, best-selling mystery and urban fantasy fiction as themselves, J.J. Cook, and Ellie Grant. They have written and published more than 70 novels for Harlequin, Penguin, Amazon, and Simon and Schuster along with hundreds of non-fiction articles for national and regional publications. They live in rural North Carolina with their family, their rescue animals, Quincy - cat, Stan Lee – cat, and Rudi - dog.

Visit them at:

www.joyceandjimlavene.com
www.Facebook.com/JoyceandJimLavene
Twitter: **https://twitter.com/AuthorJLavene**
Amazon Author Central Page:
http://amazon.com/author/jlavene

19980587R00152

Made in the USA
Middletown, DE
10 May 2015